D1058246

Amanda was lost in thought.

Phipps's kiss after he'd licked the strawberry juice from his finger was something she had never encountered before. His previous kisses had been sweet and enjoyable—but that kiss…it had shaken her to the very core of her being, arousing such a whirl of fierce passions that she had been for a moment swept quite away. She'd seen something in his eyes: an answering need that had made her feel he wanted to lay her down in the sweet meadow grass and…

There her mind stopped, for to imagine those sensations brought to fulfilment was shocking.

She realised that it was going to be harder than she'd imagined, hiding her feelings for Phipps once they were married. If his kiss could arouse such fire in her—a blazing inferno that had threatened to sweep away all barriers—what would happen on their wedding night?

CHOSEN BY
THE LIEUTENANT

Anne Herries

First published in Great Britain 2015
by Mills & Boon, an imprint of Harlequin (UK) Limited,
Large Print edition 2015
Harlequin (UK) Limited, Eton House, 18-24 Paradise Road,
Richmond, Surrey TW9 1SR

ISBN: 978-0-263-25543-0

Anne Herries lives in Cambridgeshire, where she is fond of watching wildlife and spoils the birds and squirrels that are frequent visitors to her garden. Anne loves to write about the beauty of nature, and sometimes puts a little into her books, although they are mostly about love and romance. She writes for her own enjoyment, and to give pleasure to her readers. Anne is a winner of the Romantic Novelists' Association Romance Prize. She invites readers to contact her on her website: www.lindasole.co.uk

Previous novels by the same author:

THE RAKE'S REBELLIOUS LADY
A COUNTRY MISS IN HANOVER SQUARE*
AN INNOCENT DEBUTANTE IN HANOVER SQUARE*
THE MISTRESS OF HANOVER SQUARE*
THE PIRATE'S WILLING CAPTIVE
FORBIDDEN LADY†
THE LORD'S FORCED BRIDE†
HER DARK AND DANGEROUS LORD†
FUGITIVE COUNTESS†
BOUGHT FOR THE HAREM
HOSTAGE BRIDE
THE DISAPPEARING DUCHESS**
THE MYSTERIOUS LORD MARLOWE**
THE SCANDALOUS LORD LANCHESTER**
SECRET HEIRESS
BARTERED BRIDE
CAPTAIN MOORCROFT'S CHRISTMAS BRIDE
   (part of *Candlelit Christmas Kisses*)
A STRANGER'S TOUCH†
HIS UNUSUAL GOVERNESS
PROMISED TO THE CRUSADER
COURTED BY THE CAPTAIN††
PROTECTED BY THE MAJOR††
DRAWN TO LORD RAVENSCAR††
THE REBEL CAPTAIN'S ROYALIST BRIDE†
RESCUED BY THE VISCOUNT◊

A Season in Town
†*The Melford Dynasty*
**Secrets and Scandals*
††*Officers and Gentlemen*
◊*Regency Brides of Convenience*

**Did you know that some of these novels
are also available as eBooks?
Visit www.millsandboon.co.uk**

Prologue

Amanda Hamilton looked at her reflection in the long mirror in her dressing room and sighed, for she was no beauty. Of what use to be an heiress and have three proposals from fortune-hunters in the last month when she was what could be indelicately described as overweight? And at a time when the fashion was for sylphs and girls who looked as if a puff of wind would blow them away!

If only she did not have such a sweet tooth or was some inches taller! On a taller girl her inches might have looked impressive, for she had a well-formed bust and good hips, which many gentlemen liked, but Amanda was tiny. Papa was at fault for he had spoiled her when she was a small child, giving her sweetmeats and cakes and petting her, forming her appetite for the sticky sweet things that had proved her downfall.

Although her dark hair was glossy and her grey eyes bright and fearless, what man could truly want such a dumpling for a wife? Her face was too plump and had therefore lost the pretty shape that should be hers and she thought herself plain and dowdy, despite all the money spent on her clothes. So how could she ever expect to find the man of her dreams?

Oh, there were several who paid court to her and she'd received many offers this Season, but none of the gentlemen who had spoken wanted her for herself. Nor would they have been acceptable to Papa. Lord Neville Hamilton required a gentleman who could give his daughter the lifestyle she was accustomed to, though she knew that if she'd cared for any of her suitors Papa would have given in to her wishes in the end. None of them had caused Amanda to lose a wink of sleep and that was because her heart was already given to a man she'd loved from the first time he'd smiled at her.

Lieutenant Peter Phipps: the second son of Lord Richard Piper, and quite the kindest gentleman that Amanda had ever been privileged to meet. Phipps, as his friends called him, was kind enough to dance with her at a country-house ball when she'd been sitting for more than an hour, unnoticed by most of the gentlemen present. At that time her fortune had been modest, for Amanda had an elder brother, Robert, who would naturally inherit Papa's estate. However, just a year after that fateful affair when Amanda had lost her heart, Great-aunt Mariah Howard had died and left her entire fortune to her favourite great-niece, much to the chagrin of several other nieces and nephews who might have had hopes of Lady Howard.

It seemed that some gentlemen who had found Amanda invisible a year ago were now eager to engage her attention. Several had already proposed marriage and, if she were not mistaken, another young man was about to do so. But, perversely, the one gentleman she would have married, regardless of whether he truly loved her or not, had given her no indication that he was preparing to make her an offer—even though he was unfailingly kind and always stopped to speak to her or stood up with her if she lacked partners.

Amanda was a clever girl, something she did her best to keep hidden, because as Mama had once told her, gentlemen did not care for knowing girls. Papa might be proud of her skills at drawing, French, Latin and mathematics, as well as some knowledge of the sciences, but Mama said it was all useless learning. Mama preferred her daughter to be skilled at needlework, which she was, and to be able to quote from various poets; to play the pianoforte and the harp, and to sing prettily were all essential for a young lady of her class. Amanda could do all those things. She also had a keen sense of humour, as did Papa, though Mama could not always see why they laughed at something, for she did not share their amusement in the absurd.

Mama said ladies needed a husband to provide them with children and a good home, but after that it was sensible to find one's own interests and leave the gentlemen to pursue whatever course they chose.

'Oh, you foolish, foolish girl,' Amanda said to her reflection and amusement lit the grey eyes. 'To be hankering after a man just because he is kind and always thinks of your feelings. It is ridiculous and you should put him right out of your mind. He may be kind, but he is not in love with you.'

How could he be in love with the girl she'd seen

in her mirror? No man wanted a dumpling as his wife—especially one as tall and handsome as Phipps. She was an idiot to think about it and must accept that she would probably be an old maid and stay at home to look after Papa—and he would not mind at all.

Amanda felt better and laughed, her face lighting up as she saw the funny side of her predicament. Lieutenant Phipps was in financial difficulty. She had always known that as a second son he would inherit only a small estate from his grandmother, which was situated not more than sixty miles from Papa's estate, and his younger son's portion from his father. If he wished to continue the lifestyle he so clearly enjoyed, visiting the clubs and mixing in society, he must marry an heiress. So why not her?

'Because you are fat,' Amanda told her reflection severely. 'If you were not so greedy, you would be like a waif and he would fall in love with you!'

She must renew her efforts to lose weight. Always her own worst critic, Amanda told herself off regularly, and indeed, she did try, but when one went to so many parties and was offered such delicious trifles, it was so hard to refuse. Besides, even if she did manage to lose weight, she could never look like the beautiful Miss Cynthia Langton. Lord Langton's daughter was the latest heiress to come to London and was quite the haughtiest of all the beautiful young ladies this Season. Most of the unattached gentleman had flocked to her train and Amanda had seen several young ladies give her glances that, had they been daggers, would undoubtedly have slain the new arrival.

Strangely, Miss Langton had taken a fancy to Amanda. She did not have many female friends, even though her cousins Sara and Jennifer were in town and included her in their party as a matter of course. However, Amanda had been of assistance to the beauty when a flounce on the hem of her expensive Paris gown had been torn. Always equipped with a needle and thread at parties, Amanda had advised her of the tear, taken her into a private salon and repaired it so neatly that no one could see it had ever been torn. Miss Langton had attached herself to her saviour at every possible occasion after that, calling her *my dearest Amanda* and begging her to call her Cynthia.

Thus, Amanda was always invited to any parties her friend's family gave, was invariably taken on all the outings to theatres, to Vauxhall and the park for a balloon ascension, to every picnic, every drive to Richmond and all the balls, routs or fêtes that Miss Langton attended. It meant that when the two heiresses entered a room together, within minutes at least half the gentlemen present would gravitate to their sides.

Amanda received her share of the attention, but she was not such a fool as not to notice the difference in the homage offered to her friend and the polite attentions given to herself.

None of which she minded at all—indeed, she drew a deal of amusement from watching the various gentlemen try first for Miss Langton's good graces, and then, when they perceived they were not favoured, for her own. However, her mild amusement had suffered a blow recently when Lieutenant Phipps had entered the fray.

Phipps was one of many suitors the beauty kept in her train, but she did seem to favour him sometimes and that made Amanda's heart sink. If Cynthia wanted him, she would have him, as she took anything else that caught her fancy, expecting and receiving slavish worship as her right. On the day of a ball, Amanda might expect five or six posies from would-be suitors, but Cynthia was like to receive as many as twenty. She was all the rage and the queen of the Season, and accepted the gentlemen's homage as her right.

Amanda bore with it all patiently, for she begrudged her friend none of her success, but if Phipps made her an offer and was accepted it would break her heart…

No, how foolish! Amanda laughed at herself. She was no tragedy queen and had always known that in the end she might have to settle for second best. Only if Phipps felt drawn to her, found her necessary to his comfort, would he ever look at her as a prospective bride. It was unlikely to happen, but, since she knew that Cynthia was hoping for at least an earl, he would probably find himself dropped once the right suitor presented himself. If Amanda happened to be around at that time… She shook her head once more.

If it were not so sad, it would be most amusing. Why would the tall and handsome Phipps ever look at a dumpling like her?

Chapter One

Phipps looked through the letters on the silver salver in the hall of his family's house in Gower Street. Half a dozen letters were waiting for him, but he judged that most of them would be polite reminders from his creditors. He was properly in the suds for the moment, because a sure thing at Newmarket had let him down and he'd lost five hundred guineas, which made it quite possible that he might have to leave town soon for lack of funds.

He was a damned fool, of course. Phipps glanced at his reflection in the gilt-framed mirror on the wall. His father had warned him to mend his ways and he'd managed it for a few weeks, because there was no point in applying to Lord Piper for extra funds when he knew full well that that gentleman was having trouble balancing the books on his own account. Phipps's elder brother, Alexander, was quite as expensive as Phipps himself and, had he not inherited a large estate from his grandfather, would doubtless have bankrupted his father. However, despite his fortune, there was not the least hope of asking Alex for a loan, for he normally exceeded even his generous income.

Picking up the letters, Phipps carried them to his desk and deposited them in a neat pile to examine when he could find the determination to tackle the situation. Had he last week come across an earlier pile of debts that had escaped his notice, he might never have placed that reckless bet.

Oh, well, there was no point in dwelling on the mess he was currently in. He must find some way of extricating himself from a pit of his own making. It was not a new situation; he'd always known that as the second son his affairs must trail behind those of the heir. It was the way in all good families, where the estate was entailed. Besides, Phipps knew that his elder brother outshone him in so many ways. Had he been a brilliant scholar he might have made his way in Parliament, but he had little taste for such a life and had joined the army, spending several happy years serving under Wellington. His career had been solid, but without the lustre of having distinguished himself by dying in a death-or-glory charge and instead escaping virtually unscathed. Had he only been able to wear his battle scars with pride, he might have occasioned more of a stir, but he was merely one of many brave officers who had done their duty.

How he was to make a distinguished career now that the wars were over, at least for the time being, he could not say. An officer in peacetime spent most of his life lounging around or parading his men for want of something better to do, which led to boredom and quite often excessive gambling or drinking. Phipps's father might well demand some improvement in his situation—but how? Phipps knew that in his father's eyes he was a disappointment, for which he felt deep regret, but it was not easy to match up to a brother who bestrode the world like a young god.

Calling for his valet to lay out his evening clothes, Phipps went into the dressing room to wash and shave. Maggs had put out his shaving things and there was warm water in the blue-and-white bowl. He was a good man and had served with Phipps in the army throughout the troubles with Napoleon.

It would be a huge wrench to let the man go, as it would his grooms—and his horses…

Lord! Surely things were not as bad as all that? Phipps felt slightly sick as he remembered that the sum of his debts was almost five thousand pounds. How had he allowed them to mount to such a sum?

Of course there was the generous wedding gift of silver for Jack and Charlotte's wedding…but that only accounted for a few hundred guineas. Letting his thoughts drift away for a few minutes, Phipps remembered how happy his friend had been on his wedding day. He'd stood as Jack's best man and it had been a real pleasure to make that speech and see the delightful pair emerge from church…of course Charlotte was beautiful.

Most of his particular friends were now either married or engaged, Phipps reflected as he scraped the soap from his chin, studying his face in the mirror Maggs had set for him. Phipps supposed marriage might be the answer to his problems, though he would have preferred some other way of settling his debts. It was rather demeaning to offer for an heiress, knowing that at some time soon after the wedding one would have to dip into her fortune to settle his wretched affairs. Although in theory a woman's fortune became her husband's on marriage, there was normally a contract securing an income to her and the most part of the capital to her children. To stipulate that a large portion be allotted for his personal use would make Phipps feel like a beggar.

Besides, having once offered for a lady he had believed to feel some affection for him and whom he had loved in return, only for her to marry a rich man twice her age, he was apprehensive of making an offer to any lady.

What had he, a mere second son, to tempt any lady of fortune?

Phipps had delayed looking seriously for a bride for months. Had he been able to find some gainful employment he would surely have done so before this, but it was not easy. He'd offered his services to Lord Piper, but his father had good agents and did not trust him to replace them. His army pay in peacetime was scarcely enough to keep him in boots and certainly not enough to set up a family.

Unless he could find employment as an estate

manager—or perhaps a political secretary?—he must marry an heiress, Phipps admitted with a deep sigh. The devil of it was that he knew of only two who were likely to look on him with favour and were rich enough not to bother that he needed a large sum almost immediately.

Miss Cynthia Langton and Miss Amanda Hamilton: one beautiful and proud, the other a pleasant little dumpling who might have been passably pretty had she been a stone lighter.

He had formed a part of their court for the past two months or more. Miss Hamilton was always to be seen with her beautiful friend, which meant that most of Miss Langton's suitors ended up sitting at her side and talking to her, quite often of her friend's beauty. Phipps had found himself relegated to that position less often than most, for, wonder of wonders, Miss Langton seemed often to smile on him. She would accept a cup of iced lemonade from his hand, allow him to dance with her twice at balls, take her walking in the park—with Miss Hamilton and another gentleman—take her driving to various places of interest, with Miss Hamilton following behind in the curricle of another gentleman.

Had Miss Langton been less beautiful and not so universally admired, Phipps would probably have offered for her long ago, but he doubted that she would take him. Her fortune was sufficient not to look for it in her husband, but she did look for rank and it all came back to the fact that Phipps was a younger son. His brother Alex was just a year older and in the best of health, which meant that he had no hope of ever stepping into his shoes—nor would he wish to since it would mean his brother's demise. They might not be bosom friends, but were fond enough as a rule.

Only by making a distinguished career for himself could he hope to engage the interest of a lady wealthy enough to pay his debts and keep them both in the luxury he and she would enjoy.

Phipps looked himself squarely in the eyes and admitted the truth. Miss Langton might flirt with him, she might encourage him to dangle after her, but she would not marry a younger son with few prospects.

Which left him with the alternative. Miss Hamilton might not be a beauty, but she had many fine qualities: a sense of humour, a ready mind and a generous heart. In short, Phipps liked her, but that was a part of the problem. He knew that he was not in love with either of the heiresses. He did not know of a lady who made him want to die for love of her, to swoon at her feet or fight to protect her. There had been that one unfortunate experience, when he was a green youth, but that had taught him to look beneath the surface, if one did not wish to be burned.

Indeed, rather like his friend Jack, he'd thought that romance was grossly overrated. A man should look for comfort in his home and take a beautiful mistress for his other needs. Given this, it hardly mattered what this proverbial wife looked like, providing she was good-hearted.

So, why had he not asked Miss Hamilton to marry him weeks ago?

Phipps was not a vain man, but he knew that her smile lit up her eyes when he went to sit next to her and she always seemed happy to dance with him—so why not ask her to be his wife? He was pretty sure she would take him if he asked.

A rueful grin touched his mouth. His wretched sense of honour had made him hold back. She might not be beautiful, but she was a thoroughly nice girl and it would be wrong to take advantage of her good nature. Had she been in need of protection from the fortune-hunters, Phipps might have persuaded himself that by asking her he was protecting her from men who would run through her fortune in a year and treat her abominably. He himself would do no such thing. If she gave him her hand, Phipps would do all he could to make her happy and try to increase her fortune—but would it be enough?

She was entitled to be loved for herself. Phipps was too honest to lie, and to admit that he would marry her because he could see no other way out of his debts would be to insult her. She did not deserve to be so shabbily treated! He believed that more than one unscrupulous fellow had already made the attempt and been sent away with his hopes dashed.

Phipps would find that extremely humiliating!

Suddenly, the funny side of it struck him. He could not insult Miss Hamilton by asking her to wed him, and, though he might attempt Miss Langton, he believed his efforts would be doomed to failure.

No, he must simply make some economies. Perhaps if he sold both his horses and his commission, and returned to the country for a few months he would come about—and who knew, he might fall in love with a girl who just happened to be rich. Jack had fallen in love despite the odds, why not Phipps?

He had no time to dwell on his problems now, for he was engaged to Brock for an evening at his house: dinner, cards and music was promised and it would be a popular event, for Lord Brockley's elder son was much sought by hopeful mamas, though they hunted in vain. Brock was an avowed bachelor and had recently won a large bet with Jack Delsey over which of them would marry first.

Brock's aunt was hosting the party at his large town house that evening. She was a cheerful, hearty widow who laughed loudly and resembled a horse, but was a good sort who neglected nothing in the comfort of her guests.

Emerging from his dressing room clothed in shirt and evening breeches, Phipps allowed his valet to help him struggle into a velvet coat that fit like a second skin. His hair combed into a style that was known as windswept and suited his dark locks to perfection, he allowed his valet to hand him snowy-white cravats that he then, by dint of lowering his chin, formed into perfect creases. It was not quite a waterfall, Phipps thought, but a very creditable arrangement of his own design and beginning to be followed by the young dandies that desired to be all the crack.

As he thanked his man, then left for the evening, Phipps thought that he might sell his commission. The sum it raised would not settle his debts by a long way, but he might pay the most pressing and then perhaps some clever ploy would present itself.

Phipps did not cast a look towards the small pile of letters awaiting his attention. Time enough for that tomorrow…

Amanda saw Lieutenant Phipps enter the salon. She and Miss Langton had positioned themselves on a small sofa at the far end of the room so that they might see the guests as they arrived and also be seen. However, the room had filled up considerably and their view was sometimes blocked by ladies and gentlemen lingering to talk in the centre of the room.

Her heart beat very fast as she saw Phipps look

about, his gaze finally coming to rest on her. He smiled and began to walk leisurely towards them, his intent obviously to greet Miss Langton and Amanda. She schooled her features to a polite smile as he came up to them, refusing to let her pleasure leap into her eyes as she was sure it must if she did not keep them lowered.

'Miss Langton.' Phipps bowed. 'Miss Hamilton. I look forward to the music this evening. Shall you play cards later?'

'I do not much care for cards, unless it be whist,' Miss Langton replied, giving him a smile of welcome. 'What do you play, sir?'

'Oh, I do not think I shall play this evening,' Phipps said. 'I came merely for the music and the company…'

'I love to play whist for small stakes,' Amanda said. 'I do not see the need for huge pots when it is the skill of the game that counts.'

'Then perhaps we should make up a set,' Phipps said. 'If Miss Langton would play—and who might make a fourth?'

'I say, do you speak of whist, Phipps?' a man's voice asked from behind him. 'If you play for small stakes just for amusement, then I'm your man. I see no point in risking a fortune when, as Miss Hamilton says, 'tis the skill of the game that counts.'

Amanda smothered a sigh as she saw Lord Johnston. The young man was a pompous bore, but admitted everywhere in society on his infrequent visits to town. He lived in the country and bored everyone by talking about his Jersey cows that produced such rich milk. The prospect of hours spent in his company was not appealing, but what could Phipps do other than bow his head?

'Splendid,' Lord Johnston said and sat down next to Amanda. 'I hear the guest singer this evening is Madame Bonniceur, a remarkable soprano. I believe her voice to be unmatched by any.'

Amanda held her groan inside. Whenever the young man was present at one of these affairs he would find his way to her and monopolise her company for as long as he could. She'd hoped that Phipps might take the seat beside her, but he had moved to sit beside Cynthia and she was left to make the best of Lord Johnston's company.

He was one of the few gentlemen not in need of a fortune to regularly seek her out at parties and she was always a little apprehensive, for she could not be unaware that he was showing some partiality towards her. If given the least encouragement, she feared that he would propose to her—or, worse, approach her papa and ask for his permission. Lord Johnston was exactly the kind of gentleman that her parents would welcome as a suitor. If not as rich as some here this evening, he was not in want of a fortune. Precise to a fault, well bred and the owner of a large country estate, where he spent most of his time, Papa would not object to his making her an offer.

She must be very careful not to give him the least encouragement. Yet she was a polite and generous girl and she could not be rude or imply boredom and thus hurt his feelings.

At that moment Lady Mellors called her guests to attention, asking them to gather in the music room for the recital. Amanda rose, as did Miss Langton, Phipps and Lord Johnston. Caught in the general movement towards the music room, Amanda was forced to take her companion's arm. He would of course take a seat near to her and that meant she must endure his company for the whole of the evening. However, Miss Langton led the way to a small two-seater sofa, which left the gentlemen with no choice but to stand behind them or move away. To Amanda's relief Lord Johnston bowed his head, murmured that he would see her later and moved away to find a seat.

Phipps was more resourceful. He saw a single chair and whipped it up before anyone else could take it, bringing it back to place it just by the side of the sofa. Miss Langton nodded to him and smiled, clearly approving of his action.

Amanda caught his eye and the triumph in it made her laugh. He inclined his head, a look of mischief passing between them. She wished that she might have been close enough to congratulate him on the adroit move, but the music was about to begin.

As the liquid notes of the beautiful aria filled the room, Amanda's throat seemed tight. It was a song of love…of a young man pining for a girl so far above him that he could never hope to possess her. The achingly tender words and the thrilling music made tears come to her eyes. She thought that she would give every penny of her fortune to be so loved, but knew that it would never happen, and the pain of realising that she would never feel a man's love made tears slide down her cheek.

Flicking them away with the finger of her white gloves, Amanda found her glance going towards Phipps and the look in his eyes made her feel hot all over. She would swear that he understood her feelings and was sorry for her. A surge of despair followed by anger surged through her. How dare he pity her?

She turned away, concentrating on the music. It had changed now and was a rousing song of war and honour, which soon swept away her foolish sentimentality.

After the recital was finished and the soprano enthusiastically applauded, their hostess asked them to take refreshments, and everyone moved towards the supper room. A large table was spread with all manner of treats: pastries and mousses, trifles and dainty cakes, as well as cold meats, pickles and bread for the gentlemen. Normally, Amanda would have relished such a feast, but she discovered that she had no appetite—even a champagne syllabub held no appeal for her.

'May I serve you with something, Miss Hamilton?'

She turned to discover Phipps at her side and

forced a smile. It had hurt her to see that look in his eyes, for it told her that he had no idea of offering for her, but thought her an object of pity.

'No, thank you. I am not hungry this evening.'

'Then a glass of champagne?'

'Yes, thank you, sir.'

Amanda accompanied her friend to a table. By the time Phipps arrived with a tray of delicious treats, followed by a waiter bearing two ice buckets with bottles of champagne, four gentlemen had joined them. Smiles and jests greeted Phipps and, good-naturedly, he sent for more glasses so that they might all enjoy the wine he'd provided.

'Well, this is a merry party.' Lord Johnston had seated himself beside Amanda. 'I do not know that I have ever enjoyed an evening as much.' He gave her an arch look. 'I believe you know why it is so pleasant to me, Miss Hamilton.'

Amanda lowered her gaze. His hints were becoming bolder and she could not doubt that he was working up to asking her to marry him. For a moment she was tempted. After all, if there was nothing more in life for her, she might as well take what was offered. She enjoyed life in the country and if she had children… The thought of what must pass before she could forget herself in the care of her children caused her to shiver.

'Are you cold?' her companion asked. 'I thought it hot in here and was about to ask if you would like a stroll on the terrace?'

'I thank you, no, sir,' she replied and sipped her champagne. 'I'm neither cold nor overwarm—I think someone just walked over my grave.'

'What a terrible saying that is,' Miss Langton put in. 'I should not like to think of you in your grave, Amanda dearest. We were just speaking of a jaunt to Richmond for a picnic and you must come with us, Amanda, for I shall not go if you do not.' She held her head to one side and looked naughtily at the gentlemen hanging on her every word. 'What must I do to persuade you?'

'There is not the least need to persuade me,' Amanda said and laughed, feeling grateful for the interruption. 'I am always willing to oblige you, Cynthia.'

'Well, I think you have your answer, gentlemen,' Cynthia replied and threw a challenging look at one of the men. The Marquis of Shearne was a new admirer who had only that evening become one of her court, having been in the country until the previous day. 'We shall expect to be royally entertained, sir. The success of the day must fall on you, since it was your suggestion.'

'Your wish is my desire,' the marquis answered gallantly. 'We have two ladies and five gentleman, we must find more ladies...'

'Then you may include me, and my sister will chaperon us,' Harry Brockley spoke from behind the marquis. 'I dare say Miss Langton's cousins will make up the party?'

'I am certain of it,' Amanda said, looking at him in surprise for he had not hitherto paid Miss Langton the least attention, even though he was Phipps's friend and often with him. 'I think Mama would like to come—and perhaps Miss Jane Field...'

Miss Field was a rather shy young lady, pretty but modest, who blushed easily and was quite often left sitting on the sidelines at balls and dances, unless a kind lady introduced her to a partner. Amanda had invited her to all her mama's parties and the girl was painfully grateful.

'There, Miss Hamilton takes us all in charge,' Brock said. 'It is all arranged, so when do we set out on this famous expedition?'

It was agreed for the following Friday and Amanda undertook to ask Miss Field. Phipps gave her an approving nod, his eyes steady on her face in a way that made her heart flutter.

'It was kind of you to think of Miss Field,' he murmured as their hostess reminded them that card tables had been set up. 'She is not here this evening, I think?'

'Jane does not always receive an invitation to smaller parties, though she makes up the numbers when there are to be many guests.'

'I believe she is not in as fortunate circumstances as yourself and Miss Langton?'

'I am not certain of her circumstances,' Amanda replied, though she knew well that Jane's father had little fortune and she was here only to bear her richer cousin company during her Season. 'But I care little for that—I like Jane. She is a kind girl and shy.'

'You are a generous young woman,' Phipps said. 'Miss Langton is to be my partner. Does it content you to partner Lord Johnston at whist?'

'I could not object,' Amanda said, though she wished she might have reversed the pairing. 'Lord Johnston is an adequate player, I believe.'

'We shall see,' Phipps said, glancing over his shoulder. 'Miss Langton seems taken with Shearne. I think he has but recently returned to town?'

'Yes, I believe so…' Amanda glanced at her friend and saw the way she was sparkling up at her new admirer. She felt a pang of sympathy for Phipps and her anger with him vanished as she understood that he must be feeling cast out. 'I dare say she is flattered by his attentions—they are marked.'

'Yes, indeed,' Phipps murmured, 'and our fortunate friend has both title and fortune to offer—a temptation for any lady.'

'Perhaps,' Amanda replied. She could make no comment for she had not yet spoken directly to the gentleman, but there was something about him that set her teeth on edge. The way he looked at Cynthia…was not quite what she thought proper. His smile had the eager sharpness of a predator and she thought him a rake. 'I believe Miss Langton to be a woman of sense, sir. She may not be distracted for long.'

'You may be correct,' he murmured softly in her ear. 'Brock hates him. I was surprised that he agreed to be a part of an expedition got up by Shearne.'

'Major Brockley hates the marquis?' Amanda looked at him in surprise. 'Does he have good reason?'

'If he does, he has not spoken of it, but I know he distrusts and dislikes the man intensely.'

'If Miss Langton is in any danger...'

'Oh, I do not think he would dare to try to seduce such a popular lady; he would be ostracised by society if he did her some harm...yet if I were her I should think twice before accepting an offer from him.'

'Why?' Amanda asked, but they had reached the card room and the others were waiting for them, the marquis still hovering at Cynthia's side as if he meant to watch their game and perhaps advise her.

'Another time,' Phipps said and smiled at her, making Amanda's heart leap for joy. Even though she'd been hurt earlier, she was powerless in the face of that smile.

Approaching the table, Amanda took her seat and looked across the table at her partner, suddenly realising that she would not find it so boring after all. Phipps sat to her right and Cynthia to her left, Shearne and two other gentlemen lounging against the wall and making comments as the players settled down to cut the cards.

No, she thought, it might be a pleasant enough evening after all and smiled inwardly as she saw that the marquis was not having things all his own way. Cynthia might enjoy his flattery, but she had more sense than to exclude her former suitors, and since Phipps was her partner he received his fair share of smiles and warm looks, especially as they took trick after trick.

Lord Johnston was not a competent player at all; indeed, he made so many foolish discards that Amanda was hard put to hold her tongue. However, she managed it and by the time the party was about to break up received a look of understanding from Phipps that quite restored her mood of despair.

'We shall see you in two days,' the marquis said, taking his leave of Miss Langton, though he hardly bothered to glance at Amanda.

Phipps took her hand and bowed over it, giving her another of his devastating smiles. 'Please forgive the tedious evening you have endured, Miss

Hamilton. I truly believe you have the patience of a saint.'

'Oh, do not say so,' she murmured and blushed. 'I was able to observe the skill of your play, sir, and that was entertainment enough.'

'You must be my partner another evening,' he said, pressed her hand and departed, leaving Amanda to sigh and wish for a future she knew was quite impossible.

Why could she not be tall and willowy like her friend Miss Langton? Just another two inches in height would have made all the difference. But she was being a fool, for did the Bible not say that a woman should be judged by her heart and not dwell on her vanity—or some such thing? Her vicar at home was fond of preaching on the evils of vanity and indeed it had never occurred to Amanda to worry about her looks until she came to London and was taken up by Miss Langton. She was a fool to long for her friend's looks, just because she feared that the man she wanted was preparing to ask Miss Langton to wed him.

In two weeks Papa would think of returning home. Mama would be disappointed that her daughter had not accepted an offer of marriage, for she had not spoken of those she'd dismissed without a thought—but Papa would not mind. Amanda believed that her darling father would not mind if his daughter never left home.

Chapter Two

The following morning Amanda received a note from Lady Langton to tell her that Cynthia had a sore throat and would not be able to keep an appointment to walk with her that afternoon. Amanda immediately wrote to sympathise, promising that she would call another day and enquire after her friend's health.

'Since you are free for one afternoon, you might like to come visiting with me,' Mama said, arching her brows. 'Your time has been so occupied with Miss Langton that we've hardly been out on our own for an age.'

'Yes, I should like that, Mama,' Amanda said. 'I do hope that Miss Langton will be well enough for the picnic on Friday, for everyone would be disappointed if she were to cry off.'

'Yes, though I see no need for you to disappoint

anyone and I am certain Jane Field will be looking forward to it.'

'Yes, of course I shall go,' Amanda said, 'though I fear some people will think it a waste of time if Cynthia is not there.'

'I dare say some gentlemen would think exactly that, but others would be quite content with their company.' Her mama smiled at her. 'Lord Johnston likes you very well, my dear—and Lieutenant Phipps has been attentive, I think?'

'Oh, Mama...' Amanda sighed '...Lieutenant Phipps will not offer for me—and I should refuse Lord Johnston for I should not be happy as his wife.'

'You must not be too particular,' Mama said and looked sad. 'It is unwise to give one's heart until one is married—that way one does not have it broken.'

'Do you believe that love comes to order, Mama?'

'Certainly, if one schools one's mind to it, at least affection,' she replied and patted Amanda's hand. 'Do not fret. Neither your papa nor I wish to force you to marry anyone you don't like. You may discover a gentleman you could marry sooner than you think...'

Amanda accepted her mother's suggestion, though she thought it fanciful, for she knew her heart to be given irrevocably. However, she would wish to marry in time and perhaps someone would appear magically who would make her forget her love for the handsome lieutenant.

She spent the morning going through her wardrobe, for it was surprising how many pairs of silk stockings were needed on an extensive visit to town and she had already worn out two pairs of dancing slippers. She had one new pair of long white gloves, but judged she might well need another before they left for the country. It would be better to make any purchases she might need in the near future, rather than sending for them when they were at home again, and made out a list of shopping.

By the time she'd finished her calculations, it was time for a light nuncheon, then Mama called for her carriage. Dressing in a gown of light peach with white-kid boots, short lace gloves and a white shawl, Amanda discovered that the gown was a little loose around the waist. Since it was the first time she'd worn the dress, she realised that the seamstress had made an allowance for her to put on weight. No doubt the lady understood that attending so many parties caused one to expand.

It was not loose enough to return it, but she would have to ask her maid to make a small adjustment before she wore it another day. The slight annoyance was not enough to spoil her day, for she tied her sash a little tighter and glanced in the mirror. She looked her best, even though she could not compare to the beautiful Miss Langton.

She went downstairs to join her mama and soon they were bowling along in the direction of one of the most fashionable squares. Mama seemed happy to have her daughter's company and talked of all the enjoyable times they had had since they came to London. Just as the carriage drew to a halt, she gave Amanda a look of approval.

'That gown suits you, dearest. I have not seen you looking so well in an age. The air of London must suit you.'

Amanda groaned, for when people said she looked well it was usually because she was plump in the cheeks, which some elderly gentlemen actually seemed to admire—at least, they enjoyed pinching them.

'Thank you, Mama,' she said and followed her

mother from the carriage, not forgetting to smile at the groom who assisted first Mama and then Amanda down.

She murmured a 'thank you' in a soft voice Mama could not hear, because it was not really done to thank servants for every service. People of consequence accepted instant obedience as their right, but Amanda felt grateful for kindness shown her from any direction.

They were admitted to the house by a very correct butler who said they were expected and bowed them into a charming sitting room. A lady was sitting by the fire, a light blanket thrown over her legs. Her smile was welcoming and, as Amanda looked into her face, she saw that she had once been beautiful, but there was a fragility and vulnerability about her that immediately touched her.

'Horatia, my dear friend,' she greeted Mama warmly. 'You have brought your daughter to see me, as you promised.'

'Susanna dearest.' Mama bent to kiss her cheek. 'I was surprised to hear you were in town. It is such an age since we met and I am delighted to see you again.'

'As I am to see you,' the lady said and turned

her soft blue eyes on Amanda. 'Forgive me, I cannot get up to greet you, dear child. Pray come and give me a kiss.'

'Yes, ma'am.' Amanda moved forward willingly. 'I am pleased to meet you.'

'Susanna is married to the Earl of Sandown,' Mama told her. 'We were brought out together and she is my very dearest friend—though we have not seen each other since just after…'

'I had an unfortunate accident when out riding,' Susanna said to Amanda. 'It robbed me of the power of my legs, as you see—but in all other aspects I do very well. My son is so good to me. When I said I should like to visit London, he moved heaven and earth to bring me here.'

'How long do you stay?' Mama asked.

'Oh, for three weeks or so if I keep well and there is no reason why I should not. Nathan fusses over me, but I am determined to see as many old friends as I can—though in most cases they will have to come to me. I am able to drive out in the park, or to sit at the table when we give a dinner, but I fear that it would be too much trouble to inflict on a hostess if I were to attend a ball, for I must be carried everywhere in my chair.'

'Now, Mama,' a strong voice spoke from the doorway. 'You know most of your friends would not consider that the least trouble…and if you will only allow them they will make all the necessary arrangements for your comfort.'

Amanda turned to look at the man who had spoken. At first glance she did not think him handsome, for he was of a dark complexion with heavy brows, black hair that was brushed back from his temples and a rather long nose. However, as he bent over his mother's hand, his smile transformed him. Most would undoubtedly think him handsome, though something made Amanda remain a little aloof.

'Will you not introduce me to your delightful company?' His eyes flicked to Mama and then to Amanda.

'This is Lady Hamilton and her daughter Amanda, dearest. You have heard me speak of Horatia many times, I think.' Susanna smiled at him lovingly. 'My son Nathan—you see what a scold he is!'

'I have heard so much about you,' Mama said, looking at him with interest. 'I am sure you speak the truth, Lord Armstrong. I should be happy to make any arrangements necessary to have my dear Susanna at Amanda's dance next week. It will be our last engagement in town, for after that we must think of returning home.'

'Oh, surely not so soon?' Lord Armstrong said, coming to take Mama's hand and bow over it before turning to Amanda. 'Miss Hamilton, I am delighted to meet you.'

Amanda smiled up at him, for he was tall and she barely reached his shoulder. 'As we are to meet you, sir. We have been in town for a month now, you know, and Papa took the house for six weeks, so I fear we shall have to leave at the end of that period.'

'Not at all,' he said. 'This house is far too large for the two of us. You must stay with us after the lease of your present house has expired. Mama must not be deprived of your company too soon.'

'Nathan, my love. You may command me, but you must not marshal our guests into manoeuvres of your making.'

'I fear Mama thinks me domineering, but indeed I am apt to see the easy route from difficult situations. Do you not think it is always best to cut to the chase, Miss Hamilton? People make heavy weather of things when if you simply ride straight at the obstacle you may clear it with ease.'

'You are a hunting man, sir,' Amanda replied with a teasing look. His manner was easy and since it was impossible to feel shy or reserved with a man who was so direct, she began to let down her guard a little. Clearly this gentleman scorned the polite conventions and meaningless compliments so loved by polite society. 'I see no reason to scold you, for if it were possible I am certain Mama would wish to stay with the countess...but I know that Papa cannot extend his stay.'

'Then I dare say Lord Hamilton is generous enough to allow us the pleasure of your company for another week or two, if I promise to see you safely home.'

'I believe he would,' Mama said, looking pleased. 'I should certainly enjoy being here with Susanna as my hostess, sir. I thank you for the invitation—and it will give Amanda another two weeks in town.'

Mama was hopeful that two further weeks would give her daughter a chance to receive a proposal she could accept and the thought brought a flush to her cheeks. She saw the countess and her mama exchange knowing glances and felt hot of a sudden; they were plotting something together, she was sure of it. Mama must have told her that she had not yet received an acceptable offer.

They stayed to take some refreshment at the countess's invitation and Lord Armstrong stayed with them for another twenty minutes, before excusing himself on a matter of business.

'Nathan is my stepson,' the countess told Amanda after he had left them. 'He was but a year old when I married his father and I am the only mother he has ever known. I gave my husband a daughter, who died in infancy, and another son. However, Charles is a delicate boy and remains in the country with his father. He is seven years old and a little naughty, but Nathan adores him, and spoils him as much as he spoils me. Had we not engaged a wonderful nurse to help dear old Nanny, we should never have left him for this trip to town.'

'You are fortunate to have Lord Armstrong,' Mama said. 'He could not be more fond of you if you were indeed his mother.'

'I am fortunate,' Susanna replied with a little smile. 'Nathan is a determined man, but kind and generous. His father has not been entirely well of later years and Nathan runs everything to do with the estate. Indeed, he has been so busy looking after us that he has had no time for his own affairs. His father wishes him to marry, but he shows no sign of being interested in any lady of his acquaintance.'

Amanda sensed an understanding between Mama and the countess, and saw a look of speculation in that lady's eyes. Was she being considered as a bride for Lord Armstrong? Perhaps the countess was here to find him a bride, though she felt sure that he knew nothing of her scheming.

When it was time to leave, Amanda thanked the countess for her hospitality and the invitation to stay with her another week or so in town and was instructed to kiss her.

'You are as lovely and charming as your mama told me,' Susanna said and patted her hand. 'I have oft wished my daughter had lived—and I should wish her to be just like you, my dear.'

Amanda thanked her and they were escorted to the door by the stately butler. Once in the carriage, Mama turned to look at her.

'Well, that was a surprise. I have so wished that I might spend more time with Susanna, but it was never possible, though I visited her at her country house soon after her accident—but since then somehow it was never thought of, though we often write to one another.'

'You have not spoken to me much of the countess, Mama.'

'Have I not?' Mama looked at her. 'I dare say I did not think the subject would interest you. At that time I thought it unlikely we should meet often.'

'I liked her—and Lord Armstrong. He is very direct, Mama.'

'Yes, almost overbearing,' Mama said thoughtfully. 'But kind—so very considerate. Some gentlemen are like that… I believe his father was much the same. Now your papa has always been so easy-going…'

'Papa is a darling,' Amanda said. 'I dare say Lord Armstrong has found it easier to organise everyone for their own good…since his mother and brother are delicate.'

'His father, too, has been unwell for a couple of years. I imagine that Nathan has had to bear more than his fair share of responsibility for some years.'

'I suppose that is why he has formed a habit of taking command.'

'Yes, indeed. He is barely three years older than your brother, Amanda, and Robert is but twenty-one…but he seems older.' Mama frowned. 'I had thought…but I see it would not do…'

Amanda glanced at Mama's profile. She looked disappointed, and Amanda guessed that she had been hoping her old friend's son might appeal to her as a husband.

'I do not dislike Lord Armstrong, Mama,' Amanda said and saw her mother's frown disappear. 'At least he is not pompous or foolish—and I think him a man one might rely on in a crisis. However, it would be presumptuous to think he might look at me. There are so many pretty girls in London. Even if he admired me, I should soon fade from his mind once he saw Miss Langton.'

'Susanna so wants him to marry a nice girl who will be content to live in the country with her and her family.'

'Yes, Mama, I realised that you had hopes, both of you, but you must have seen that it is quite ridiculous. Why would a man who might have anyone he chose look at me?'

'You may be a little plumper than I should like,' Mama said, 'but because you have been so much in Miss Langton's company you have come to think yourself unattractive, but that is not so. Indeed, I thought you looked very pretty today and I know Susanna thought the same.'

Amanda pealed with laughter. 'Oh, Mama, I do love you,' she said. 'I know you want the best for me—and I am sure that one day I shall receive an offer I can accept with equanimity, if not with ecstasy.'

'Well, there is no hurry after all,' Mama said and patted her gloved hand. 'I suppose Susanna and I must give up our dream, but that does not mean we cannot enjoy our stay with her.'

Her mother was incorrigible! Amanda believed that Mama would go to any lengths to see her well suited.

'No, of course not. I liked the countess very well,' Amanda said. 'But will Papa mind going home alone?'

'Your papa never minds if something makes me happy,' Mama said, a little smile curving her mouth. 'If I were you, dearest, I should choose an amiable man as your husband when the time comes—for I think you have too much spirit to be dominated.'

Amanda smiled and nodded, but made no reply. She was relieved that Mama was not set on a match between her and her friend's son, for she was certain such a plan was doomed to disappointment.

'I do hope Miss Langton will have recovered from her chill tomorrow,' she said. 'I shall visit her in the morning to see how she goes on.'

Lady Langton was hesitant when Amanda called the next morning, but took her into a small sitting room and made a full confession.

'We have given it out that Cynthia has a chill,' she explained, 'but the truth is much worse—she has contracted chicken pox and the rash has come out all over her this morning.'

'Oh, that is awful for her,' Amanda said. 'She will miss the picnic tomorrow—and that will disappoint several people.'

'Yes, I believe it will.' Cynthia's mother smiled complacently. 'However, it cannot be helped. I shall be taking her down to the country as soon as she is able to travel—but she does not wish it to be generally known that she has chicken pox. I know I may rely on you to keep the true reason for her illness private.'

'Yes, of course, ma'am. I should not dream of speaking of it. May I go up to see her?'

'Are you not afraid of taking the infection?'

'My brother brought it home when I was but six years old, ma'am. I am unlikely to catch it again.'

The marchioness nodded thoughtfully. 'I think her too unwell today—but perhaps you will call after the picnic to tell her of it?'

'Yes, certainly,' Amanda said and took her leave.

She was walking home with her maid when she saw someone she knew coming towards her. Lieutenant Phipps was bearing a posy of flowers and, since they were but one street from Miss Langton's house, Amanda guessed the tribute was for Cynthia.

'Miss Hamilton,' Phipps said and took his hat off to her. 'Have you been to visit Miss Langton? How is she?'

'Still quite unwell, I believe,' Amanda replied. 'I believe she will not be able to accompany us to the picnic tomorrow, sir.'

'How unfortunate for her. I hope you will not let it spoil your pleasure in the outing?'

'I had already invited Miss Field,' Amanda said. 'It would be a shame to disappoint her—and indeed, I am looking forward to it.'

'Then I shall not cry off,' Phipps said gallantly. 'I fear Shearne will be a little put out, but he can hardly cancel the affair when so many have been invited.'

'No, indeed. I am convinced that Miss Langton would not like to think that her friends had been disappointed simply because she could not attend,' Amanda said. 'Are you taking her that lovely posy? I should think it must cheer her up.'

'It is but a poor tribute,' Phipps said, looking conscious. 'But I thought it right to visit and enquire how she goes on.'

'Yes, I believe her mama must be pleased to see all Miss Langton's friends make such a gesture.' Amanda inclined her head. 'We shall see you tomorrow then, sir?'

'Of course. I shall call for you, as we had decided,' he murmured. 'I believe we shall have a pleasant day.'

Amanda agreed and they parted. She was

thoughtful as she walked home, because although the lieutenant was always charmingly polite to her, she could not bring herself to believe that he had any intention of asking her to marry him. As yet she was not sure what he intended for Cynthia—he had not given her any indication that a proposal from him was imminent. Amanda knew that her friend had received any number of flattering offers, some from determined fortune-hunters, but some from very acceptable gentlemen.

'I have not yet found the right person,' Cynthia had confided to her once, but that had been before the Marquis of Shearne had joined her court. It must be frustrating for her friend to be forced to retire to the sickroom at such a moment.

Some people found Miss Langton proud and cold, but Amanda knew that she could be charming and considerate to people she liked—it was only that she had perhaps been reared to remember her position. Amanda herself had received nothing but kindness from Cynthia and her sympathy was all with her at this time.

Amanda felt for her, because it was unlikely that the marquis would dance attendance on her in the country and Lady Langton was determined to carry her off there as soon as she was well enough.

She could only call to see her friend as soon as she was well enough and hope that her admirers would not be put off should there be a few blemishes from the illness. Amanda had one or two small scars on her body, but she did not regard them; she'd been lucky that only one tiny one had marked her face at her right temple and hoped that Cynthia would be as fortunate. She was so beautiful that she would be distressed should the illness leave her scarred, especially on her face.

'I have been so looking forward to this,' Jane Field said when she arrived at Amanda's house the following morning. 'When I heard that Miss Langton had a chill I was afraid the picnic would be called off.'

'Oh, no, I am certain it could not,' Amanda soothed her. 'Lieutenant Phipps assured me that it would go ahead—and the marquis could not disappoint so many people, of course.'

Amanda was certain she must be speaking the truth, but she could not know how close the expedition had been to being cancelled. Had Phipps

not insisted that it must go ahead when he spoke
to Shearne the previous evening, the ladies might
indeed have found themselves disappointed. However, his offer to take over the arrangements if the
marquis should feel it too much trouble reminded
that gentleman of his social duties, and to all ap-
pearances he was the gracious host when the company assembled in the park later that morning.

Phipps had arrived punctually and driven them
to meet up with Brock's carriage, and that of the
Misses Ramsden, cousins to the beautiful Miss
Langton. Lord Johnston, having taken up Lady
Hamilton, drove behind Phipps and Amanda,
looking glum, for he had hoped to drive her himself.

However, once the party had assembled and the
carriages were removed by servants, leaving the
ladies and gentlemen to enjoy their picnic, he attached himself to Amanda's side and would not
yield to any other's claims.

The gentlemen had decided on a spot close to
the river, a pretty place close to a bend where the
willows hung down to caress the water. While the
ladies sat in the shade of a tree, some of the gentlemen indulged in an impromptu game of cricket.

A stray ball chancing to fly Amanda's way, she shot up her hand and caught it, to cheers from the bowler who declared that Shearne was fairly caught and out. He glared in Amanda's direction, for she was not officially playing.

'Perhaps Miss Hamilton would care to take my place in the field since I have no aptitude for catching and she is clearly proficient.'

Amanda ignored the veiled sarcasm and got to her feet, declaring herself willing to take his place. She was used to such games, having played with her brother for years, and soon proved herself worthy, preventing the new batsman from running as often as he might have wished.

'I say, Miss Hamilton...' Major Brockley applauded her as she once again made a splendid catch and Phipps was also out '...you should play for our team at home.'

Laughing at the compliment, she shook her head and was ready to retire, but when she turned to look she saw that one of Cynthia's cousins had come forward and was claiming that she was good with a bat. The gentleman handed it over to her and then proceeded to bowl a gentle underarm ball, which was contemptuously sent flying into the river and lost.

A few groans went up, because no one had thought to bring a replacement, and the game broke up.

'It's time we had our picnic.' Lady Hamilton beckoned to them. 'Come, gentlemen, the food is ready…'

Amanda rejoined the party of ladies under the sheltering tree, as did most of the gentlemen. It was only as she reached for a small pastry that Amanda realised that Jane Field was not with the other ladies. Looking round for her, she saw that the young girl had wandered some distance from the others—and, to her dismay, Jane was not alone.

The sight of Shearne standing so close to Jane sent shivers down Amanda's spine. There was something so predatory about his manner that she feared Jane might be in danger—especially if they disappeared round the bend and were lost to sight.

She put down the pastry and was about to rise, when she saw that Major Brockley had also noticed. He looked straight at Amanda, inclined his head and set after the others instantly.

Phipps sat down next to Amanda, leaning towards her to speak softly so that only she might hear. 'Do not be alarmed, Miss Hamilton. Brock will see that your friend comes to no harm.'

'Thank you. Her mother entrusted her to our care...'

'And she ought to be safe. I fear our host is a little put out because the lady he desired to please could not come today. Miss Field would not have received a second glance had Miss Langton graced our party.'

'Miss Langton is quite unwell. Her mama thinks she may need to take her home in a few days.'

'That would be a pity,' Phipps said and raised the glass of cooled wine to his lips. 'I dare say there will be several disappointed gentlemen when they hear that she has left town.'

'Chills can be very draining...'

'Yes, indeed. I am sure...'

'I am sure Miss Langton will be pleased to receive visitors in the country when she is feeling better.'

'I imagine so. Shall you visit her?'

'Perhaps—though we intend to stay in town a week or so longer than we had planned. Mama's friend, the Countess of Sandown, has invited us to join her for a few days. Papa will go home, but Lord Armstrong will escort us home if need be.'

'Pray allow me to offer my services,' Phipps said. 'Your home is not so far distant from my own and I shall pay my father a visit in a few weeks. I could quite easily escort you there—and take you home when your visit is done.'

Amanda looked at him steadily, trying to understand what he was thinking. His attentions were more marked today—was she wrong? Was he in fact thinking of making her an offer after all and how would she answer him?

Her heart raced for a moment, then he directed his attention to Jane Field, who was walking back to them with Major Brockley by her side. There was for the moment no sign of the marquis.

'I am so sorry,' Jane said, looking flustered as she came up to them. 'I hope I have not kept anyone waiting?'

'The picnic is quite informal,' Major Brockley said kindly. 'No need for embarrassment, Miss Field.'

The company had taken little notice, interested only in the delicious food being served to them by the marquis's servants, and only Amanda seemed to be aware of the flush in the shy girl's cheeks or the fact that the marquis did not immediately come to join them.

When he did return he studiously refused to look at either Jane Field or Major Brockley, and soon after the food was devoured the company split up to stroll by the river. Jane stayed close to Amanda's side and Major Brock accompanied them, though Phipps had joined some of the other ladies and gentlemen.

It was not until they were on the way home that Jane confessed that the marquis had been a little too ardent in his attentions for her liking.

'He wanted me to walk further down the bank with him and the way he looked at me—I was ready to die,' she whispered to Amanda. 'Truly, I was afraid he meant to—to seduce me, but then Major Brock came and the marquis went off alone.'

Since Amanda had expected something of the sort, she was not surprised. She had instinctively disliked the marquis from the start and guessed that he had turned his attention to her shy friend because he was angry that Miss Langton had not come to the picnic he had arranged especially for her.

It was perhaps as well that she had not, for if he was not to be trusted Cynthia must be warned.

Chapter Three

Much to Amanda's surprise when she next went into society, she discovered that most of the ladies and gentlemen who had flocked to join her and Cynthia continued to pay her attention. She had taken Jane Field under her wing and the girl accompanied her to most of the balls, routs, card evenings, soirées and other diversions society was pleased to hold for the delight of its friends.

Only Shearne and one or two other gentlemen, who were particular admirers of Miss Langton's, had deserted to the side of another rather pretty young girl freshly come to town. Moreover, Amanda found that another gentleman of some importance had joined her court. Lord Armstrong was often to be seen at the *ton* parties, sometimes accompanied by his mama, at others alone. He invariably spent time sitting or standing next to

Amanda and danced with her at least once on every occasion, taking her into supper at one very splendid affair.

'Mama is so looking forward to your company,' he told her one evening when the countess had not appeared. 'She has been dining with friends most evenings and was too tired to come tonight—as she says, balls make her long to dance and it is a little sad only to watch when one was accounted good at something.'

'Yes, sad indeed,' Amanda agreed warmly. 'I think her very brave to attempt this visit to London, for it must be so much easier to stay at home and have everyone come to you.'

'Yes, though a little boring. Mama was a lively person until her accident.'

'I imagine so. It is unfortunate for her.'

'She does not speak of it, but is often in pain. One of her main reasons for coming was to see a doctor she had heard of who may be able to help relieve at least some of her discomfort.'

'Then I hope she has good news from him.'

'You are truly a kind girl,' Lord Armstrong said. 'As an heiress in your own right, and widely admired, you might have become spoiled or self-ish, but you retain a pleasant manner and seem to show true interest in your friends. I have noticed your kindness to Miss Field.'

'Jane is a little shy,' Amanda replied. 'I do not think I betray a secret if I tell you that she was not at first invited everywhere—but that is no longer the case. Now she has several admirers and friends of her own.'

'Due to your generosity in taking her everywhere with you, I dare say.'

'Oh...' Amanda blushed. 'Until recently, it was I who was taken everywhere in Miss Langton's train. However, she has been unwell and her mama takes her home the day after tomorrow.'

'Miss Langton is your particular friend?'

'We are good friends,' Amanda agreed. 'I shall visit her tomorrow to take my leave of her—and I believe she may wish me to visit her at her home in a few weeks.'

'After your visit with my mother, I dare say?'

'Perhaps, though I must go home first. Papa will not wish me to be lost to all sense of duty. At home there are people—cousins and friends—who will wish to hear all about my trip to town. To keep them waiting too long would be unfair. I visit some of our dependants most weeks to take them comfits and keep them company for an hour or so; Papa would think me lost to anything but pleasure if I neglected them too long.'

'As I said before, you are a generous girl—but these people will have to learn to do without you when you marry, you know.'

'Yes, of course. Mama or my cousins will take over my duties then—but if and when I marry, I shall pay proper farewell visits and so satisfy their wish to say goodbye.'

Lord Armstrong inclined his head and said no more on the subject, but he had a small smile on his lips and, when Amanda was asked to dance next, she saw him seek out Jane Field. The thought crossed her mind that if he were looking for a companion for his mama, he could not do better than Jane—but she was not certain how the girl would feel, for he was a very strong-willed man.

Amanda danced almost every dance that evening and it was not until supper that she had a chance to talk to Jane.

'Are you enjoying yourself? I saw you dancing with Lord Armstrong, Mr Pearson and Major

Brockley. I do not think you have often sat out this evening.'

'Oh, no, everyone has been so kind, especially Lord Armstrong,' Jane said. 'He admires you so much, Amanda, and talked to me of you in such tones that I think he is falling in love with you.'

'Oh, no,' Amanda denied, her cheeks heating. 'I am sure it is not so, Jane. He speaks of me because he knows we are friends. You would make him a much better wife than I should.'

'No…' Jane's cheeks went hot. 'I am sure he would not look at me. I am such a little mouse… and you are so clever and bright, and pretty too,' she added loyally.

Amanda pealed with laughter. 'Jane, you must not tell fibs! I may have a quick mind, but I am not pretty. You cannot truly think it?'

'Oh, I know that beside Miss Langton you may appear merely attractive,' Jane replied earnestly. 'She is a diamond of the first water, of course, and few ladies can compare to her. When she is not here you are as pretty as most other girls.'

'If I were not quite as plump, or a little taller, I suppose I might be thought quite attractive,'

Amanda said with devastating frankness. 'I am trying not to eat quite as much.'

'You are a little plump, but it is the style of your gowns that make it noticeable,' Jane said, looking at her thoughtfully. 'But not so fat that you look ugly or unpleasant. Besides, a lot of men prefer plump girls and find thin ones intimidating. My uncle thinks you...' Jane blushed again. 'Forgive me, Amanda, but he said you were a delightful armful. If he were ten years younger, I think he would offer for you...' She looked at Amanda awkwardly, but her doubts fled as Amanda burst into laughter.

'I am most grateful to him,' Amanda said, amusement dancing in her eyes. 'One of the nicest compliments paid me, I think, because it was honest.'

'May one share the jest?' Phipps asked, coming up to them with his friend Brock. 'You have danced with me but once this evening, Miss Hamilton. I fear I must have offended you?'

'No, indeed, you have not,' Amanda said. 'If you wish, I have the waltz after supper free?'

'I thank you. We should go now, for I think the musicians are about to start.'

Amanda had been so busy laughing and talking that she had left most of her supper untouched, but she did not regret it for she loved to dance, and since Major Brockley had once again solicited Jane's hand, she had no qualms about leaving her.

'I am getting up a little party at my country house for August,' Major Brockley said as the two couples returned to the ballroom. 'I should be happy if both you and your mama—and Miss Field—would make up part of the company, Miss Hamilton.'

'I should like to come,' Amanda replied. 'I am not certain whether I shall be at home before that—or the guest of Miss Langton.'

'Oh, Miss Langton will naturally be included,' Brock said. 'I shall send the invitations to your home. I dare say either your papa or your mama will let you know the precise details, if you are not at home.'

'Thank you, I look forward to it,' Amanda replied.

The two couples parted to take their places on the floor and the music struck up. Of all things, Amanda loved to waltz, and to do so with the man who made her heart beat faster and her feet as light as a feather was such a delight that the music was over too soon. However, Brock then solicited her hand for a country dance and Phipps partnered Miss Field.

After the set was finished, Lady Hamilton came in search of them and said it was time they left. Told of the scheme for a house party at Lord Brockley's country seat, she appeared flattered and agreed instantly that she would be delighted to bring her daughter and to chaperon Miss Field.

'We shall arrange for Jane to stay with us for two days before we come to your father's estate, sir—and that way I may chaperon them both.'

Jane was flushed with pleasure and, on the way home, thanked Lady Hamilton so many times that that lady laughed and told her she had been thanked enough.

'It is no trouble, my dear. You are a delightful girl and I am glad to see Amanda making friends that she may keep throughout her life.'

Jane afterwards contented herself with making plans for the visit. Her parents were not rich and, had she not had a generous aunt, the visit to town would not have happened. She confessed that she intended to make herself some new gowns for the promised treat, for the prices charged by London seamstresses were much too high for her pocket.

Amanda, having a generous dress allowance, felt as if she ought to offer some kind of help to her friend, but Mama intervened and spoke of Jane's talent in dressmaking.

'Did you make the gown you are wearing?' she asked.

Jane smiled and inclined her head. 'I have been asked for the name of my dressmaker several times, Lady Hamilton, but I make them all myself. Mama's maid helps me cut the patterns, but the needlework and designs are my own.'

'Amanda needs two new gowns,' Mama said. 'If you were to help her choose them, I dare say the silk we buy could be ordered in a sufficient quantity for you to make yourself a gown to match. Think how pretty that would look—the two of you in the same silk, but different styles.'

'I should love to help Amanda choose her new gowns,' Jane said, 'but I need no payment, ma'am.'

'Oh, but I think that is a lovely idea,' Amanda cried, thinking how clever Mama was. 'You could help me make some adjustments to my gowns,

Jane. I have discovered that at least three of my new dresses are too big around the waist. I think the seamstress made too much allowance…'

'No, I think you have lost some weight,' Jane corrected her. 'I have an eye for these things and you were rounder at the beginning of the Season than you are now—at least that is my observation.'

'Do you think so?' Amanda was puzzled for she had not noticed anything. 'I thought the seamstress believed I might grow into the extra size.'

'No, Jane is right,' Mama said. 'I thought you might have lost a couple of inches about your waist, my love. I dare say it is all the dancing you've been doing…but will you help us, in return for the silk, Jane?'

'Of course, if you wish it,' Jane said. 'I should like to redesign a few things for you, Amanda, if you trust my judgement.'

'You must come with us when we remove to the countess's house,' Lady Hamilton announced. 'I do not wish to see you girls parted and I know Susanna will be delighted to have you stay. You will prolong your visit to town, Jane, and then come home with us for a week or two. Unless your parents are desperate for you to return?'

'No, ma'am, they will be only too pleased for me to stay with friends for a while.'

Having arranged the future to her satisfaction, Lady Hamilton allowed the girls to talk together, closing her eyes until Coachman stopped outside Jane's aunt's house, and they took leave of one another, after arranging for Jane to accompany Amanda to the dressmaker two days hence.

Continuing their journey, Amanda's mother was silent for a moment, then, 'Do you think Major Brockley has taken a fancy to Jane, my dearest? I noticed he danced with her at least twice this evening.'

'Yes, Mama, he did,' Amanda agreed. 'However, he danced with several pretty girls twice—and with me also.'

'You *are* a pretty girl,' Mama said. 'You put yourself down too much. I have noticed that you are even more popular of late, which proves that it was not just because you went everywhere with Miss Langton.'

Amanda shook her head, laughing a little in the darkness inside the carriage. Her mama was prejudiced, of course, and Jane was always so sweet to her. Amanda's opinion of herself would always be that she had too many faults, for she did not notice the shine of her hair or see how her eyes lit up when she smiled. Obsessed by her wish to look more like Cynthia Langton, she could not think herself more than vaguely attractive. Yet she had not noticed that many gentlemen had defected and believed that her fortune had always been much sought after. Though several of the young men who had solicited her hand for a dance that evening could not be said to be in want of a fortune: of course, a dance was not an offer of marriage...

'I must call on Miss Langton in the morning,' Amanda said as the carriage came to a halt. 'I am so sorry that she is being forced to leave town. She will miss the last weeks of the Season.'

'I wish Mama would not insist that we go home,' Cynthia complained when Amanda visited her in her room the next morning. There were some red patches on her face, though they seemed to be fading, and it was unlikely she would be permanently scarred. 'It will be ages before we can go anywhere again and I hate the country.'

'Major Brockley is getting up a house party for August,' Amanda said. 'You, Jane and I have been invited—and I know Phipps is going. I dare say a lot of your admirers will be there.'

'Mama has not yet had the invitation,' Cynthia said, but she brightened up and sat forward, but then frowned. 'I dare say he will not have invited the Marquis of Shearne, though. I believe they do not much like each other.' A wistful look came to her face, as if she regretted that she would not meet the marquis at Major Brockley's house party.

'No, I believe there is an old quarrel,' Amanda said. She hesitated, wondering whether to tell her friend about Shearne's behaviour at the picnic. It seemed not quite nice to blacken the gentleman's name, and the probability that the two would not meet again before Cynthia was safely engaged or wed made her think it unnecessary.

Cynthia sighed, but cheered up as Amanda told her that Jane was going to make a new gown and had promised to help her adjust hers. She was always interested in clothes and soon the conversation passed on to a promised visit to Bath in the autumn.

'Mama says she shall take me to Bath at the end of September,' Cynthia told her, sitting forward eagerly. 'You will come with us, Amanda?

I was going to invite you to stay before, but you already have so many engagements.' She pouted. 'You must not desert me because you have so many friends.'

'Of course I shall not,' Amanda said and smiled in sympathy. 'You have more than I, I am sure. I imagine most of them have called to see how you go on and brought you small gifts?'

'A few gentlemen, yes,' Cynthia agreed, but sighed. 'I've had flowers and a book of poems, but no ladies have called—apart from my cousins, of course. You are the only one to visit me and actually sit with me, Amanda.'

Amanda was shocked, though she did not let it show. 'I suppose the young ladies are afraid of contracting your illness.'

'One or two send notes, but they do not know I have had more than a wretched chill. Mama has told no one but you, Amanda. She said you were to be trusted, but she did not want the news spread all over town.' Cynthia pleated the white linen sheet between her fingers. 'I am so miserable. I thought the marquis liked me, but apart from one posy, I have heard nothing from him.'

Amanda hesitated. Should she tell her friend

that he was a desperate flirt and not to be trusted? Yet she was already feeling low and Amanda had no wish to distress her.

'I believe he may have gone out of town,' she offered uncertainly. 'I have not seen him for a few days.'

'Oh—well, perhaps he has,' Cynthia said with a dismissive shake of her head. 'Lieutenant Phipps has sent me several lovely bouquets and a box of bonbons. He is very kind, I think.'

'Yes, he is,' Amanda said, her heart sinking a little. If Cynthia decided that she would have him, her own faint hopes would founder immediately. 'He has enquired after you several times, I believe?'

'At least twice this week and the same last week,' Cynthia said, her brow creased in thought. 'Sometimes I think I would do anything to be married and my own mistress. Mama is good to me, but she smothers me—and I have been driven to distraction these past few days. I do not know what I should have done without your visits.'

'I was happy to visit. It is such a shame that you should have caught the chicken pox at such a time when you had been enjoying your visit to town so much.'

'Mama says we shall go to Bath in September, as I told you—but it is not the same as London. If I do not find a husband soon, I must wait until next spring.'

'Oh, I should not despair,' Amanda said in a rallying tone. 'I am certain once it is known that you are out and about again, you will have visitors.'

'Do you think so?' Once again Cynthia looked wistful. 'I'm not sure people like me as much as they like you. Everyone always looks pleased when you walk into the room, while…some ladies dislike me, I think.'

'I suppose some are jealous,' Amanda admitted. 'You are very beautiful, Cynthia, and so many gentlemen choose to form a part of your court. You cannot wonder if a few girls resent you—you have both wealth and beauty.'

'As do you,' Cynthia retorted. 'You have lots of women friends, and gentlemen, too. They all genuinely like you. My aunt told me that you are now the most popular lady at all the best affairs.'

'I'm sure that isn't true,' Amanda replied. 'Most of the people I know became my acquaintances when I went everywhere with you. Had you not taken me up, I dare say I should hardly have been noticed.'

'That is what Mama says,' Cynthia said and blushed. 'I told her she is wrong. Oh, at first, perhaps, people might not notice you, but when they know you—they like you and want to be your friend.'

'How kind you are to me,' Amanda said. 'Everyone asks me how you are. I tell them you are a little pulled down by the chill, which was severe, and they all tell me to send their good wishes.'

'Matrons and friends of Mama's,' Cynthia said. 'Shearne did not ask you how I went on, did he?'

'The marquis never notices me,' Amanda said. 'To be honest, I do not much like him, Cynthia. He is a rake and I think he flirts with lots of young ladies and means no good to any of them.'

Cynthia looked away and did not answer. After a moment, she began to talk of fashions, showing Amanda a magazine her aunt had brought her.

They spent the next hour or so poring over various fashion plates and Amanda told her that Jane Field was going to help her design her new gowns.

'Jane has a real eye for style,' Amanda said. 'She thinks I would look better in a simple cut without the knots of ribbons Mama likes for me. I think I shall take her advice.'

'You always look nice to me,' Cynthia replied, a wistful expression in her eyes. 'Do not become so fond of Jane's company that you forget me.'

'I should not do that, Cynthia. You are my friend and I have so much enjoyed my visit to town— and that is very much due to your kindness in taking me up.'

'You make me ashamed,' Cynthia said, her cheeks pink. 'When I first took you up, Amanda, I did so because I thought I showed to advantage in your company.'

'Yes, I was little competition for you,' Amanda said and laughed, her eyes bright. 'I believe I re-alised that, my dear friend, but I think that after a while you came to value me for my wit, despite my lack of height and too many inches about my waist.'

'It's strange,' Cynthia replied thoughtfully. 'When one comes to know you, my dearest Amanda, one no longer notices. You were such good company, and everyone laughed and smiled when you were there.'

'As they do when you are,' Amanda reassured her. 'You are much missed, believe me.'

'Thank you for remaining my friend.' Cynthia clasped her hand emotionally. 'I know I have been proud and cold...'

'Towards some I believe you may have,' Amanda said, 'but not to me. What is this, Cynthia? You must not doubt yourself. When you are feeling more yourself, you will soon have all the friends and admirers you could wish for.'

'I believe I shall always have your friendship,' Cynthia said. 'You will come to Bath with us later in the summer?'

'We shall see each other at Lord Brockley's estate. Major Brockley is one of your admirers. I know that you will receive his invitation soon— and now I must go, for I have a fitting this afternoon.'

'How I wish that I could come with you.'

'I shall call again as soon as I am able,' Amanda promised and took her leave.

She was thoughtful as she made her way home, her maid walking silently at her side. Cynthia had ruled supreme in the drawing rooms for some weeks, but it seemed she'd had fewer visitors than might have been expected. Her lack of female friends had clearly made its mark on her and she had realised that her aloof manner had brought its own reward.

Amanda would speak to Jane and ask her to visit Cynthia. Jane had not thought she would be welcome to the proud beauty, but she would go if Amanda asked it of her—and take a little gift, which Amanda would provide.

Perhaps she ought to have told Cynthia of Shearne's behaviour to Jane, and also that the last time she'd noticed him, he'd seemed to have a new flirt. Yet she knew that her friend was feeling low in spirits and it was obvious that she liked the marquis, too much for her own good. If Amanda told her something she would not like, she might think she was being spiteful. Hopefully, she would enjoy herself at Major Brockley's house and forget him.

After spending a pleasant afternoon with Jane at the fashionable seamstress's establishment and choosing two new gowns, one in pale blue silk and the other in sea green, Amanda left feeling pleased. Jane's suggestions had seemed sensible to her and, after draping various silks against her, she felt that her new gowns would be an improvement on some that she'd had made earlier.

'Because you are so tiny, full skirts make you look dumpy, but a slim skirt would emphasise your waist, which is good, Amanda. I can alter the neckline on two of your gowns, make them fit you tighter at the waist and take off those awful ruffles at the back that make you look bigger than you are.' Jane looked at her. 'That dove-grey walking dress you tried on really suited you. I could take the fullness out of your green walking gown and then it would look the way the grey did.'

'I do not want you to spend all your time working on my gowns,' Amanda said. 'You must make your own new gowns, too—and have time for reading and walking.'

'I love to sew,' Jane told her. 'When we are in the country you may read to us as I work. I enjoy hearing you read, Amanda—you put such meaning into the words.'

Amanda was about to reply when they found their path obstructed. Looking up into the hostile face of the Marquis of Shearne, Amanda felt a chill down her spine. He was clearly brooding about something and she knew that Jane had shrunk closer to her, seeming afraid of him.

'Miss Hamilton, Miss Field,' he murmured silkily. 'What a delightful picture you make—the sparrow and the plump dove, what tasty morsels for the taking.'

Jane gasped and clutched Amanda's arm. Glancing at her face, Amanda felt a spurt of anger, for his taunt had taken all the colour and pleasure from Jane's cheeks.

'And you, sir—are you a hawk or a wolf?' she asked, her voice sharp and her eyes shooting a challenge at him. 'How dare you address us in such a manner? Whichever you see yourself, let me assure you that neither of us are yours for the taking.'

'You think not?' Shearne leered at her, a cold malice in his eyes. 'I would not be denied if I truly wished to have either of you, but to tell the truth neither is worth the trouble. I am after more enticing prey.'

'If you mean Miss Langton...I think you despicable and shall certainly inform her of your true nature, when next we meet. Perhaps I should write to her…'

His hand shot out, gripping her wrist so tightly that it was all she could do to stop from crying out. She felt a cold fear grip her as she saw hatred in his eyes and knew she had made an enemy.

'If you do not allow us to pass, I shall call for help, sir.'

'You are a sight too proud for your own good and one of these days…but you are not worth the trouble. I shall allow you to pass, but remember, if one word passes your lips concerning me to Miss Langton, I shall take my revenge.'

'You do not frighten me, sir.'

'Do I not?' For a moment the look in his eyes was so evil that Amanda felt faint, but then a gentleman crossed the road towards them and he flung her away from him. 'You are less than nothing to me—just a fat little frump—you and that mouse you take about with you.'

'We are much obliged to you, sir,' Amanda replied, holding back sharper retorts for she had already said too much. 'We shall bid you good day, sir. Come, Jane, we must not keep this…*person* dallying.' She gave him a look of disdain that was calculated to make him squirm.

Seeing the flash of fury in his eyes, Amanda wished she had not made her tone quite so insulting. She had implied that he was not a gentleman and, a little to her surprise, it seemed to have touched him on the raw.

'Think yourself fortunate that I have other business, Miss Hamilton. Had I the leisure I might take the time to teach you a lesson...'

Deciding that retreat was the better part of valour at this moment, Amanda propelled Jane past him, ignoring the temptation to tell him that nothing he could do would tempt her to spend a moment longer than necessary in his company.

'Oh, Amanda,' Jane whispered once they were safely out of reach. 'Ought you to have answered him so? I think he is a cruel man. He would delight in punishing you, if he could.'

'I do not fear that slimy creature,' Amanda said. 'Besides, I have only to tell Major Brockley what was said and he would...'

'What?' Jane looked at her curiously, but she shook her head.

'I believe the marquis to be in need of a lesson

himself,' she said. 'If I thought either of us truly in danger, I should beg Major Brockley to help, but I do not think him interested in either of us. He needs neither fortune nor wife—and if he did he would more likely look at Miss Langton than either of us. Indeed, I fear she may be in some danger...'

Amanda felt a chill at her nape. The marquis was the kind of man who would look for revenge if anyone offended him. Phipps had told her that Brock hated him and there must be a good reason for that... It might be as well to tell Phipps when she next saw him that the marquis had tried to intimidate them. However, in another ten days or so she would be leaving town and would probably never see Shearne again.

Chapter Four

Although they met at a card party and again at a dinner, with readings of poetry afterwards, Amanda did not have the opportunity to speak to Phipps privately until the morning of her own dance. He called then to bring her a posy of beautiful white rosebuds. She happened to be at the top of the stairs when he was admitted and went down to greet him and take the flowers from his own hand.

'It was so kind of you to bring me these,' she said. 'As it happens they will be perfect, for my gown this evening is pink and white. Thank you so much, sir.'

'You will save me two dances,' Phipps said with a caressing smile that made her heart jump for joy. 'You are looking very well, Miss Hamilton. Are you anticipating this evening with pleasure?'

'Yes, very much,' Amanda replied. 'I think it may be our last big engagement before we leave for the country. You know we are to stay with Lord Armstrong and the countess for another few days, but I think we shall attend only small affairs, though the countess will give two evenings of music and cards herself.'

'I hope I shall be invited?'

'I was asked who I would like to invite, sir. I gave the countess your name, also Major Brock's and Jane Field's. Jane is to stay with me after we leave town, just for a week or so…'

'I am glad you made friends with Miss Field. I think her a nice girl and Brock likes her. He was angry when Shearne frightened her, you know.'

'I meant to tell you,' Amanda said. 'We encountered him in the street a few days ago and his behaviour towards her was predatory—and to me hostile, because I'm afraid I gave him a set-down. He made what I considered a threat towards Miss Langton and I said something unwise. Indeed, I warned him that I should inform her of his true nature when I next see her—I fear I may have made an enemy of the marquis.'

'And do you intend to say anything to Miss Langton?'

'When I see her I shall attempt to warn her…but one must be careful of such things. To write hints of what I suspect in a letter would be slander.'

'No, you must not do that, for you have no proof.'

'That was my own thought, but when I see her I may hint a little. I spoke thoughtlessly, out of anger at his manner towards us, and I think it was unwise.'

'If he should do anything at all to upset you, Miss Hamilton, you have only to tell me or Brock.'

'I should not wish to cause trouble for anyone. Mama did not invite the marquis this evening—and I dare say I shall not see him again before we leave for the country.'

'I heard that he was leaving town for his estates this weekend. If he took himself off and never returned, it would not be a bad thing,' Phipps said. 'Had I known he'd upset you, I should have given him a thrashing.'

Amanda pealed with laughter. 'Please do nothing of the sort, sir. I fear you would make an enemy for life. I may have piqued his pride, but he will soon forget me—if you took a horsewhip to him he would not cease to look for his revenge.'

'I am more than a match for his ilk.'

'But I could not bear to cause harm to you...' Amanda blushed, for she had said too much and she saw his gaze narrow in thought. 'Or Major Brockley either. It would be very foolish of either of you to call him out for such a trifle.'

'Oh, Brock has his own reasons. No, I may not tell you, for it is not my secret,' Phipps said and smiled at her, warmth in his eyes. 'But if Shearne harmed you, I could not answer for his safety.' He bowed over her hand, then raised it to his lips. 'I look forward to our dances, Miss Hamilton.'

Amanda bid him a shy farewell, hardly daring to look at him lest she betray herself further. Was it her imagination, or had he grown more particular in his manner to her? She had tried not to let him or anyone else see how strong her partiality for him was, but she feared she had let the mask slip just for a moment.

Oh, well, if he had guessed her secret it could not be helped. It would either bring him up to scratch or make him retreat in good order. Amanda was not certain which she would find more painful—

to be asked to marry, because she had a fortune, or to lose all hope of the man she loved.

Phipps was thoughtful as he left Amanda's house and continued on his way to an appointment with Brock at one of the clubs they both patronised. He had from the start sensed that she liked him more than most of the gentlemen that formed her court, though of late she had shown a certain friendship towards Lord Armstrong. She tolerated Lord Johnston, but there were others she had a warm rapport with—including a couple of older gentlemen who had no need of her fortune and who, Phipps suspected, liked her very well.

Was he in fact arrogant to believe that she might accept a proposal of marriage from him? His thoughts on the matter veered from being confident to the realisation that he would be presumptuous to ask her. He had nothing to offer... nothing that a dozen other gentlemen could give her. What right had he, a second son, with no prospects to offer for a girl with all Miss Hamilton's advantages? Perhaps she wasn't as beautiful as Miss Langton, but few girls were. Phipps had noticed of late how Amanda's eyes always had the glow of laughter, a way of teasing that was vastly pleasing, and her soft curves felt rather pleasant in his arms.

The fact that she'd included Brock on her list of friends to be invited to the countess's house meant little. She was on easy terms with him, but Phipps knew that he had no intention of making her an offer. His main rivals—if he had intentions towards her—were Armstrong and Lord Johnston, but he believed he could dismiss the latter.

When she spoke of Shearne's hostility toward her, Phipps had felt oddly protective. It would take little provocation from the marquis to have him issue a challenge. Should the man actually seek to harm her…? Phipps frowned, because he did not know why he should feel that quiver down his spine, or the coldness at his neck.

He had no liking for Shearne, though the man was accepted everywhere. Had Brock chosen to reveal what he knew, Shearne would speedily find himself being ostracised by the people he claimed as friends. He was not particularly popular with the gentlemen, but he easily charmed most ladies. However, that would change if they knew what he truly was.

Brock would never betray a confidence. Phipps knew the truth only because he'd happened to be staying with his friend when the scandal was narrowly avoided. Brock had a lifelong friend, a certain Miss Mary Smith, a girl of some beauty, but very shy. She had been barely sixteen when Shearne came upon her in Lord Brockley's woods, where she had been gathering primroses on her way to visit Brock's old nurse.

What had happened then had been so shocking that it did not bear repeating, especially to a lady. The marquis had tried to seduce poor Mary with sweet words, but meeting with a firm refusal, he'd pursued her through the woods, raped and beaten her, leaving her, after his brutal attack, to lie in a state of near unconsciousness until Brock had stumbled on her some minutes later.

Mary had been unable to whisper more than a name before losing her senses. She had fallen ill, lying sick and silent in her bed for weeks. When she did leave her room, she had walked about like a wraith and a shadow of her former self. She would tell her anxious parents nothing, giving Brock only the barest details, and begging him never to reveal them to another.

Brock had given his word, while vowing to teach the marquis a lesson he would not forget. He'd tracked down his quarry and thrashed him with his whip, leaving the marquis to crawl home and lick his wounds. When he had recovered, Shearne had left England for the Continent and not been seen for some years, but the enmity between the two men was as fierce as ever. Brock had been unable to repeat the story that would have seen the marquis shunned by decent society, for the girl he protected had retired to a nunnery to live out her life in solitude and seclusion.

'That devil ruined Mary's life,' Brock had told Phipps once in a rage. 'Yet he flaunts himself in society and I can do nothing to stop him without betraying Mary's secret. If I could, I would shoot him down like the dog he is, but that would bring me down to his level. Instead of thrashing him, I ought to have challenged him to a duel—but the coward would not meet me.'

'He thought he would lose,' Phipps said. 'Yet your skill with the pistols is not as good as Jack Delsey's or mine. Would you like me to call him out for you, old fellow?'

'Had you a good reason for doing so, I should be

glad of it, for that would not involve Mary, nor yet endanger her secret,' Brock said, 'though whatever we do we cannot give Mary back her life.'

'Does that hurt you so much?'

'It hurts me that a beautiful shy creature should be so hurt that she can no longer bear to face the world,' Brock told him. 'She was as a sister to me, Phipps. It was not a romance between us, yet I loved her. Something died in me after she went into the convent. I felt that I had failed her—and I can never deserve to be happy. I should have seen Mary to her home that day, but I never expected that she would come to harm in *our* woods.'

Phipps understood his friend's guilt. It was the memory of what had happened to Mary that had made him spring to Jane's defence that day at Richmond. He had protected a girl he scarcely knew, even though it recharged the enmity between him and Shearne.

If Phipps told him of Amanda's encounter with the marquis, Brock was likely to accost the man and force a duel on him. It might be better for the moment to let sleeping dogs lie. Shearne was going out of town and by the time he returned Amanda and Jane would have left for the country…or might even be planning their weddings.

That thought brought Phipps back full circle. Did he mean to make Amanda Hamilton an offer or not?

He had given much thought to the matter in the past weeks, but was still uncertain. Phipps thought that of all the heiresses he'd met that Season, he would prefer to have Amanda as his wife than any other. She had a lively wit, a ready smile and a generous heart. Of late her popularity had been rising and Phipps had wondered if he'd let his chance of her slip. Lord Armstrong's manner towards her was quite definitely that of a suitor, perhaps because he thought her a perfect companion for his invalid mother. He might be content to marry for his mother's sake, and the hope of heirs…and yet he seemed to like her very well.

If the man were in love with Amanda, Phipps would be doing her a disservice if he proposed too soon. He liked her very much, had come to find her excellent company—and there was that odd feeling of wanting to protect her from Shearne.

What a fool he was not to know his own mind! Phipps laughed at himself, for surely it was an easy decision to make? Amanda might be a little plump, but she was in all other ways a perfect wife

for any man: an attractive smile, kind and generous to her friends. Was he so hard to please? Some
ladies became plump after bearing children—
and men sometimes took a mistress in town if it
pleased them, leaving their plain comfortable wife
in the country to care for the children.

No, he would not serve Amanda such a turn!
The idea revolted him. If he were to ask her, he
would be good to her and cause her no harm. In
Phipps's opinion, it was all very well for a single
man to keep his opera dancer, but marriage should
be for the comfort and happiness of both.

What could he offer her that would compen-
sate her for all he would gain? To be always feeling himself obliged to his wife was something
he could not quite bring himself to accept. If he
married Amanda for her money alone, he would
be a kept man—and much less a man in his own
estimation.

If there were only a way that he could be of true
value to her…

Amanda's dance was one of the last big events
of the Season. Lady Hamilton had planned it so,
hoping that by this time she could announce her

daughter's engagement, but unfortunately no one who had approached the girl's father had been accepted. It did cross her mama's mind that Amanda might have discouraged more than one suitor, but as a proper gentleman would first approach the father of the girl he wished to marry, she supposed that only fortune-hunters had made the attempt and been discouraged. Much as she would have liked to see her daughter happily married, Lady Hamilton would rather take her daughter home still unattached than see her fall for a rogue.

When Amanda emerged from her room that evening, Lady Hamilton was a little surprised to see how well the girl looked. Wearing a gown of white silk with an overdress of pink gauze, a band of pale pink embroidered with red rosebuds about her waist, and puffed sleeves, she looked rather pretty, thought the fond mother. Several unnecessary knots of ribbons had been removed from the skirt and Amanda's hair had been swept into a cluster of curls at the back of her head, held by pearl pins to match the bracelet about her wrist and her eardrops. The curls were a new style suggested by Miss Field and suited Amanda well for they made her neck look longer.

Was she imagining it, or did her daughter appear slimmer than she had been before they came to London? Lady Hamilton could not be sure, but something had improved Amanda's looks; her skin looked clearer and her eyes shone, and her mama was grateful for it. Perhaps that young man the girl liked too much for her own good might speak this evening? He really was a very provoking man, for if he did not mean to speak, why was he always at Amanda's side, paying her very flattering attention?

Lady Hamilton wondered if she ought to have given Lieutenant Phipps a nudge before now. She had thought about it, for she was well aware of the reason for Amanda's attraction to many of the young gentlemen and Phipps was but a second son. Amanda's fortune was not to be sneezed at, and if he were hanging out for an heiress why not her own obliging daughter?

Compared to the beautiful Miss Langton, even a doting mama could not think Amanda much of a lure, but the beauty had retired from the fray for this Season. There were other heiresses, of course, but none with quite such a large fortune, and Lady Hamilton had truly expected to find herself planning her daughter's wedding before the summer was out.

However, she had given her daughter no hint of her frustration and went to her with a smile of welcome on her lips, kissing her cheeks and exclaiming over her scent.

'What a lovely fragrance, dearest! Is it a new perfume?'

'Yes, Mama. Jane and I discovered it when we were shopping and I decided to purchase it.'

Mama nodded her approval. 'I think Jane has benefited from your friendship, dearest, but she has certainly been a help to you, too.'

'I have become very fond of her,' Amanda said. 'She is always so shy in company, but when we are together she is so bright—and her taste is excellent. This dress never fitted me so well or looked so good. I should have sent it back to the seamstress to be altered, for it looked too fussy and the bodice never fit properly, but Jane saw just what it needed.'

'Well, it certainly becomes you now, my love,' Mama said. 'I feel proud of you this evening, Amanda. I do not think I have ever seen you look better.' She glanced at the posy her daughter carried. 'Are those the roses Lieutenant Phipps brought for you?'

'Yes, Mama. Was it not lucky that they matched my gown? I have had as many as twelve floral tributes today, but these are my favourites.'

'Yes, I know,' Mama said, perfectly understanding why equally lovely tributes had been set aside in favour of this simple posy. 'Well, it is time to greet our guests. Are you ready?'

Amanda said she was and they went to the head of the impressive staircase to join Lord Hamilton and prepare to greet their guests.

Amanda was conscious of how very kind people were to her that night. Her gown was admired, and she was asked who had made it for her, but her hairstyle was much remarked on.

'I declare I should not have known you, so elegant as you appear,' one matron said a little rudely. 'You are much in looks tonight, Miss Hamilton.'

Amanda smiled and made a slight curtsy to thank her, but other ladies were kinder and told her that she looked both elegant and pretty. Some of the gentlemen went further and made her the kind of compliments she had been used to hearing Cynthia receive, but, realising that Jane's cleverness in altering the gown to flatter had made the difference, Amanda merely smiled. Since she knew she was not beautiful, it was clearly the gown that had made the difference. She wished that she might place the credit where it belonged, but to do so would embarrass her friend, for the girl would not wish it known how clever she was with her needle.

However, when Jane arrived Mama released her to take her friend into the reception rooms, though she herself remained at the head of the stairs to receive the latecomers.

'You do look lovely,' Jane whispered to her. 'I'm glad you decided to sweep your hair up in that way; it is so elegant.'

'I *have* been told I look elegant this evening,' Amanda replied with a laugh. 'That is to your credit, Jane. Had I been able, I could have sent you a dozen ladies eager for your services tonight.'

'I have often thought I might become a stylish dressmaker,' Jane said, looking thoughtful. 'For I shall not have another chance to visit London and I dare say I shall not marry—unless I take old Colonel Ruston, and he is too stout and too pompous for me to care for him as I ought if we were to marry. I feel as if I should be a nurse before ever I was a wife.'

'Yes, you *shall* come to town again,' Amanda said generously. 'I will ask Mama to bring you next year, if we come, and, if I should marry before that, you shall be my guest. In any case, we are sure to visit Bath before then and you shall come with us there, too. It is my hope that we shall see each often in future, dear Jane.'

Jane squeezed her arm gently. 'You have been so kind to me. Oh, do look, Lieutenant Phipps and Major Brockley are coming this way.'

'Yes, I see them,' Amanda said. 'Is he not handsome?'

'They are both handsome,' Jane said and giggled. 'You meant Lieutenant Phipps, of course.'

'Yes, I confess I did. Major Brockley is a little too stern for my taste, though when he smiles— then he is handsome, too.'

'He can be very kind and has been to me,' Jane said with a little blush.

The two gentlemen came up to them, their mission to secure dances. Phipps asked Amanda which waltzes she had allotted him and was told the first and the last. He smiled and thanked her, then solicited Jane's hand for the next set of country dances. Brock asked Jane for a waltz and a country dance later and then enquired if Amanda would stand up with him. She gave him her card and he wrote in his name against the second waltz of the evening.

'Who have you chosen to open the dancing with?' he asked.

'Papa,' Amanda said and smiled as her father came towards her. 'Here he is now... I think that means the dancing is about to begin.'

'Do not forget my dances,' Phipps said and offered his arm to Jane, following Amanda and her father into the ballroom.

The musicians struck up a tune and Lord Hamilton led his daughter on to the floor as the couples began to form lines.

'You look happy and quite lovely, my dear,' Papa told her. 'I was saying to your mother earlier that this visit has done you a great deal of good, Amanda. I like to see my daughter with so many charming friends about her. I must say that until this evening I had not quite understood how popular you have become. I have been complimented on your manners more times than I can count. Your mother may wish you had more beauty, but I am content to know that you have a beautiful nature.'

'Oh, Papa,' Amanda said and trilled with laughter. 'I shall never be vain while I have you to guide me.'

He looked bewildered and then gave a great guffaw of laughter. 'I did not mean that you were not well enough in looks, my love. You have always been beautiful to me.'

'I know that, my very dear Papa,' Amanda said. 'You have spoiled me from the moment I was born.'

'And why not, pray?' He gazed down at her indulgently. 'I shall be sorry when you marry, for the house always has sunshine in it when you are at home.'

'I do not think you need to worry just yet, Papa.'

'I am not so sure. Three gentlemen have already asked to call on me before I leave town. Since all are young men, I cannot think they have such fondness for my company that they need beg me for an interview—unless they have good reason.'

'No, Papa!' Amanda stared in astonishment.

'No one has spoken to me...well, no one you would have granted the time of day and I sent *them* packing.'

'These gentlemen are not fortune-hunters,' Papa told her with a warm smile. 'However, we shall talk of this later. I dare say I may have further news before the evening is out.' He looked so pleased with himself that she was hard put to it not to giggle. 'I'm sure I never expected to find myself so much in demand!'

Amanda was silent for she had not expected anything of the sort. Papa's words had taken her by surprise and she longed to ask if one of the gentlemen was Phipps, but dared not. For a moment she was so distracted that she almost missed her step, but then recovered. Papa might be mistaken and the gentlemen had something other than marriage on their minds.

After Papa conducted her back to the spot where the matrons had gathered to watch the proceedings and gossip, Amanda had no more time to speculate. All the gentlemen she knew as friends gathered about her to ask for dances, as well as several with whom she was only slightly acquainted. It was her dance, of course, and accounted for the sudden surge in her popularity.

Having been swept into one of the country dances that were universally liked, Amanda did not speak to Jane again until the interval when they both found seats and waited for their chosen partners to bring them cooling drinks and ices.

'Are you enjoying yourself, Jane?' Amanda asked her. 'Did I not see you dance twice with Lord Armstrong?'

'Yes, I did,' Jane said. 'I danced the first waltz with him—and then a promenade later.' She smiled. 'You have danced every dance, Amanda— and you looked so happy, especially when you waltzed with Lieutenant Phipps.'

'He is a wonderful dancer and particularly good at waltzing,' Amanda replied. 'Besides, he is so considerate of his partners. Did you not think so when you danced with him?'

'I like him very well,' Jane admitted. 'Of course, he only asked me because I am your friend, Amanda. Indeed, several people ask me because they think I have influence with you.'

'You have, but I am sure that most—the sensible ones—ask you for yourself. Major Brockley would not ask you because he thought you had influence with me. He likes you, Jane. I am sure he does.'

'Yes, perhaps,' Jane admitted, her cheeks pink. 'Oh, they are starting up the music again. Shall we take supper together?'

'Yes, of course. Enjoy yourself...'

Neither girl had time to speak again until they were taken into supper. Jane was on Brock's arm and Amanda had promised Phipps that pleasure— or perhaps, she corrected herself mentally, she had promised the pleasure to herself.

However, the four of them were not left long to their intimate circle for five other gentlemen and three ladies gravitated to their table, and the men were forced to draw up more chairs.

'Miss Hamilton,' Lord Johnston murmured, sitting as close to her as he could manage. 'I must tell you, I have Lord Hamilton's promise that I may call on him tomorrow.'

'Oh...' Amanda determinedly kept her smile in place, though her heart sank. She knew well enough that her father was about to receive an offer for her hand from Lord Johnston, despite all her efforts to prevent him coming to the point. It would mean an embarrassing interview for she must out of politeness do him the honour of refusing in person. 'Yes, I see, sir. I must thank you for your kindness...'

'Indeed, any other young lady would have guessed long ago that I meant to ask for her,' he said. 'Your modesty is one of the things I particularly like in you. But we shall not speak of this again until I have spoken to your father.'

Amanda thanked heaven for his manners, which would not allow him to speak to her more openly until he had formally offered for her to her father. She prayed fervently that his was not the only offer Papa would receive for she was determined to decline it and did not wish to cause offence or disappointment to her family.

'Miss Hamilton.' Phipps came to her rescue almost immediately. 'I believe it is our dance next. Shall we return to the ballroom?'

'Yes, I thank you, sir,' she replied and stood up, once again leaving her supper almost untouched. Since she'd eaten only a bite of one little pastry, she was surprised to discover that she was not in the least hungry, even though she had eaten nothing since nibbling on an apple and a slice of bread and butter for luncheon.

'What did Johnston say to you?' Phipps asked as he took Amanda's hand and led her to the dance floor. 'Did he distress you?'

'Only a very little,' Amanda murmured, her cheeks warm. She hesitated, then decided that this was the time for speaking out. 'It was nothing… only that he—he means to speak to Papa for me.'

Phipps glanced at her, a hint of alarm in his eyes, which made Amanda's heart jump. 'Is he likely to succeed?' he asked.

'No, not at all,' she said faintly, hardly knowing where to look. Her behaviour in provoking this outspoken remark was really quite shameless. 'I should not wish it.'

'I am glad,' Phipps murmured, in a husky voice that set her spine tingling. 'I had hoped to speak to your father before he leaves town myself.'

Amanda's eyes flew to his and she knew that he must see her question. Indeed, it was imperative that she forced him to answer, for her happiness depended upon it. 'Is it truly your intention to…to ask Papa…?'

'It is,' he replied a little awkwardly. 'I have been slow, but I was not sure that I had the right... I have little to offer...'

'You have everything to offer,' she replied impulsively, then, as a fiery blush rose in her cheeks, 'if you truly want to...?'

Phipps laughed down at her and her heart caught. 'I should not have spoken if I did not,' he replied. 'I have been tardy only for your sake, Amanda.'

'Oh...' She breathed and was lost for words. 'I thought... I hoped... But...'

'I wish I might take you off somewhere so that we might be alone,' Phipps said, a hint of frustration in his voice. 'But I know that you are engaged for every dance.'

'Yes, I am,' Amanda said and she might have swooned for sheer happiness had she been the kind of girl inclined to such fancies. 'You have said enough for now, sir. We have an understanding. Speak to Papa at the end of this dance and I shall expect you tomorrow.'

'Amanda...' Phipps seemed as if he could hardly contain himself. 'You know I... But, no, I shall speak to you tomorrow, my very dear Amanda.'

The music was drawing to a close. Amanda felt his hand clasp hers in what she could not but feel was an intimate gesture and which was accompanied by a look that made her want to melt into a puddle of pure pleasure.

When Phipps released her to her next partner, she knew a violent wish that he would cast convention to the winds and sweep her off to a private room where he could embrace her and tell her everything she wished to hear, but it would not do, of course. He was a complete gentleman and that was one of the things she so admired about him. Only a violent passion on his part could have prompted such action and Amanda was not so lost to dreams that she had forgot the likely reason behind his sudden declaration.

He was asking for her hand, but she could not expect him to love her, as she loved him. The thought swathed through her with a slash of pain that almost caused her to cry out, but she resolutely controlled it.

Phipps was her friend. Amanda knew that she could rely on both his friend Brock and Phipps if she needed help, but she had not seen any sign of warmer feeling than friendship on his part. Indeed, she knew that she had deliberately prompted him, urged on by a sudden need to provoke him into speaking. She felt a little prick of guilt, but banished it immediately. Had he not been intending to speak, he would not have reacted as he had.

It would be fatal to allow herself to doubt the wisdom of making a marriage of convenience—for that was what it must be on his part, Amanda knew. Yet many people found happiness in such a marriage, and she believed she could—if she were sensible.

Banishing both her doubts and her surging excitement to the backwaters of her mind, Amanda gave herself up to the enjoyment of the dance and smiled sweetly at her partner, who happened to be a young subaltern on leave from the Army.

'I say, Miss Hamilton,' he confided to her. 'I was told you was a bit stuffy, but I think you a jolly decent girl, and I'm glad I came this evening even though he said I should find it a bore.'

'Oh, dear.' Amanda could not help laughing up at him, for he was a rather shy young man with ginger hair that stuck out at all angles and a freckled complexion. 'Who did I upset, sir? I must have done so for I am not generally thought stuffy, I believe.'

'Oh...' A blush rose up his neck. 'I think he was put out because he did not receive an invitation... He is a cousin of mine, you see. Shearne...'

His awkward confession betrayed his youth for he should never have told her. Amanda felt coldness at her nape, because she knew that she had made an enemy out of the marquis. Mama had decided not to invite him, partly because they already had so many guests that the house could not hold any more and partly because of his unsavoury reputation. He had the entrée almost everywhere, though a few of the high sticklers steadfastly refused to receive him. Papa had told Mama something that made her take against the marquis, though she would not repeat it to Amanda for she said it was shocking.

'I see...' Amanda was a little uncertain. 'Yes, the marquis and I are not friends, for he distressed a friend of mine, you see.'

'Yes, I do see,' her partner replied. 'I should not have mentioned him, Miss Hamilton; he is a shockingly loose screw, to own the truth, and Mama does not care for him. Though she is obliged to acknowledge him, she warned me not to trust him.'

'Well, no harm done,' she said and forced herself to smile again. 'When do you return to your unit, sir?'

'Next week,' he said. 'Mama is holding a dance herself next week—just a small affair, nothing on this scale. I suppose it is too late to invite you and Lady Hamilton?'

'We are committed to friends all next week and then I fear we leave town,' Amanda told him. 'Why do you not ask Miss Field? Have you met her?'

'I'm not sure,' he replied. 'Perhaps you would introduce me?'

Amanda promised she would and when their dance was ended, she took him to meet Jane, who had just returned from dancing with Lord Johnston.

Glancing round the room as she waited for her next partner to arrive, she saw that Phipps was talking with Papa and, to her relief, they seemed to be getting on well.

The next set of dances was the last of the evening; Lord Armstrong, who had written his name in the space on her card, arrived to claim her. He smiled down at her as he led her into the set of lively young people who were still eager to dance.

'I think you may say that your dance has been one of the most successful this Season, Miss Hamilton.'

'Oh, do you say so?' Amanda glanced up at him. 'How kind you are, my lord. I have seen rooms more crowded than this, I do assure you. Mama invited only those people she thought our friends so that it should not be too much of a crush. I think that perhaps some of them brought guests of their own, for I had not thought we possessed so many acquaintances.'

'My mother was sad to miss your dance, but she has some friends to dine this evening, you know. Small intimate gatherings are more to her taste these days, though at home we entertain more than forty families at Christmas, for the great hall is large enough to accommodate them. Mama has nothing to do but sit and be a queen amongst us.'

'Do you have a very old house, sir?'

'Yes, positively medieval and boasts a priest hole and secret passage, perhaps a ghost—though

I have not seen it. Very uncomfortable parts of it can be in the winter, too,' he said with a laugh. 'However, the family rooms are more modern and the chimneys do not smoke so we can be cosy on chilly evenings.'

'I love to visit old houses for they are full of nooks and crannies,' Amanda replied. 'But I do not think I should care to live in one—unless part of it had been modernised. Secret rooms and gloomy passages are very well within the pages of a Gothic novel, but less so in reality, I believe.'

'You are not a romantic, Miss Hamilton?' He sounded a little disappointed, which made her smile inwardly. Had he thought his description of his home and a possible ghost would make her shiver with anticipation and delight?

'No, I fear I am much too sensible—even prosaic,' she said and sighed. 'I do envy girls who can faint at the sight of blood and cry to order.'

'Why should you envy anyone? It seems to me that, as popular as you are, you have no need to regret your lack of these things.'

'No, and that was a foolish thing to say,' Amanda admitted. 'It was thinking of those foolish novels that are so much the rage these days that made me say it.'

He laughed and shook his head, but seemed reflective, as the dance demanded that they pass on to another partner. By the time the elaborate set of steps had been executed and Amanda once more found herself with his large hand clasped about hers, he had changed his manner once more and was full of a titbit of gossip he had heard about the Regent's wife.

When the musicians had put down their instruments there was a general move to fetch cloaks and greatcoats. Waiters circulated with cups of a warming nightcap to see the guests on their way.

Amanda went to stand by her mother and wish her guests a safe journey home and hope they had enjoyed the evening. As it was a fine night and no one had far to go, most people had stayed to the very end and seemed reluctant to leave.

Phipps and Brock were amongst the last. Brock was talking with Miss Field, who was to stay the night and go home in the morning. Phipps made his bow to Lady Hamilton and thanked her for a wonderful evening, then drew Amanda a little aside.

'I have spoken to your papa,' he said softly. 'I am to see him at ten tomorrow. I shall be the first of five gentlemen who have sought appointments, Amanda. Will you see me afterwards, if your father permits?'

'Of course,' she said and gave him her hands. 'Papa would never refuse me, Phipps. He has always spoiled me.'

'Then I shall see you tomorrow,' he said and raised her hand to his lips, kissing it softly. 'Goodnight, my dearest.'

Amanda bid him goodnight. She stood, feeling a glow of happiness spread through her as the last of their guests departed, and then Mama turned to her and kissed her cheek.

'Papa has told me he has promised Lieutenant Phipps an interview in the morning—has he spoken to you, Amanda?'

'He—he has said enough to lead me to understand he means to ask for my hand, if Papa admits.'

'And is it your wish that he should?'

'Yes, please, Mama.'

Mama smiled at her. 'I thought so. I am glad he has spoken at last, dearest. Take Jane up now and try to get some sleep, for you would wish to be at your best in the morning.'

Chapter Five

Well, the die was cast and Phipps did not regret it. He had dallied long enough and was pleased that he had decided to speak, though, in truth, he had not intended it until he realised that something had changed. If pressed, Phipps could not have said what was different, but he had been aware from the first that several gentleman had cast interested glances at their hosts' daughter that evening. Amanda was certainly looking very well, but then, he'd always thought her an attractive girl, if a little plumper than he normally admired. However, for a long time he'd found her excellent company, charming, witty when she chose and genuinely kind-hearted.

Realising from a chance remark that Lord Johnston meant to ask for her—and to be told later that four other gentlemen were bent on the same mission—Phipps had been spurred on. His unguarded words to Amanda had been an impulse, but having spoken he discovered that he was satisfied with the bargain he'd made, perhaps more so than he'd expected to be. Lord Hamilton had told him in an open, frank manner that his was not the only offer his daughter might expect, but was surprisingly welcoming. Whether he would feel the same once he knew the exact nature of Phipps's circumstances remained to be seen. It was certain that at least one of the offers made would be of a more substantial nature than Phipps could hope to make. Amanda was sure her father would oblige her, but he could only hope that she was not mistaken in his indulgence of her wishes.

Walking home with Brock, he was inclined to be thoughtful and discovered that his friend was also in a reflective mood. He offered Brock a bed for the night, but was refused and they parted on good terms, Phipps to seek his own bed and Brock to walk the silent streets for longer than Phipps guessed he intended.

It was a little after seven the following morning and Phipps was just thinking of calling for his shaving water when the knocker sounded urgently. He left his bed and had just put on a rather splendid crimson-and-black-striped silk dressing gown when a footman knocked and entered.

'Yes, Hardy, what is it?'

'A message, my lord. Major Brockley was attacked last evening as he walked home. As I understand it, an attempt was made on his life.'

'Good grief!' Phipps was stunned for a moment, then, 'He lives?'

'Yes, indeed, sir. His message was to tell you that he has a wound to his left shoulder and is bidden to keep to his bed this day, but is in no danger. He would like you to call on him at your convenience for he has something of import to tell you.'

'I shall certainly do so later,' Phipps replied, frowning. 'Send a message back. Tell Major Brockley that I have an appointment this morning at ten, but I shall wait on him no later than noon.'

'Yes, sir. The messenger waits. I shall give him your answer at once.'

'Thank you—and send up my man. I shall shave and dress immediately, then come down for breakfast.'

Phipps was thoughtful after the man left him.

The streets of London could be unsafe late at night, for there were footpads and young fools on a wild spree after a night spent drinking and gambling. However, Brock was no unwary pigeon for the plucking and for him to fall prey to one of these persons was odd…indeed, it sounded as if Brock thought it more than an attempt to rob him.

He almost wished that he had gone to his friend's side at once, but if Brock's message had been urgent he would have said as much. Brock merely wanted to apprise him of what had happened and to speak to him later.

He took his time shaving and preparing for his interview that morning, making a light breakfast of some ale, cold beef and fresh bread, and then changed from his dressing gown into a pair of pale dove pantaloons, a dark grey coat that fitted him like a second skin and a pair of gleaming Hessians with silver tassels. After pinning a diamond into the snowy folds of his neckcloth, he saw that it wanted but half an hour to his appointment. Just time for him to walk there.

Phipps was aware of nerves in the pit of his stomach as he strolled towards Lord Hamilton's town house. His own family was of equal lineage, to be sure, but his fortune, as a second son, could not compare with Amanda's. He would not be able to afford to keep his future wife in the manner she was accustomed to and felt his position keenly, for it would be within Hamilton's rights to send him smartly about his business.

Once again, Phipps was assailed by his doubts. What right had he to ask for a girl whose fortune was so far above his, though he was her equal in birth if not in consequence? He wished he might at least have had a promising future, but although a brave and sometimes reckless soldier, he had few talents to help him make a fortune.

Phipps was a modest man and perhaps not aware that his manners, caring attitude and genuine goodwill made him universally popular. Had he received more of his father's approval and affection, he might have realised that he could look as high as he pleased for a wife, because there were many young ladies in society who would have been glad of his interest.

Feeling his neckcloth unaccountably tight, he arrived outside Amanda's home and was assailed by a craven urge to take flight. However, he knew that she was expecting him and gathered his courage, raising his hand to knock sharply once. The door was opened almost instantly and the stately butler, who had been in evidence the previous evening, admitted him.

'Good day, Lieutenant Phipps,' Craddick said pleasantly. 'His lordship is expecting you. I shall take you up to him.'

'Thank you,' Phipps replied and cleared his throat nervously. He was vaguely aware that the hall contained rather more servants than usual at this time in the morning and heard a woman's laughter. However, he retained a dignified manner and refused to look for the source of the mirth. No doubt Lord Hamilton's servants were aware that this was an important day for the daughter of the house.

Craddick conducted him up the magnificent staircase and then led him to the far end of the passage, before knocking on a door and opening it to announce him.

Phipps entered, feeling rather like the condemned man on his way to the hangman's noose, but when his host looked up from a letter he had been studying, he saw that there was only welcome in the gentleman's eyes.

'Do sit down, sir,' he invited.

'I think I should stand for the moment, my lord.'

'Well, please yourself. You asked for an interview, Phipps?'

'I wanted to ask…for the honour of Miss Hamilton's hand in marriage.' Phipps blurted the words out, forgetting the speech he'd meant to make. 'I know she is far above me in fortune, but I care for her deeply and I hope to make her happy.'

'Yes, I'm sure you do,' the doting father said and beamed at him. 'I understand you are the second son of your father and entitled only to a younger son's portion?'

'Yes, sir.' Phipps surreptitiously tugged at his neckcloth, which was somehow much tighter than before. 'I have a small estate that is my own and four thousand a year from my father—I believe he may give me something, perhaps a thousand or two as a gift, when I marry. There is a trust fund to bring me an income of five thousand when my father dies.'

'Yes, I see,' Lord Hamilton said. 'Not very much for an expensive young man to live on, is it? I imagine you may have a few debts?'

'Yes, sir.' Phipps swallowed hard. 'I believe I

may clear my debts by selling my commission. I would not expect Miss Hamilton to follow the drum, sir.'

'No, neither her mama nor I should care for that,' Lord Hamilton said and looked thoughtful. 'You are prepared for a civilian life? I know you young chaps like the army way of doing things.'

'It is for young and mainly unmarried men,' Phipps replied. 'I shall take my wife to my estate and do what I can to make it prosper. We have the use of my father's house here in town and I should bring Miss Hamilton up to visit when she wishes.'

'As to where she wishes to live, you must consult with her—if I agree,' the father went on, his gaze narrowing. 'She is a considerable heiress and has a large estate of her own, besides what I choose to settle on her. There is no town property and my country seat, along with the property in Scotland and Devon, will go in its entirety to my son, but my daughter has always been happiest in the country. I own a decent house in Bath, which will always be available to Amanda, and, on her mama's demise, will be wholly hers. They have been accustomed to visit at least twice a year, you understand.'

'I had no notion of it, sir—but I should wish to accommodate my wife's wishes in these things.'

'I shall settle thirty thousand on her when she marries. Another twenty is in trust for her and becomes hers when she takes a husband—that capital will be available to her husband should he wish it. Much of her fortune is tied up in property and land, and was bequeathed her by a great-aunt. She has capital of fifty thousand pounds invested in blue-chip shares, left to her by yet another aunt, which shares I should not like to see sold for they bring in a good income—and there is another twenty thousand bringing her in around five per cent annually, which is what she has been accustomed to using for pin money. Together with the various land, property and capital, she has somewhere in the region of two hundred and fifty thousand pounds, give or take a few thousand…and an income of some five-and-twenty thousand a year.'

'Good grief,' Phipps said and sat down suddenly in case his legs should not support him. He felt overwhelmed and aware of his inadequacy. Had he realised, he would probably not have dared to ask. 'I had no idea of the extent of her fortune, sir.'

'What are the extent of your debts, Lieutenant?'

'Five thousand,' Phipps answered, too shocked to realise what he was saying. 'But I told you, I can cover them with the sale of my commission and my next allowance.'

'If we agreed on a contract, I should think it only right to make you a gift of say…ten thousand pounds. Would you find that satisfactory? You see, I prefer that my daughter's land and property remain her and your property and would not like to see them sold and the money wasted on the payment of large debts.'

'Five thousand is all I owe… Good grief! Do you think I ask for Miss Hamilton only to cover my debts?'

'I am aware that several have tried to win her heart for that purpose, but my daughter is a sensible girl. She sent them packing without my help, though I should have done so had they got as far as addressing me.' Lord Hamilton paused. 'Amanda is not a great beauty. Had she no fortune, we might have had difficulty in finding her a husband she could like, but I want her to be happy, sir. I know that she likes you very well and, for that reason, I am happy to overlook the disparity in your fortunes. However, if I thought you did not care a button for her, you would not be standing here now. Do I make myself clear?'

'Perfectly,' Phipps said a little stiffly. He'd known this interview would not be easy, but had not thought it could be quite so humiliating. Lord Hamilton's kindness was making it worse, for Phipps felt shamed. 'May I ask you to arrange the contract so that Miss Hamilton and I continue to enjoy the income from her property, for I should not wish to deprive her of anything she is accustomed to command—but I do not wish her capital to be available to me. Once my debts are paid, and I have the gift you so generously offered, I shall not need more.'

'Well said, sir, and I am glad of it,' Lord Hamilton said. 'But Amanda must have the last say. Some of her capital is tied up in various trusts, but I think she might wish the twenty thousand I spoke of to be available to you both. As her husband you will have control of the whole, should you wish to make changes.'

'I shall need no more than the income you have mentioned,' Phipps said. 'I hope and expect to increase my own once I take charge of my estate—small as it is—and shall not touch her capital. However, it shall be available for her use. For myself, I would see the rest of her fortune in trust for her heirs.'

'Well, well, I see you are a sensible fellow. There is no need for that—though we may set a part of the property aside for that purpose if Amanda wishes it. However, I see no reason for haste. It is clear to me that my daughter's affairs will be in good hands, sir—and if she accepts you I shall wish you both happy.'

Phipps rose at the same moment as his host and they shook hands. Feeling a little dazed, Phipps allowed himself to be escorted to another parlour where he was assured Amanda would soon join him. He stood looking out at a pleasant garden, his mind still reeling from the shock of discovering just how vast was her fortune. Phipps doubted that anyone had been aware of the full extent of it, perhaps even Amanda did not know herself, for her father was a shrewd man. He might appear a bluff good fellow, but when it came down to business he was not behind the times. His stewardship of Amanda's fortune had clearly been exemplary and Phipps could only hope to follow in his footsteps.

Lost in his thoughts, he did not notice when the door opened behind him, and it was not until he heard a small cough that he turned to see the lady who had entered. Amanda was attired in a simple gown of primrose, her hair caught loosely back by a ribbon; she looked very young, innocent and pretty, her cheeks pleasantly plump, but her features well defined, and he drew a sharp breath, assailed by feelings he could not place. Why had he not realised how very attractive she was before this—but surely there was a new glow in her eyes, an air of confidence that had not always been there?

'Miss Hamilton...' He moved towards her, holding out his hands. 'I can scarce believe it, but your father has approved my suit. I have the honour to tell you that I consider myself a truly fortunate man and to assure you of my deep regard. You may look for me to be a constant husband, who will have your best interests at heart—if you will consent to be my wife?'

Amanda slid her hands into his, her clear eyes seeking his. She seemed to find what she was looking for, because she smiled and blushed rosily.

'I thank you for your kind offer, sir, and I do

most readily accept you. I am very happy that you have done me this honour.'

'It is an unequal match, my very dear girl,' Phipps said, then bent his head to kiss her softly on the lips. He made no attempt to hold her to him, but the kiss held for several seconds. 'I am a very happy man…and I hope to deserve you.'

'Fustian!' she said calmly and startled him out of the daze he had been in. 'If you speak such nonsense to me, Phipps, I shall be cross with you. I am rich, I know that, but I do not consider it. Money does not make anyone happy, though it makes life very much easier, especially for those unfortunates who have none. I give away what I can afford to those who need it, did Papa tell you that? Here in town I have been used to spending a fortune on my clothes, but in general, you know, I spend little on myself. I prefer a simple life in the country with my horses and dogs—though I shall be happy to visit both London and Bath when it is time for a change. I do not expect you to live in my pocket. You must consider yourself at liberty to visit the town on business whenever you choose.'

Was she giving him *carte blanche* to enjoy himself with a mistress if he chose? It sounded very like it, but the idea revolted him coming on top of her father's revelations about her fortune.

'What, would you get rid of me so soon?' he teased. 'I believe I am content in the country for the most part and, if my understanding is correct, we will have vast estates and property that will take up a considerable amount of my time, for I mean to care for them for you.'

The realisation that her fortune would bring great responsibilities was a revelation, a bright light that gave his life purpose and reason. Amanda needed a competent steward and he intended to be more than that—he would be scrupulous in all his dealings with her and make her richer than she was, if it were possible.

'Thank you, it is all I could ask,' she said. 'I have no interest in business, though I like to see my estate in good heart, and I take an interest in my people. Papa has always overseen things for me, because my main estate is only twenty miles distant from his own, and I am in the habit of staying there with Mama sometimes. In truth, I do not know what my fortune amounts to and I have no wish to know. My income is more than

I should ever spend and I want you to do as you wish with it, Phipps. You must think of the estate as ours and do as you consider fit. I give somewhere in the region of five thousand pounds to good causes each year, but I shall leave that to you to decide in future.'

'You are very trusting, Amanda.'

'Not at all,' she replied and her eyes twinkled up at him. 'Had I thought you a fortune-hunter I should have asked Papa not to hear you. I have been obliged to listen to the ranting of more than one gentleman wishing to convince me of his undying love. I did not listen and I did not bother Papa. I am a sensible girl, Phipps, not at all romantic.'

'Oh, Amanda, my love,' he said and gave a shout of laughter. 'You are quite delightful and I am very glad we met.'

'Mama has asked if you would wish to stay for luncheon—or would perhaps prefer to dine with us this evening?'

'I have an appointment at noon,' he said and glanced at his watch, the smile fading from his eyes.

'Is something wrong? Please tell me.'

He hesitated, then, 'Brock was attacked last night after he left me. I have not the details yet, but I am promised to him for this afternoon. I shall be delighted to dine with you, dearest, but I must go to him first.'

'Yes, of course you must,' she said, at once concerned. 'I do hope he is not badly hurt.'

'I believe it is but a slight wound, though his doctor has advised him to rest.'

'Do you think it was an attempt at robbery?'

'I am not certain. I shall be able to tell you more this evening.' He hesitated, then, 'When would you wish the wedding to be?'

'It might be pleasant in September,' Amanda said. 'If…that would suit you?'

'Following our visit to the Brockley estate?' He inclined his head. 'Yes, that will give you time to have your bride clothes made. We shall discuss the details with your mama this evening.' He held her hands once more, gazing down into her face a little uncertainly. 'You are happy, Amanda?'

'Perfectly,' she said. 'I look forward to being your wife—and the mother of your children. I see no reason why we should not be comfortable together—do you?'

'None at all. It is my intention to make you happy.'

'Then I shall be,' she said and gave a gurgle of laughter. 'I am easy to please, Phipps. Just keep your word to me—and do not forget to bring me flowers on my birthday.'

He saw she was teasing him and smiled. 'You shall have a house filled with flowers,' he promised and raised her hand to his lips. 'I must speak with Lady Hamilton for a few moments and then I must leave—but I shall see you this evening.'

Chapter Six

'You have no idea who attacked you?' Phipps asked, looking anxiously at his friend, as he lay propped against a pile of fresh linen pillows. 'I suppose it was an attempt at robbery.'

'I should rather doubt it,' Brock said. 'There were three of them and I am certain they meant to kill me, but were instructed to make it look like a robbery. Had I not been in the habit of carrying my swordstick, they must have succeeded in their aims. Fortunately, once I had it unsheathed I made short work of them. Two were cut and the third made off like the cur he was.'

'If that is so, it was a cowardly piece of work,' Phipps said in disgust. 'You must have an enemy who hates you, Brock—as Jack Delsey did, when he was twice set upon. Do you think Shearne paid those rogues to murder you?'

'I can think of no one else with good reason,' Brock admitted and sipped the posset his man had made him with distaste. 'This stuff is awful, but better than the physician left for me.'

'If we had proof, we might lay information against him,' Phipps observed. 'However, knowing and proving something are two different things.'

'Yes; besides, it would only dredge up the past and I've no mind to tell the world of Mary's sorrows. I was a fool to wander about alone so late at night and should have stayed at your house the night, as you asked.'

'That is all very well, but he cannot be allowed to get away with this, Brock. Next time you might not get off so lightly.'

'I shall make arrangements to have my back watched, though since I shall be going into the country presently I dare say this will all blow over soon enough.'

'The man is a menace to society,' Phipps said. 'He threatened Miss Field and Miss Hamilton the other day in the street... Oh, by the way, will you wish me happy?'

'You've spoken to Miss Hamilton?' Brock inclined his head, a broad grin banishing the frown. 'That's excellent, my dear fellow. I like Miss Hamilton and think her the very wife for you, Phipps. You are in general an easygoing fellow and you should have a lady who will take care of your interests. She is both clever and kind—an unusual combination, for clever women often have a sharp tongue.'

'Miss Hamilton does not scruple to say what she thinks,' Phipps assured him. 'But she says it frankly and without malice—and she is the most generous girl.'

'Miss Field tells me she has been invited to stay after they leave town. I dare say you will escort them home and stay a few days or so before visiting your parents. I must speak to my father and make the arrangements for our house party.'

'Tell me to mind my own business, if you please—but have you intentions towards Miss Field?'

'Mind your own business, there's a good fellow,' Brock said, but without the least malice. 'To be honest with you, I am far more concerned about sorting this business out with Shearne.'

'Yes, of course. Just thought I'd ask, because

that Armstrong fellow has been nosing about. I've a notion that he was after Amanda, but when he knows he isn't going to get her, he may go after Miss Field. I think he wants a quiet girl to care for his mother.'

Brock murmured something, but the subject was dropped there. Phipps visited with him for a couple of hours, but apart from making an appointment to dine together in two days' time little more of substance was said.

Phipps was thoughtful as he left his friend to saunter down to Bond Street. He had been giving the matter of a ring for Amanda some thought and had decided that he would buy her a personal gift of some sort and give her a rather splendid diamond-and-ruby ring that had been left him by his maternal grandmother. It and several other pieces were kept in the bank for the time when he should marry. Phipps had at one time considered whether he should sell some of the items, but a natural reluctance to part with family pieces had made him hesitate. Now he was glad he had not yielded to temptation, for the pearls were good. He would have the diamond clasp cleaned and the pearls restrung as a wedding gift, but for now he would buy Amanda a gold-and-pearl bangle he'd noticed a few days earlier.

Amanda felt as if she were in a dream. She had spent most of the day after Phipps left in changing the flowers, helping Mama write out a guest list and looking through her clothes. Mama was determined that they should have the wedding at home so that all their friends in the country could attend.

'Any of our town friends who care to come down may do so,' she said. 'But our special friends at home might not wish to travel, either to town or to Phipps's country house. So I believe we shall have the wedding at home. We must discuss it with him, naturally, but his family might like you to stay for a week or two prior to the wedding and if they wish to give a ball for all their neighbours—but of course we shall invite anyone dear Phipps wishes for to the wedding. I think a marquee in the grounds, my love, for the overflow—but the evening reception must be in the house for September nights can be cold.'

'I think a marquee is a lovely idea,' Amanda

agreed. 'I want to invite all the people I know and it will mean a huge number of guests, Mama.'

'I should be most disappointed if it did not,' Mama said, smiling fondly. 'We only have one daughter and Papa has already told me that no expense is to be spared.'

'I should have my gown made in town, I suppose…unless Jane would undertake it for me. It is a lot to ask, for she has to make herself two new gowns.'

'You must ask her when she calls tomorrow,' Mama said. 'And then we shall repair to Susanna's house for the rest of our stay in town.'

'Yes, Mama.' Amanda carefully avoided her mother's gaze for she could have wished that they were going straight out of town when Papa gave up the house he had leased for the Season. She liked the countess, but Lord Armstrong had been one of those gentlemen that Papa had been forced to tell that his daughter was already spoken for. If he made anything out of it, she might find his company awkward. 'You will enjoy that, I think?'

'Yes, to own the truth, I shall,' Mama admitted. 'It is years since we saw one another and there is no time to talk at social events. We shall be able to sit and chatter without interruption.'

Amanda made no comment, for she knew that it would suit her mother after having spent the past five weeks escorting her daughter to all the *ton* parties. For Amanda it would seem quiet. She would have preferred to go home with Papa and Phipps for escort and spent the time discussing the wedding preparations. However, Mama deserved some time with her old friend and Amanda was pleased for her that she was to have it.

When Phipps dined with them that evening it was a quiet family affair and the conversation was all of the wedding. Phipps was agreeable to whatever suited Amanda and her mama, and said that he would prepare a list of his family and friends for them. He thought that the relatives he ought to invite and the handful of friends he wanted to have with him might amount to the region of a hundred.

'I shall be inviting many more than that,' Amanda told him. 'Many will be neighbours and elderly friends, and they will not stay for the evening. I dare say there may be upwards of three hundred at church and the reception in the garden, but in the evening perhaps less than two.'

Phipps did not seem surprised that she had so many friends, for the people from her own estate must be invited, as well as those from her father's—and all their friends in town, though many of them were mutual.

Amanda was allowed to take Phipps to the door when he left that evening and it was then that they were able to have some private conversation.

'Was Major Brockley able to leave his bed when you saw him?'

'No, he was advised to rest for the day, but he was perfectly able to talk. I imagine it was most likely footpads.'

'If he has an enemy, he must take great care,' Amanda said, looking up at him anxiously. 'You, too, Phipps. I should not wish harm to come your way.'

He frowned down at her. 'What are you saying, Amanda?'

'I think it may have been Shearne who paid those rogues to harm Brock. He is a vindictive man, Phipps—and you have both crossed him in recent memory.'

'It is possible. I shall not hide it from you, Amanda—but I am fairly sure Shearne left town in a hurry. His creditors were dunning him.'

'I thought he was a wealthy man?'

'It may be merely a temporary awkwardness, but someone told me at the club that Shearne had been badly dipped at Newmarket and the tables. If he's taken a bolt to the country, he may not yet know that his attempt on Brock was unsuccessful. I do not fear him, for I believe he hardly notices me—his quarrel with Brock is of long standing.' He shook his head as she looked enquiringly at him. 'A private matter and one I am sworn not to reveal, my love.'

'Well, as long as you are not concerned. I hope he *has* been forced to seek his estates in the country for a time and we may not be troubled with him again.'

'I doubt he will bother his head with any of us. Brock is another matter—but I assure you, he is taking precautions and is well able to protect himself.'

With that she had to be content. They formed a plan of taking a drive in the park the following afternoon, after which he would call on her at

Lord Armstrong's house before taking leave of her for a few days.

'I should go down and speak to my father,' he told her. 'I shall return to escort you home, Amanda, and then I hope to visit with you—and to meet some of your friends. After that, I must visit my own estate and set some matters in hand for us.'

'And then it will be time for our visit to Lord Brockley's home,' she said. 'Brock's father must be an easygoing man to keep open house for his son's friends.'

'Lord Brockley is a generous host and enjoys nothing more. He often has house parties and Brock knows that he is at liberty to fill his father's house with guests whenever he chooses. Brock is the heir, of course, though he has three sisters and a brother fifteen years his junior.'

'You have but one brother, I believe?'

'Yes. He is one year my senior and was always more interested in politics than the army. He may well rise in his profession for he has a safe seat for the Tories and my father is hale. There is no need for Alexander to think of the estate for years yet.'

'And no sisters?'

'None, unfortunately. Mama wanted a daughter, I believe, but it was not to be.'

'Well, she may yet have two daughters-in-law.'

'As yet Alexander is not married.' Phipps frowned. 'He shows no sign of it, which is a source of irritation to my father.'

'Well, let us hope he will be pleased with your marriage.'

'He cannot fail to be pleased,' Phipps replied and smiled down at her. 'I must let you go now, dearest. I shall see you tomorrow.'

'Miss Field comes in the morning and stays for nuncheon. I shall see you at three.'

With their plans made for the near future, Phipps went off and Amanda returned to say goodnight to her parents. Mama was still chattering about the wedding when they went upstairs and parted for the night.

The morning brought a letter from Cynthia with the post. It was filled with complaints. Miss Langton was thoroughly bored and looked forward to seeing her friend again at Lord Brockley's estate. She wrote that her rash had gone and she was free of infection.

She wished that her mama had not brought her home, for she missed all her friends and Amanda in particular. It would suit her if Amanda could come and stay with her when they left town, for it would be no trouble to Lady Langton to chaperon Amanda when they travelled to Lord Brockley's home.

Amanda felt a spasm of disquiet, for she knew that she must write at once to tell Cynthia that she was now engaged to Phipps. Cynthia's letter was mercifully free of any mention of him, which relieved Amanda's mind a little, because she had thought her friend was thinking of him favourably.

It was not until the last few lines of her letter that she wrote a hint of what might now be occupying her mind.

It was on the way home that we were forced to stop two days at an inn to have a repair made to the leading pole of Mama's carriage. At first the foolish man said it would take a week to repair it, but fortunately the Marquis of Shearne happened to arrive and prevailed upon the blacksmith to mend it at once.

Mama was delighted and she invited him

to call on us at home, which he has done. I
must tell you, Amanda, he is the most delight-
ful companion...

There was some more in this vein, which caused
Amanda a few qualms. Knowing what she did of
the marquis, ought she to write a warning to her
friend? She had threatened the marquis with it,
though she had not meant to follow through on it.
Would Cynthia see such a letter as an act of kindness or think it spiteful? Her conscience told her
she ought. Yet what could she say? He had annoyed Miss Field by the river, made veiled threats
to her—and Brock suspected him of having paid
some rogues to set on him. It would be so much
better to speak to Cynthia as a friend rather than
write what must be a libellous letter. Yes, she must
wait until she saw her friend before giving her the
warning that was needed.

Amanda had no proof that the marquis was a
rogue, even though he was suspected of having
had an attempt made on Brock's life—and the rest
of it could be put down to mere impoliteness. She
could make no assertion that was strong enough
to deter Cynthia—and to write of what she did

not know would be libellous and morally wrong. Therefore she decided to keep her doubts to herself, at least until they met. Cynthia's parents were her guardians, and it must be for them to keep a watchful eye on her.

In this way she was able to ease her conscience and to write a friendly letter to Cynthia, telling her of her engagement to Phipps and inviting her and her family to the wedding. She said that she was also looking forward to the visit at Lord Brockley's estate, but apologised for not being able to visit Cynthia at her home.

Cynthia must forgive her, but after she left the countess, Phipps was to escort them home. She did not know for certain, but rather thought that his parents might invite her to meet them in the interval between their return home and the promised visit to Major Brockley's home.

It is not certain yet. Phipps said we must go at some time prior to the wedding, but he means to ask his parents when it will suit them to receive my family.

I fear this means I shall not be able to accompany you and Lady Langton to Bath, but I am sure we shall arrange something in the future, for I shall still have the use of the house in Bath and I should love you to be our guests...

Amanda sat for a while over her letter, frowning, but she could see no way of improving it. If Cynthia felt that she had stolen Phipps from her while she was unwell there was little she could do to soothe her friend's ruffled feathers. She did not think that Cynthia had truly cared for Phipps, because while she held court he was only one of many she had smiled on. Besides, Phipps had asked Amanda and he would not have done so if he preferred Cynthia Langton—would he?

Amanda tried to forget that she had prompted him to speak, because to allow a shadow to intrude on her happiness would be foolish. She had never misled herself into thinking that Phipps loved her, for she knew that she was a little dab of a thing and not remarkable in any way, though she did think that perhaps she might have lost a little weight recently. Yet she thought that he was content in her company and she meant to make him a good wife. Amanda would not dissolve into tears the first time he went off in a pet and she would not hang on his sleeve at every turn, even though she suspected it would be painful to her. He'd promised that he would be a good husband to her and care for her interests, and she must be content to know that he was her husband—and to centre her love upon her children when they came.

She must not and would not expect romantic love for that was too much to ask of him. Even if that hurt a little, Amanda was able to subdue it, because her love for him must be enough for them both. She must never allow herself to mourn something that she had always known could not be hers.

The morning also brought Jane Field, who declared herself delighted at the news of Amanda's wedding, and asked her what she intended to do about her wedding gown.

'I'm not sure what to do,' Amanda told her. 'Madame Arlene made most of my clothes this Season, but I shall have to be strict with her for I do not want something with miles of silk that makes me look like a balloon.'

'If I accompanied you, I could help you choose the style that will suit you very well, and if there are any last-minute alterations I shall be happy to undertake them. I would make the gown myself, but I'm not sure I could finish everything in time.'

'No, no, Jane,' Amanda said. 'It will be enough if you come with me and make her understand what I need—and if she should make it too big as she has all my other clothes, you may take it in for me, as you did before.'

The arrangement was made and the conversation turned to other topics, though mostly concerning the wedding. Jane was looking forward to staying in the country with Amanda's family and they spent the morning talking contentedly. After nuncheon Jane took her leave and Amanda changed into a pale green carriage gown, a straw bonnet with darker green ribbons and York tan gloves. Her kid-leather boots were fastened with black buttons at the sides and the latest fashion. She barely had time to take a glance at herself in the mirror before the knocker sounded.

Phipps was waiting in the hall for her and looked up with a smile of welcome that made her heart catch.

'You are exactly on time,' he said approvingly.

'It makes you an example to your kind, for my mother is never ready when she promises.'

Amanda laughed, went to kiss Mama's cheek and told her that she would see her at the countess's house.

'I feel that I should have been with you,' she said. 'There is so much to see to and I was with Jane all morning...'

'I have little to do but change my gown,' Mama said. 'The trunks we need for a few days have already been delivered to Susanna's house and your papa is having everything else sent off home. He, of course, will stay here tonight and leave in the morning for the country, as we planned.'

Amanda knew that her papa had organised everything, as he always did, and her mother had only to issue her orders to the servants. Indeed, she was better out of the house, for Mama would fret as the time to leave approached and only Papa's resolution would see her on her way across London to her friend's house.

Amanda had overseen most of her packing herself early that morning and now had nothing to do but to enjoy a drive with her fiancé. Phipps escorted her to his curricle and helped her up, then drove her to the park, talking all the while of mutual acquaintances. It was only when they were in the park and he could draw the horses to a halt in a quiet spot that he turned to her. Taking a small box from his coat pocket, he offered it to her.

'This is the ring my maternal grandmother left to me for my wife,' he told her. 'I believe it is rather fine, but if you should dislike it I can buy you another.'

Amanda opened the box and gasped as she saw the magnificent ruby-and-diamond ring. The centre stone was large, oval and a deep glowing red; surrounded by a circle of fine diamonds, it was very beautiful.

'This is wonderful,' she murmured. 'How did you know that I love rubies?'

'I fear I did not,' he answered truthfully. 'Had I been a rich man, I should no doubt have bought you something new—but although I have another present for you, which is new, I could not have managed something to equal this.'

'But I could not want for anything other than this delightful ring,' Amanda said at once. 'I love it. Will you slip it on for me?'

He transferred the reins to his left hand and

leaned across to slip the ring on to her third finger, finding to his relief that it went on easily.

'I feared I might have to have it altered, but it fits well, I think.'

'Perfectly,' she said and her eyes sparkled up at him. 'Thank you so very much, Phipps. I should like to thank you properly, but there are people staring and I dare not.'

'I am in the way, I dare say,' Phipps told her and took up the reins once more, coaxing the horses into a gentle walking motion as they circled the road leading through the park. 'I am glad you like your ring, Amanda. When I have made my estate prosperous I hope to buy you as many jewels as you wish for.'

'Then you need not work too hard,' she said with a teasing laugh. 'You may perhaps have noticed that for the most part I wear only my pearls, a diamond necklet Papa gave me and some matching bracelets now and then. It is not because my jewel box is empty, but that I am not concerned with such things and wear only the pieces that I love or that mean something to me.'

Phipps shot a curious, slightly rueful glance at

her. 'If I may not give you jewels, what may I do for you?'

'I need only affection and kindness to make me happy,' she answered and laughed up at him. 'Papa has spoiled me with trinkets of all kinds from the moment I was born. As a child I had only to ask and I was given whatever had taken my fancy. When I was old enough to realise, I refrained from asking too often.'

'It is a wonder that your nature has not been spoiled,' he said, amusement in his eyes. 'How did you remain so level-headed?'

'I fear it is a sad lack of romance in me,' she answered on a gurgle of laughter. 'I have a fondness for my dogs and my horses, Phipps. If you truly wish to spoil me, then you must find me a pair of bang-up-to-the-mark carriage horses that I may purchase, together with a light phaeton—and then you must teach me to drive them with style. I like that trick you have of catching your thong with your whip hand.'

She saw an answering spark in his eyes and knew that she had struck the right note. This was something he could do for her and was, besides, an ambition she had cherished for a while.

'I've not had the privilege of seeing you on a horse yet,' he said. 'But I shall be delighted to look for horses that will suit a lady and to commission a light phaeton for your use. I might begin your lessons when I escort you home, Amanda.'

'Only if you have horses I may drive,' she said. 'For Papa has no more room to stable my horses. It is the reason I have said nothing to him, because he would have to build on to the stables to accommodate them—our hunters and carriage horses are already too many, you see. I could keep them at my own estate, but then I should not be able to drive them when I wished so I have waited until the right time.'

'I see no reason why you should not drive one of my teams,' Phipps said. 'I fear I am extravagant when it comes to my stables—and we may well have to enlarge ours once we are wed.'

'Do you breed your mares?' Amanda asked, leading him into a conversation that she knew would last throughout their drive.

By the time that he had taken her twice round the park and then conveyed her to the countess's house, Amanda felt that they had made progress.

In discovering a shared interest—for she was closely involved with the breeding regime at her father's stables—they had moved insensibly to a firmer footing. She felt that the slight awkwardness that had hung between them since her father revealed the extent of her fortune to Phipps had somehow melted in the warmth of a shared enthusiasm.

It was exactly what she had hoped when she told Phipps that she preferred horses to jewels, though she did not fail to thank him again for the lovely ring he had given her before they parted. However, she had every hope that now, instead of worrying what he could give her with his limited resources, he understood that she was relying on him to manage her stables. He would naturally oversee the finances of their shared estates and in this way Amanda hoped to found a sensible working relationship. She had given him to understand that she thought of him as a partner in her life, someone to share the small things that made life of interest and pleasure to her. If Phipps were content with that, they might go on excellently together.

Being a very well brought-up young lady,

Amanda had enjoyed their brief kiss and known a curious longing for something more, but she had not yet given the bedroom a second thought. Although perfectly aware of what happened between mare and stallion, and being able to work out the differences in humans from once having seen her brother swim naked as a young boy with two of his friends, Amanda gave little thought to that part of marriage. She knew that ladies were not supposed to be curious, and some of the young matrons she knew had told her that *it* was nothing to make a fuss over.

'Really, one has so much else to enjoy that an hour or so of one's time is less than nothing…and afterwards one can be comfortable in one's own bed, of course.'

The young woman in question was a flighty young madam, who had not given up flirting with any gentleman who appealed to her, even though more than a year married to a man twice her age. She was his spoiled darling and spent his fortune recklessly, for he doted upon her, and clearly whatever passed between them in the bedroom meant nothing to her.

Amanda was innocent enough to imagine that

bedroom matters could not be so very important, for ladies never spoke of these things—and Mama said that a wife must do her duty as best she could, but that making a man comfortable in his home by ensuring everything was to his liking was of far more consequence.

Amanda thought that she liked Phipps very well and, since she had enjoyed his kisses, it followed that she would not dislike whatever else he chose to do. She hoped to win his trust and his friendship, and, not being given to flights of fancy, expected that they would go on well enough providing that each was willing to give and take a little.

Therefore, it was with no particular misgivings that she made her farewells to Phipps when he handed her down in front of the countess's town house.

'I shall be no more than a few days in the country,' he told her and kissed her hand. 'You may depend on me to return before you are ready to leave town—and I shall do my best to set in hand your commissions.'

Amanda thanked him, told him there was plenty of time, and they took a cordial leave of one another. Since Phipps waited to see her safely inside the house before he drove off, she was not privileged to see him glance back at her.

Once the door was closed, she felt a slight pang because she had been used to seeing him most days and several must pass before he came to visit her again. However, she banished the thought, gave her bonnet and gloves to the hovering footman and was conducted upstairs to the countess's favourite parlour.

'Ah, there you are, dearest,' Mama greeted her. 'I fear you are too late for tea, for we have had ours—but I dare say Mrs Goombridge will bring you a tray upstairs when you change if you are in need of something.'

'Thank you, I am not in the least hungry. A glass of water will suffice until dinner, I think.'

'Oh, but that will not do,' the countess said and rang the bell. 'I shall ask Goombridge to take a tray up to your room, just tea if that is all you require.'

'Yes, my lady, thank you,' Amanda said, for she did not wish to make a fuss. 'I trust you are well, Lady Sandown? We shall be happy to stay quietly with you and do not expect you to entertain for our sakes, do we, Mama? Phipps has gone into the country and will return in six days' time.'

'Oh, but I should not want you to be dull,' Susanna said with a bright smile. 'I have arranged two small card parties and three dinners, so we shall be blessed for guests, though not this evening. I thought we could all settle down to become better acquainted, my love.'

Amanda thanked her and then Mama said she would show her up to her room, for they were sharing a suite of very comfortable chambers and perhaps Amanda would like to rest and change her gown for dinner.

Amanda said that she would and they went upstairs together. It was a beautiful house in the older style and had been in the Earl of Sandown's possession for many years. As honoured visitors they had been given the best guest apartments.

'Susanna is so pleased to have us,' Mama told her. 'She is disappointed that you chose other than her son, but she will make nothing of it, dearest. You need not fear embarrassment on that account.'

Amanda murmured something appropriate and they parted, each to their own bedchamber, to refresh their *toilettes* before dinner.

Chapter Seven

Susanna was indeed the perfect hostess, making her friends feel quite at home in her lovely house. Lord Armstrong was perfectly polite, but had withdrawn some of the flattering attentions he had paid Amanda at the start, which was quite proper and very understandable. She continued to meet Jane, who walked with her most mornings in the park, sometimes stayed for nuncheon and tea, and made herself so indispensable to the company that the countess said she thought her a dear girl and would be glad to have her stay. On hearing that Jane was to accompany Amanda to her home at the end of the visit, she insisted that the girl be her guest and Jane was transferred with all her baggage to one of the best guest chambers, so after that they were not obliged to part, except to change or sleep.

Jane's company helped Amanda to keep a cheerful countenance, for she had discovered that her enforced parting from Phipps was far more painful than she could ever have imagined. Despite scolding herself, for it was very foolish to pine for him when he had been gone no more than two days, she had to fight to stop herself sinking into the dumps. She had thought she could accept such absences with complacence, but discovered that he was more necessary to her comfort than she would have thought possible.

She was perhaps more romantic than she had ever believed, for she found that her mind strayed to each and every meeting when Phipps had noticed her, and particularly to their last drive in the park—and the kisses he had given her on various occasions. She began to think about her wedding night for the first time and was nervous of what was to come in a way she had not been earlier. Amanda knew her own failings, and even if she had lost quite a bit of weight, as her visit to the seamstress confirmed, when her measurements all had to be taken again, she would never be slender. Even a man who loved her would never call her a waif or a sprite. Phipps was not in love with her, of course, though he was everything kind and generous. He was so very considerate of her since their engagement and she found herself counting the hours until his return.

However, being a polite girl, she was determined not to show that she was missing her fiancé and paid her hostess every kind attention. The evening parties the countess had set up for her entertainment seemed dull, for she could not help searching the company for the tall handsome man she loved and not finding him, was always disappointed. Yet she carried herself well and smiled at the countess's guests, taking her part in the evening with a lightness she did not feel. It was strange how she'd felt so confident when Phipps was with her each day, but now she found herself wondering and doubting. Did he care for her at all or had she been deceiving herself?

She found her appetite had dwindled to a shadow of its former self and was aware that her face looked much thinner than it once had, but as she was not given to admiring herself had no idea whether she looked better or worse. Besides, Phipps was not marrying her for her face or figure; he needed a rich wife and she had a fortune.

Yet to allow herself to think that her fortune was all to him was to court unhappiness.

One day while out walking with Jane they happened to meet Major Brockley. He had recovered from his injury and thanked them for their anxious enquiries with a brief smile. He had declined the countess's invitation to dinner with regret for he was about to leave town for his father's estate.

'I shall look forward to seeing you both at the beginning of August,' he told them, kissed their hands and took his leave.

'He is such a comforting man,' Jane said and sighed as they watched him stride away. 'One always feels he is to be relied on in a crisis.'

'Yes, he is a strong and very worthy man,' Amanda agreed, watching her friend's face a little anxiously. She was afraid Jane might have given her heart to the brave soldier and hoped she would not be disappointed. However, she knew from Phipps that Brock was not interested in marriage.

'Though of course he must one day, for the sake of an heir,' Phipps had told her. 'I doubt it will be before he is forced to think of settling down, which is unlikely to be just yet.'

They had also met Lord Johnston on their walks.

He had stopped to exchange greetings, though his look was reproachful as he told Amanda that he was leaving town the next day.

'There is no longer any reason for me to continue my visit...I have already delayed too long.'

She felt a little guilty, though she had never encouraged him to think of her, but she'd known it was in his mind and wondered if she could have found a way of dispelling his hopes sooner.

Apart from those two encounters Amanda saw few of the friends she'd made in London, and guessed from what Mama said that most people were leaving town and going down to the country for the summer.

The countess's friends were mostly older and some of them lived in London for much of the year, leaving only for a few weeks in the summer when the hot and dusty streets became unbearable.

Of the Marquis of Shearne the two girls heard and saw nothing. Amanda was relieved, for Jane's sake more than her own, because she knew her friend was afraid of him. At the back of her mind she wondered if Cynthia was encouraging his advances still, but tried not to think of it because there was nothing she could do. She had no real grounds for suspecting the marquis of evil intent and Cynthia would be justly annoyed had Amanda tried to interfere in her affairs.

At least Amanda would have no need to fear him in future. She would be in the country soon, and when she returned to London as a wife, perhaps next year, Shearne would have forgotten her. She prayed that he would have forgotten Jane, too, and hoped that her friend might also receive a proposal of marriage in the near future. Lord Armstrong had been showing Jane some kind attention and Susanna had fallen into the habit of calling her 'my good little comforter'.

Amanda was not sure of her friend's heart and did not like to question her, for she thought that perhaps Jane did not know herself exactly how she felt. If she received an offer from Lord Armstrong, she would have a comfortable life—but not if her heart belonged to the dashing Major Brockley.

How difficult these affairs of the heart were, Amanda reflected. She had been granted her wish in the matter of a husband, but not every young lady was as fortunate. Too many were forced to wed for the convenience of their family and Jane might fear to turn down an obliging offer for the sake of hers.

It was strange how long a few days could seem when waiting for the return of someone who meant so much. Amanda knew a few moments of unease, as she realised that in marrying a man whom she knew did not love her, as she loved him, she might be laying up a deal of unhappiness for herself in the years to come.

Phipps was relieved when he could at last say his farewells and return to London. He was surprised to discover how very much he'd missed Amanda. He had come to enjoy her companionship and to look forward to seeing her every day. If he had once thought that it might be a sacrifice to marry a girl who was at best attractive, but certainly would not be thought beautiful by most people's standards, he no longer had any such thought and found himself eager to begin his new life.

Having suffered from a feeling of being second-best for many years, he had discovered a strong desire to prove himself and as Amanda's husband and steward he would have ample opportunity.

Her father had been an excellent steward of her fortune and Phipps was determined to be no less. He would find it fulfilling to have large estates and various properties to manage, and had discovered that for the first time in his life he no longer felt inferior and his father's careless words could not sting him as they once had.

Amanda trusted him and that had given him a new purpose and a spring in his step. He could hardly wait to return to London and to commence his courtship of her in earnest this time. It would be his duty and his pleasure to make his wife happy and he felt a strong desire to care for and protect her to the best of his ability.

All the doubts, fears and anxious thoughts melted the moment she heard Phipps in the hall and knew that he had returned safely to her. She heard him speaking with Lord Armstrong and schooled herself to patience, waiting for him to come to her in the parlour where she sat with Jane that afternoon.

'I shall leave you now,' Jane said as they heard footsteps approaching.

'There is not the least need,' Amanda said, but

Jane only shook her head, pausing to curtsy to Phipps as she met him in the doorway. Her heart racing wildly, Amanda put down her book and stood as he entered, her eyes searching his face eagerly. He was just the same, as beloved as ever. 'Did all go well?'

'My dearest Amanda.' Phipps strode across the room to take her hands in his. A little shiver of delight went through her as she saw the welcoming smile in his eyes. As unlikely as it might seem, she believed he had missed her. 'Father was delighted with the match and Mama is eager to welcome her future daughter. They have begged me to bring you to them at the earliest opportunity. I know that Jane is to stay with you for a few weeks—she might come too, if you wished?'

'I dare say Jane will need to go home for a while before the visit in August,' Amanda said, a smile on her lips for she felt so ridiculously happy. 'We must consult Mama, for Papa has been on his own this past week and will not wish to part with us again too soon.'

'Yes, of course, my love. I thought we might go down for a few days and then continue on to Brock's for it is not far from my father's estate.'

'That sounds a good plan,' Amanda agreed. Cynthia had already asked the same thing, but her first allegiance must be to her future husband and his family. 'I must tell you that I shall be glad to go home, though the countess has been more than kind to us.'

Phipps nodded, a warm smile in his eyes. 'I have set some work in train at my own estate, for we shall visit there occasionally—but as yet I do not know where you would choose to live. You may prefer your own estate; it is close to your family and I dare say you have a fondness for it.'

'There is no need to decide just yet. Papa has been a good steward of my estate, though there is an agent and the bailiff to care for the land. I have made it my business to visit my people from time to time, but whether I need to live there is another matter. I think we should try a few months at both estates and discover which suits us best.'

'You are sensible as always,' Phipps told her. 'What have you been doing this past week? I have thought of you every day and wondered how you went on.'

'Oh, well enough,' Amanda said in a dismissive manner, for she did not want to tell him that each day had seemed an age without him. 'I have been measured for my wedding dress and a few new gowns, though I do not need so very many.'

'No, for you must buy some in Paris,' Phipps told her with a twinkle in his eye. 'Mama says there's nothing like a gown made in Paris—and she should know for she has an armoire filled with them.'

Amanda laughed at this, saying, 'I am looking forward to meeting your mama, Phipps. I hope she will like me.'

'How could she fail to?' he asked in a manner so fond that she could almost feel herself loved. 'My father is excessively pleased with me and has given me a larger allowance, as well as a present of three thousand pounds, which is more than I had expected and will provide for a wedding trip we may enjoy.'

Amanda wanted to ask so many questions, but before she could begin to ask them Mama came into the room, bearing a letter in her hand. It was obvious that she was shocked about something and Amanda's heart caught. She started forward, holding out her hand, her heart pounding with fright.

'Is something wrong with Papa?'

'No, nothing like that, my love. It is just the most shocking news—about Miss Langton...'

'Cynthia?' Amanda said, her throat tight of a sudden. 'Has something happened to her?'

'She has eloped with the Marquis of Shearne,' Mama told her. 'I have it from Lady Marlborough, who had it from her cousin, and their estate marches with her own.'

'Cynthia has run off with him?' Amanda stared at her mother. 'But why would she do such a thing? In her letter to me, she said that her mother liked him...so why run off?'

'Apparently, Lady Langton received a letter warning her of his true character and informing her that he had done something wicked in the past. She forbade her daughter to speak to him again and banished the man from her house; the next morning she discovered that Cynthia was missing—and she learned that a coach she believed to be the marquis's had been seen leaving the area at a spanking pace early that morning.'

'Who would send such a letter?' Amanda asked, feeling a little uneasy, though she could not have said why—except that she had threatened she would do so and Shearne might well believe that she had done so out of anger or spite.

She felt coldness at her nape and a shiver went down her spine.

'It does not follow that Cynthia went willingly,' Amanda said. 'He—might have abducted her and it may not truly be an elopement...'

'Lord have mercy!' Mama cried and sat down in the nearest chair, clutching her letter. 'What makes you say such a thing, Amanda?'

'Because she knows the marquis is not to be trusted,' Phipps spoke before Amanda could reply. 'He has frightened Miss Field on more than one occasion and is not to be trusted with vulnerable young ladies.'

'Oh, my goodness,' Mama said weakly. 'It makes one feel positively faint to think of it... If he does not marry her, she will be ruined.'

'It is my fault, Mama,' Amanda said. 'I knew he was a rogue and yet I did not warn her. I was afraid she might think I was interfering, but I see that I should have done so.'

'You ought to have told me if you knew she had a feeling for him, Amanda. I might then have

given her mother a hint much sooner and thus prevented a scandal and the girl's ruin.'

'Yes, Mama, I see my fault,' Amanda owned.
'I was too much concerned with my own affairs.
Besides, I did not dream that Cynthia would do
anything so rash.'

'Perhaps she did not,' Phipps said. 'It is entirely
possible that she merely went to tell him she could
not see him and was snatched out of revenge.
Shearne is a jealous, petty man and I would put
nothing past him.'

Mama looked overcome with distress. 'I feel for
her family—but what can we do now? It is too
late, for if I have learned of this shocking occur-
rence so must many others and the poor girl will
be ruined.'

'It may not be too late,' Phipps said. 'I shall
send an urgent post to Brock and ask him to look
into the situation. No one knows Shearne better
or dislikes him more. I know he will spare no effort to find them—and to rescue Miss Langton
if it is possible.'

'Oh, do you think he might do something?'
Mama asked, looking at him hopefully.

'I shall go to send the letter express at once. I

would offer to look for them myself, but Brock will know what to do—and I must see you safely to the country. Though, if I could be of help to Brock afterwards, I should hold myself at his disposal.'

'What a comfort you are to be sure,' Mama said. 'I am so glad you were here, Phipps, for I do not feel that I should worry Lord Armstrong with this.'

'Indeed, ma'am. We must keep it to ourselves as much as possible, if Miss Langton is to be rescued. Mayhap it will be possible to find some reasonable explanation for her behaviour that will restore her in the eyes of society.'

'It must be hoped so for her sake, and for her family,' Mama said. 'Oh, dear, and I had hoped this would be such a happy time for us all.'

'And so it will, Mama,' Amanda said. 'Phipps and Brock will do all they can to save her and her reputation, if it is possible, but it can make no real difference to our plans. Though it casts a shadow...'

Mama agreed that they must do what they could, though it was clear that she felt Cynthia was ruined no matter what the reason for her disappearance. However, she went off to her room to recover before joining the countess for afternoon tea.

Amanda looked up at Phipps. 'You know that Brock has gone home? Your letter will take a day or so to reach him—would it not be better to go in person to save time?'

'The damage has already been done,' Phipps said. 'My duty is to you and your mama, though it is like you to think of others first.'

'I am at fault for not warning Cynthia.'

'I doubt she would have listened. Shearne has a certain charm with ladies—even though both you and Miss Field took him in dislike, there are many that think him fascinating. Miss Langton is headstrong and might have defied you even had you warned her.'

Amanda knew he was right, though she still felt guilty and anxious for her friend. Phipps went off almost at once to send his letter express and promised to return to dine with them that evening, as expected.

Amanda joined the others for tea, feeling ill at ease. A shadow had suddenly fallen over her, for she could not think of her friend without regret and still felt some blame for what had happened. Yet there was nothing she could do but keep Cynthia's secret. The whispers would no doubt spread, but if Brock came up with a plan for her rescue, Amanda would help all she could by remaining Cynthia's friend no matter what.

She did not at first give much credence to the idea that the marquis meant to marry Cynthia, but then the thought struck her that perhaps he wanted her fortune and, if she had obeyed her mama and broken with him, then he might have carried her off to marry her by force. If he had ruined her, she would have little choice but to wed him.

It was a disturbing thought and Amanda wished with all her heart that her friend might escape her fate with her reputation intact, though, try as she might, she could see no way of achieving that favourable option.

Amanda went downstairs as soon as she was ready that evening, so she was in the parlour when Phipps arrived. She went to him at once, looking at him for reassurance. He took her hands, gazing down at her in his steadfast way and smiling to comfort her.

'The letter has gone and Brock will receive it tomorrow for the courier will ride through the night to deliver it. Brock will do what he can, I promise you that, my love—and, as far as I can ascertain, the news has not yet begun to be spoken of in town. If we can find her, we may be able to limit the damage, though she may be best to go abroad for a year or so.'

'Supposing Shearne needs her fortune and has married her?'

'Then I see no help for her,' Phipps said. 'While he lives he will control her fortune, even if she leaves him—unless we could prove that she was unwilling and we do not yet know whether she went willingly.'

'No…' Amanda caught her breath. 'I have been worrying for her, but it is to no avail until we find out for certain the circumstances of her disappearance.'

'You must not let this spoil things for you, my love,' Phipps said, then bent his head and kissed her softly on the lips. She felt herself tremble and melted into him, her heart beating wildly as he traced the line of her cheek with his fingertips. 'I want this to be a happy time for you.'

'It is. I am,' she said breathlessly. 'Yet Cynthia is my friend and I must regret this has happened to her.'

'As do we all,' he agreed. 'Rest assured that we shall do all we can. Brock will know where to find me if he needs me and we shall see how we go on.'

Amanda could only agree. She had been anxious for Jane's sake, but it seemed that the marquis had only meant to dally with her; he was looking for richer prey and it appeared that poor Cynthia had walked into his net.

All they could do now was to wait and see if Brock could find the runaways and then form some kind of plan to extricate her from the scandal into which she had fallen. Their dependence was all upon him and Amanda could only pray that he had some idea of where to find them.

'I wish you a good journey,' the countess said as she kissed Amanda's cheek the next morning. 'I had hoped to persuade your mama to bring you to us at home one of these days, but I know you have much to plan. I can only wish you happiness in your marriage.'

Amanda thanked her for her kindness and went

out to the waiting carriage. She had liked the countess well enough, but in the circumstances must be glad to be returning home. There was so much to be set in train for the wedding and the matter of Cynthia's disappearance weighed on her, for she felt herself in part to blame. Had she told Cynthia about the marquis's behaviour to Miss Field on the day of the picnic, perhaps it might have been averted.

However, there was no point in repining over something that had already happened and, being a sensible girl, she pushed the thought to the back of her mind for the moment.

Phipps had chosen to ride and Mama's maid accompanied them and Jane in the carriage, which meant that they did not feel free to discuss Cynthia's predicament. They spent the most part of the time discussing various plans for the wedding, and in speaking of their friends, the first part of the journey was soon accomplished.

Phipps had delivered them to a respectable inn where they all alighted to partake of a light meal while the horses were changed. The advantage of going post was that all the horses were of the same quality and no time was wasted behind a sluggish pair, which sometimes happened if one used one's own carriage and hired horses on the various stages.

The journey into Leicestershire was too far for it to be accomplished in one day and so they were obliged to stop at another inn overnight. The White Hart was a busy posting house and frequented by the aristocracy on their journey northwards from London. Phipps had seen to it that rooms were secured in advance for all of them, including her ladyship's maid and the grooms, and a good dinner was bespoke for them on their arrival in a private parlour.

'I am tired, Amanda,' Mama said as soon as they had eaten. 'I think we should go up at once, for we have almost as long a day before us tomorrow.'

'Yes, of course,' Amanda agreed. She stood up and went over to Phipps who had just returned after speaking to the landlord. 'We shall say goodnight, sir. Mama is very tired.'

'I am sure you must be, too,' he said and took her hands. 'Pray go up. If we leave soon after eight in the morning, we should be at your home before nightfall. I must go and speak to my grooms and make certain everything is in readiness for an early start.'

'Yes, of course, thank you,' she said and smiled. He leaned forward to kiss her cheek briefly and they parted, he to speak with his servants and she to retire for the night. Amanda followed her mama up the stairs. She had reached the top when she heard a disturbance below and glanced back. A man had just arrived and was shouting for the landlord, his voice loud and abusive, as he demanded one of the best rooms immediately; an argument ensued and voices were raised.

She knew that voice! Amanda's heart caught and she turned back to look for she was certain it was the Marquis of Shearne. Looking down, she saw him and gave a little cry of alarm and heard Jane's gasp. She touched her friend's arm in reassurance, but indeed her own nerves were on edge. Shearne was here in the inn—but was Cynthia with him?

'Go upstairs with Mama,' she whispered to Jane. 'Tell Mama that I recalled something I must say to Phipps, but do not tell her that man is here.'

'You will not go near him?' Jane said. 'You must

not, Amanda, please. Find Lieutenant Phipps and tell him, but do not attempt anything yourself.'

'Go quickly now or Mama will look for me,' Amanda urged and ran down the stairs. She was in time to see the marquis enter the private parlour, which Phipps had hired and followed him impulsively. She must discover whether Cynthia was with him!

When she entered the parlour, the marquis was standing by the fire, staring morosely into the flames. He muttered something about the landlord and wine and turned, his eyes narrowing with suspicion as he saw her standing there.

'Where is she?' Amanda demanded, too angry for caution. 'Is she in the carriage? What have you done with her?'

'Where's that damned landlord with my wine?' Shearne demanded, leering at her drunkenly. 'The plump dove to hand—have you come to see what your handiwork has done? Think you can gloat at my expense?' He glared at her, a pulse throbbing at his temple. 'I'll teach you a lesson, as I did her.'

'What do you mean?' Amanda's heart jerked, but she saw the cold anger in his eyes and realised that although he was clearly drunk, he knew her and he blamed her for Lady Langton's rejection of his suit. He must have thought that she had sent that letter telling of his base character! 'What have you done with Cynthia?'

'Damn her to hell…damn them all,' Shearne muttered and raised his head, looking as if he would like to murder her. 'Women are the very devil! We should do better to rid ourselves of the lot of them.'

'I demand to know what you've done with my friend.' Amanda's fear was lost as her anxiety for Cynthia mounted. 'Is she in your carriage—or have you hidden her somewhere?'

'What should I want with the she-devil? One woman is as good as any other: they are good for only one thing—whores and liars the lot of them.'

'You are a wicked evil man,' Amanda said. 'I know you must have abducted her—what have you done to her?'

'I would have her fortune,' the marquis muttered. 'She thinks she has outwitted me, but I'll have my revenge.'

'Where is she? Tell me what you've done with her…'

'I'll show you what I should have done to her.'

He lunged at Amanda and grabbed her by the throat. 'I'll make you pay for what you've done... you've ruined me, you hellcat...'

Amanda screamed once before his hands closed about her throat, kicking out at his shins and causing his grasp to loosen. She staggered back, realising that Jane was right; she ought to have fetched Phipps rather than confront him herself. Even as she looked for a way of escape the door of the parlour was flung open and suddenly Phipps was there.

'Stand away from her, sir!' Phipps cried. 'Touch her again and you die!'

'Come to catch your plump little dove, have you?' the marquis sneered. 'Afraid I might snatch your prize from under your nose...'

'How dare you speak of Miss Hamilton in that manner?' Phipps advanced towards him. 'Amanda, come here to me. You should not have come down.'

'He has done something with Cynthia. I know he has...'

'That bitch...not worth the bother,' Shearne said and snatched the wine bottle from the table where Phipps had left it, lifting it to his mouth to drink what remained. 'Haughty slut…wouldn't have me. Thought herself too good for the likes of me.'

'If you dislike her so, I wonder that you should care whether she accepted your proposal or not,' Phipps said, moving so that he was between the marquis and Amanda. He was gesturing for her to leave, but she could not because she was determined to watch and listen, to discover what had happened to Cynthia if she could.

'Oh, I didn't bother to ask, I just took her screaming and struggling,' Shearne said, draining the bottle of wine and tossing it into the grate where it shattered. He stood, leering at them, a mocking smile in his eyes. 'In my grasp she was, but I had to stop to change horses and while I was busy, the witch came to her senses and somehow got away.'

'You mean that your attempt at abduction went sadly wrong for she had too much spirit!' Phipps curled his hands at his sides. 'And what did you do then, sir? Did you look for her—or did you abandon her to her fate?'

Amanda stifled the cry that rose to her lips, watching in fascination as Phipps began to dominate the other man with the force of his will.

'The witch chose to leave me so why should I care what happens to her—besides, I knew that devil Brock was on our trail. I was warned he was looking for me…interfering dog. I would that he'd died when he should have.'

Phipps's eyes never left his face. 'And where did this lady get away from you, sir? How long ago?'

'Damn you, what's it to you?' Shearne demanded, staring at him in a belligerent manner. He blinked, seeming unsure of what he'd said or done and then suddenly threw a wild punch at Phipps, who had approached nearer than he liked. 'Get out of my way, you wretch. I do not answer to you…'

Phipps ducked neatly, then counter-punched and his landed square on the chin. The marquis slumped to the floor and lay there, not moving when Phipps dug the toe of his boot into his side. He was drunk and out for the count, which meant that he would answer no more questions this night, and when sober would deny everything.

'So, we have it from his own mouth,' Phipps said, looking at Amanda. 'Shearne abducted Miss Langton and carried her off, intent on wedding her for her fortune.'

'He wanted her money, but cared nothing for her,' Amanda said, her voice a little whispery. She put a hand to her throat, feeling the mark of his fingers like a bruise. 'He is such a brute. He tried to strangle me before you came—if he had Cynthia…he might have done anything to her…'

'Did he hurt you?' Phipps looked down at her face. 'It was madness to confront him alone, Amanda.'

'I know, but I could only think of her. He thought I had written that letter—the one telling her mother that he was not an honourable man.'

'You did not?'

'No, for I thought it best to tell her my opinion in person when we met at Brock's house. I have no proof of anything…he has always been accepted by society. Why should he have done such a desperate thing?'

'The only reason he could have embarked on such a wicked course must be because he'd been turned from the house and refused the chance to propose to the woman he wanted, not for herself but for her fortune.'

'Do you think he needed her money so badly?'

'I imagine he must have done.'

'What has happened to her? She is not in his carriage?'

'I think not. We must assume that she was terrified, having been abducted, perhaps drugged—though it seems that she was brave enough to escape when she had the chance. She would, however, have been stranded far from her home, perhaps without money or means of paying for transport.'

'Oh, Phipps,' Amanda cried, looking at him worriedly. 'She must be so frightened—alone and with no means of getting home. You must go and search for her…'

'My first duty is to take you safely to your home, dearest. He is sleeping off all the wine he's drunk and will be no danger to you for a few hours, but I shall not feel safe until we have you home.'

'That is so kind and exactly what Mama would wish—but I fear for her, Phipps.'

'I shall go and question his servants and then I'll send my own to look if his men will tell me where to start.' He smiled down at Amanda. 'Go up to your mother now, my dearest. I must summon the landlord and see to this scoundrel.'

'Yes, of course,' she said. 'You were so strong

and clever to knock him down, Phipps. I shall go up now—but please discover what you can, for I shall be anxious about Cynthia until we discover more of her fate.'

Chapter Eight

Amanda had slept fitfully. Mama had snored for most of the night and that had kept her awake, but it was only a minor irritant for she was concerned over Cynthia's fate. Since she was not with the marquis she had got away from him, but where was she now? Anything could have happened to her, alone and away from her home, she would be so vulnerable.

Unable to rest, Amanda got up carefully so as not to disturb her mama or Jane; she went behind the screen to wash in cold water and dress in the gown she'd worn the previous day. It would do very well for travelling, for they would be home before nightfall and then she could change into a clean one. Now that it was morning, she could surely go downstairs and see if Phipps was about, for she longed to know if he had discovered anything the previous evening.

She ventured downstairs a little cautiously, fearing that she might meet the marquis, but discovered that only the landlord and a maid were about, cleaning up behind their customers of the previous evening. He inclined his head to her with a friendly smile.

'Are you looking for the gentleman, miss? He was out at the stables first thing, but I think he is in the parlour now.'

'Thank you, I shall go in.'

'Should I bring you a pot of tea and some fresh rolls, miss?'

'Thank you, yes.' Amanda gave him a grateful look and walked on to the parlour. She knocked at the door and Phipps opened it to her, offering her his hand and drawing her in.

'Are you always an early riser or could you not sleep?'

'I was too anxious to rest,' she said. 'Did you manage to discover anything?'

'I questioned his servants and one of them was eager to tell me as much as he knew. Shearne was careless when they stopped to change horses and she got away from him… He did not pursue her. It seems that by this time he knew Brock was on his trail.'

'Oh, but…she must have been in his company for some days.' Amanda looked at him anxiously. 'Unless this can be hushed up she will be ruined—even though she was not to blame.'

'I fear that may well be the case, unless it can be covered up in some way. I doubt if it is worth questioning Shearne more closely. He was carried unconscious to his room. However, I did manage to speak to his groom, before the man left in a hurry.'

'His groom ran off?'

Phipps smiled grimly. 'There were two servants in his employ and it appears that they were reluctant to help with the abduction, but he threatened them and they obeyed him. When I represented the seriousness of their offence to them, they took fright. One of them declared he would not work for the marquis again and left almost immediately. The other said he wanted money he was owed, but would be leaving Shearne's service as soon as he was paid.'

'Did you discover where she was abandoned?'

'They had stopped at the Dog and Gin, a posting inn some thirty-five miles from her home, I believe.'

'That is terrible,' Amanda cried. 'Anything may have happened to her, especially if she had no money with her—and if she was abducted it is unlikely that she was carrying her reticule.'

'I fear that may well be the case,' Phipps said. 'One thing, however—she had not been in Shearne's power for more than two days and they had been travelling all the time, she in a drugged state. His man told me that he was furious when she escaped and has been drunk for most of the time since then. It seems he was more interested in a forced marriage than seduction. And he feared that Brock would stop him before he had her safely hidden at his estates in the north.'

'How can it be that Brock was already searching for her? Surely he would hardly have had your letter...'

'I wondered, but then it came to me that Brock may already have been looking for the marquis on his own account. You remember that he was set upon in town?'

'Yes, of course,' Amanda said, her frown clearing. 'If Brock meant to have it out with him, he might indeed have been searching for him.'

'I believe Shearne intended to slink off to his estates in the north of England before he abducted Miss Langton, and when her mama sent him away with a flea in his ear, he acted out of spite or revenge. We cannot know the whole, but it may be that Brock was nearby when the abduction occurred and set out after them within hours—we can only pray that he may have come across her soon after she escaped her captor.'

'Should you leave us and begin the search for her?' Amanda held out her hand to him in supplication. 'I cannot bear to think of her lost and alone, perhaps at the mercy of another rogue.'

'My promise was to your mama and to you, Amanda,' Phipps said. 'However, I took the liberty of involving my groom—a trustworthy man who was with me in the Regiment. He will not reveal Miss Langton's secret, but he set off to look for her after he had broken his fast this morning. He will send word to us at your home if he discovers anything.'

Amanda nodded, giving him a grateful look. 'I am truly obliged to you, Phipps. Mama has her own servants, but she is never comfortable unless she has a gentleman to escort her. I own I should have liked you to search for Cynthia in person, for I dare say she may be frightened and anxious if she is stranded some distance from her home.'

'Believe me, Jackson is to be relied on in an emergency. He once got me back to headquarters through twenty miles of enemy territory and I was in a fever for half that time. He will leave no stone unturned in trying to find her.'

'Then I am doubly indebted to him,' Amanda said warmly. 'For bringing you to safety—as well as the service he may be called upon to render Miss Langton.'

'He will tell you that he did his duty, as we all did out there, Amanda, but I assure you that he is a good man.'

She was content with this. After breakfasting on tea and soft rolls with honey, she went back to the bedchamber she'd shared with her mama and discovered that both she and Jane were awake and her maid had brought them a similar breakfast to her own, which she had partaken of in the parlour below.

'Have you spoken to Phipps?'

'Yes, Mama. He was able to tell me a little.'

She explained all that he had discovered and what was being proposed to find Miss Langton, and Mama said she was satisfied that they had done all they could.

'It is not truly our affair, Amanda, but I should not want to neglect any detail that might avert a tragedy or indeed a scandal.'

Since Mama seemed content that they could reasonably do nothing more, Amanda decided to keep her fears to herself. She hoped that she would not be forced to confront the marquis before they set out, because if she were to come face to face with the man she was not sure that she could keep a still tongue. Any fear she'd had of him had turned to a just rage and she wished that she had some means of punishing him.

Fortunately, there was still no sign of Shearne when they gathered in the courtyard and the small convoy set off in the direction of Amanda's home. She heaved a sigh of relief when the country inn was left behind and hoped that it was the last she would ever need to see of him.

* * *

Looking about her own room, Amanda thought that she was glad to be here. She had enjoyed her stay in town, but was happy to be home again and to see smiling faces all about her. Everyone seemed to know about her engagement and they had all been eager to catch a first glimpse of her fiancé and to wish her happiness.

She had left Phipps talking to Papa in his study and come upstairs to change for a much-delayed dinner. The roads had been poor on the last stage of their journey and it was well past the hour they usually dined. Fortunately, Papa had instructed Cook to prepare a cold collation and a warming soup that she could heat when they arrived.

Amanda was glad to put off her crumpled gown, and to save her maid the trouble of looking out one of her London gowns said she would wear a green silk that she had not taken with her. However, when she tried it on it hung on her and looked awful, so she was obliged to choose a gown from amongst those that had been sent back with Papa, which had been hung up but not pressed; it took another twenty minutes to shake out the creases, and by the time she got downstairs even Mama was waiting with signs of impatience.

'I am sorry to keep everyone waiting, there was a problem with my gown,' she said apologetically. 'I had thought to wear my old green silk, Mama, but it is too big for me now.'

'Yes, I dare say,' Mama said. 'I think you will need to have several of your gowns altered, my love.'

'I should be happy to do them,' Jane offered, but Amanda laughed and shook her head.

'You are here to have a holiday and enjoy your-self—making the alterations to the gowns we have already chosen is quite enough, dearest Jane.'

The evening passed swiftly, for by the time din-ner was over and Mama had sent for the tea tray the ladies were beginning to yawn and within a short time of the gentlemen joining them, they said goodnight.

Amanda was able to say goodnight to Phipps in private, but there was no time to talk for ev-eryone followed them into the hall and she was obliged to take leave of him without saying half of what she wished to.

'Perhaps you will show me over the estate to-morrow?' Phipps asked her in a soft tone that only she could hear. 'I should like to see you ride.'

'Yes, of course, I should enjoy that,' Amanda said. 'I shall be ready to ride by eight….'

He gave her an approving look and bowed to Mama and Jane, then turned as Papa invited him to take a nightcap in his study. Jane and Mama were chattering, apparently discussing the herb garden in which Jane was very interested, and Mama was promising to show her some of her rare herbs on the morrow.

Amanda accompanied Jane to her bedchamber and spent a few minutes talking to her, before seeking her own room. She had dismissed her maid and was about to get into bed when someone knocked at the door and then her mother entered.

'I just wanted to say goodnight and to ask if you are happy to be home, my love?'

'Yes, Mama. I thoroughly enjoyed my stay in London—but I love to be at home, and in a day or so I shall make sure to visit all my friends. I've bought lots of small gifts and when my trunks are completely unpacked, I shall take them round to everyone.'

'Yes, that is so like you,' Mama said and kissed her cheek. 'You know, dearest, at first I thought you might have done better than a second son—but Lieutenant Phipps was such a comfort on the way here that I am quite content. I believe he thinks well of you, Amanda, and I suspect that you will be happier than I had imagined.'

'Thank you, Mama. Phipps is very kind—and capable. I always feel that everything will be fine once he is there to protect me.'

'Yes, he is a capable young man and you are a sensible girl not to expect too much. He may not be madly in love with you, but he will be a considerate husband. It seems that you have done better than I feared and I'm pleased for you.' She smiled as she went to the door. 'I am glad to be home. I do not think that I shall venture as far as London again for a long time. I do prefer Bath...'

Why was it that Mama's speech of congratulation had made Amanda feel quashed? She had always known that Phipps was not desperately in love with her, of course, but perhaps she'd hoped that he loved her a little. Mama's words made it plain that she thought it was merely a marriage of convenience on his part, though *he thought well of her...*

Such lowering words! Amanda was almost over-set by a feeling of depression. Had she been fool-ing herself into imagining that her chosen husband would come to love her in time? Clearly, Mama harboured no such thoughts and was congratu-lating her daughter on being such a level-headed girl that she did not regard it.

If only she knew the truth! How much her daughter longed to be loved with a passion that equalled her own. The doubts and foolish long-ings that assailed her if she once let down her guard. Yet she knew she must give no sign of her feelings, either to Mama or to Phipps—especially not Phipps.

Amanda merely inclined her head in answer. Her bed was made and she did not wish to change things for she was perfectly certain that no other man she had ever met would suit her as well as the tall, charming, handsome man who had sto-len her heart the first time he had smiled at her. Yet she also knew that if Phipps was kind to her and never found her too clinging or too dull, she could be happy with her lot. She liked London well enough for a visit, but was more suited to the country. All she needed to make her happy was her horses, her dogs…and someone to care for her. Phipps was certainly to be trusted with her comfort. He had proven his abilities on the journey from London. She was putting her trust in him and hoped that, even if he never loved her in quite the way she loved him, he would not inadvertently cause her pain too often, for she was certain he would never knowingly do so.

He had certainly set himself to please both her and her mother, and she could only hope that Phipps would not grow bored with his bargain in the coming months and years.

Phipps took a cordial leave of his host and went upstairs to the very comfortable chamber that had been prepared for him. He was pleasantly tired, though unused to such early hours, for in London he had been accustomed to staying out to the early hours and despite the long journey would readily have sat up another hour or two.

He loosened his cravat and Lord Hamilton's footman pulled off his boots for him, before asking if there was anything more he needed.

'No, thank you, Jenks,' he said pleasantly. 'I sometimes like to take a stroll outside before I sleep, though I shall not tonight—but in the general way…is there a side door that I can use to let myself in and out?'

'I'm sure I could provide you with a key, sir,' Jenks said. 'Most of the doors are locked and bolted, but there is a little side door that we usually leave for those returning late to their duties… a servants' entrance, sir.'

'That would suit me very well. You may show me tomorrow. Thank you.'

After the man had gone, Phipps sat down in a chair by the fireplace. No fire was burning for he had prevented the footman setting a match to it earlier. He was not cold, used as he was to much harsher conditions when in the army.

Pouring himself a brandy, he swirled the rich liquid in the huge balloon glass and stared at it reflectively. Lord Hamilton's house was large, but of no great age, and built more with comfort than grandeur in mind, which was a blessing for both the family and friends. His own house was much older—at least one wing of it was and the others had been built on in later centuries. It had a certain charm and he was in his way quite fond of the ancient house, but he thought Amanda might find it uncomfortable after living in such a house as this. Of course they would have a choice of residences once they were married, for she had her own estate, though Lord Hamilton had told him that the house was smaller than this and nothing remarkable.

'The land is the best part of the estate,' he'd told him. 'There is a great deal of property scattered about, though none of it would make a comfortable home for a gentleman's family. You may have to consider building on another wing—or pulling the whole down and rebuilding.'

'I must discover what Amanda wishes before I think of either,' Phipps said and the subject had been closed.

He sat thoughtfully, sipping his brandy and reflecting on the changes looming. Life was certainly going to be interesting for the foreseeable future; he would find it a challenge to administer his wife's estates, because he would not be content unless they flourished. He owed it to her to give her something in return for taking him, because his fortune was nowhere near the equal of hers.

Yet despite a slight awkwardness when he first learned just how wealthy she was, he had come to accept and look forward to the challenge. Life had been a trifle dull after he'd returned to England when the war ended. To kick his heels in an army barracks was too slow for a man with an intelligent mind and a fund of energy. However, a feeling of contentment had come over him of late, for though it had taken him some time to bring himself to propose marriage to Amanda, he had discovered that he was more comfortable with his bargain than he'd imagined at the start.

He'd always thought Amanda had a lovely face, which matched her nature, though she had undoubtedly been a little on the plump side. Unless he was mistaken, she had shed several inches these past weeks, which had improved her figure, and her features were more defined somehow. There was a glow about her, her hair glossy and her skin clear. She had always had an enchanting smile and beautiful eyes, but she seemed to be so much more lively than when they first met in London. She would never of course be the equal of Miss Langton, but still he did not regret his choice, for he believed the beauty to be self-ish and, though he was outraged that a man like Shearne had sought to take advantage of her, he did not think he would wish to be her husband, even for a fortune. No, he much preferred his little Amanda, who could be a darling and aroused his protective instincts.

Phipps yawned and stretched and walked over to the window, staring out at the night sky for some time…until he became aware that he in turn was being watched from somewhere out there in the darkness.

Phipps turned and blew out the candle before looking back towards the shadows, where he had seen something move. It was almost pitch black out there, for layers of cloud hid the moon. He concentrated his gaze for several minutes, but whatever had been there had gone—perhaps he had imagined it. Yet he was sure that a man had stood in the shadows looking up at his window. He must have been clearly visible for the curtains were not drawn and the candle was lit behind him.

If someone was watching the house, they knew exactly where Phipps was lodged. Yet surely that was his imagination. Who could be watching the house—and why? It made no sense to him.

He dismissed the idea almost at once. This was England, not a foreign land at war. He did not need to imagine spies or enemy sharpshooters. If anyone had been there, it was probably one of Lord Hamilton's keepers taking a last stroll round before he retired.

Yawning, he drew the curtains, returned to the bed and began to strip off his clothes. He had arranged to ride with Amanda early in the morning and did not wish to disappoint her.

Over the next two days, Amanda divided her time between showing Phipps the estate and making Jane feel at home. However, although happy to walk in the gardens with Amanda, Jane seemed as content to sit in the parlour sewing while Lady Hamilton spoke to her about the wedding.

Mama had drawn up a wedding list, adding in those relatives and friends that Phipps particularly wished to ask, and Jane took her turn in helping to write them out, for there were more than three hundred and fifty in all. Papa said they would need to have a marquee in the garden to hold the overspill for the reception and joked that Amanda was bent on ruining him, while at the same time adding people that he'd thought of to their list and insisting that no expense should be spared.

It was on the morning of the fifth day that a letter arrived for Amanda that greatly relieved her mind.

Cynthia had written to her at some length.

My dearest Amanda,

I must tell you that if scurrilous rumours have reached you concerning my elopement with the Marquis of Shearne you must ignore them. Mama received information that made her think he was a rogue and she forbade me to see him. As I had not formed an affection for him I naturally obliged her.

Unfortunately, I met with an accident when out for an early walk and, having fallen into a deep ditch and rendered myself unconscious, I lay there for some time. When I recovered my senses it was night and I discovered that I could not climb out of the ditch for it was too deep. I called all night, but no one came near and it was the following day that I was found by a chance traveller, who rescued me and carried me home, but not before nightfall.

Mama had been so worried and erroneously believed I might have fled with the marquis because she forbade me to see him, and unfortunately one of our neighbours overheard her crying and telling Papa that I had gone off with him. We fear that rumours may have spread for the lady is an inveterate gossip, but hope that my reappearance so soon after the event—and Major Brockley's kind testimony to having found me fallen in that wretched ditch—may avert a scandal.

The major has been so kind and we have been invited to stay at his home before the house party to which you are invited. We leave almost immediately and should be there when you receive this letter. I know I may trust you to keep this to yourself, Amanda, but Brock has made me an offer of marriage. You may be surprised, as I was myself, for I had not thought him truly one of my suitors, but it is so and I have accepted him.

I am looking forward to seeing you in August and I must congratulate you on your own marriage and hope that we shall continue as

friends, as seems likely since our future hus-
bands are the best of friends.
   Your devoted friend,
   Cynthia Langton

Amanda read the letter twice and then took it to Mama, who puzzled over it and then shook her head in disbelief.

'You may depend upon it that this is the tale they have put about to save her reputation, for Phipps had it from Shearne himself when he was in his cups—but of course you must pretend to believe it, Amanda.'

'Yes, Mama, of course. I would not harm Cynthia for the world. It is clear that Major Brockley found her and took her home. Do you suppose he truly cares for her?'

'One must suppose so. It would be extreme to marry her simply to repair her damaged reputation, I think.'

Phipps was undecided, frowning over the letter for some minutes in silence. 'Brock is a law unto himself, Amanda. If he thought he was in some part to blame for what happened to Miss Langton, he might act out of chivalry—but who knows what was in his mind?'

'Mama says I must accept her story as true, Phipps.'

'Yes, of course, for she will tell you the truth if she believes she can trust you, but in all courtesy you must appear to believe her.'

'I should not dream of doing otherwise,' she said, 'though I might have wished she had trusted me enough to know the truth.'

'She may well confide in you when you meet,' Phipps said and touched her hand, 'but to write it in a letter…which might be read by anyone…'

'Yes, of course.' Amanda's brow cleared. 'I am so glad it has all come well for her. Now I can stop worrying about her and think only of the future.'

'Yes, much better,' he agreed, looking at her. 'You are dressed for walking. I had thought I might take you for a drive—perhaps begin your lessons?'

'I should like that very much if you would do so this afternoon, but it is my intention this morning to begin my visits…to people living on the estate. They will be eagerly waiting to hear news of my sojourn in town, Phipps, and of course my marriage.'

'Then I must not hinder you—but you will not go alone?'

Amanda looked at him in surprise. 'I have walked these fields since I was ten years old quite alone. Indeed, I often walk as far as the village. I cannot think I shall come to harm where I am everywhere known—and liked. Mama does not mind at all, you know.'

'I do not suggest that it is in any way improper, just that...' He shook his head, but looked anxious. 'Would you accept my company, Amanda?'

'Yes, of course, if you can be bothered. Most of them are Papa's old servants, men and women who have either worked in the house and gardens or on the estate. They live in a hamlet of grace-and-favour cottages that Papa built at the edge of the estate. It is a long tramp for...' She laughed and looked up at him with mischief in her eyes. 'You are accustomed to town living, I think?'

His caught fire and he gave a shout of laughter. 'You wretch, Amanda! Do you think me soft from town living? I will have you know that we often marched twenty or more miles a day in pursuit of the enemy.'

'Oh, but that was some time ago,' she said with a provoking look.

Phipps inclined his head, much amused. 'It would be quite improper of me to list my sporting achievements, my love, but I shall take leave to tell you that I am able to walk quite as far as you.'

'Now you put me on my mettle,' she said. 'Very well, I shall give you one of my baskets to carry and I warn you they are heavy—but will be lighter on the way home, I promise.'

Phipps smiled, looking at her with a challenge in his eyes and something more that made her heart race. He had never looked at her in just that way before and she could not help feeling pleased that she had captured his interest.

'I shall be down in a moment,' she promised and headed towards the stairs, meeting one of the maids as she came along the corridor carrying two baskets packed with small gifts. 'Oh, Janet, I shall not need you to help me after all. Lieutenant Phipps is to accompany me.'

Amanda smiled to herself as she took the baskets, wondering what had prompted her to allow Phipps to believe she intended to walk alone—

but some devil had got into her and she could not regret the impulse, even if she was becoming a little devious.

Had she not allowed Phipps to imagine she intended to make the long walk entirely alone, she doubted that he would have wished to visit Papa's elderly dependants. It was a trifle wicked of her to be sure, but even here in the country there was very little chance for them to be alone.

Chapter Nine

All of Amanda's friends had been delighted to receive a visit from her *intended* and everyone invited them to sit down and partake of homemade wine and cakes. Indeed, if they had drunk more than a sip of every glass of elderberry, parsnip or elderflower wine, and even a half of the glass of sloe gin pressed on them by old Mr Greene, who was almost, Amanda had told him, like a grandfather to her, they would have been very merry indeed.

Phipps had spent an amusing and informative morning. Any small barriers that remained had fallen as he watched Amanda in her element. He'd known in London that she was prettily behaved and a generous girl, but here in the midst of people who worshipped her, she was a young goddess. It was apparent that a visit from Miss Hamilton was much to be prized and each of the elderly recipients of the gifts she brought were as much delighted by the fact that she'd brought her fiancé to visit as by the expensive treats of chocolate mints, Turkish Delight, tobacco and French brandy, which she had bestowed on Mr Greene, who had once been a footman at the Grange. He was a keen gardener in his retirement and pressed a bowl of early strawberries on her, saying that he knew she was partial to them and he had plenty more in his garden.

They were warm from the sun and fresh picked, and on their way home Amanda and Phipps had shared them, eating the plump, soft, ripe fruit with much enjoyment and laughter. Once the juice had dripped down Amanda's chin and on a sudden instinct he caught it on his finger and then sucked it. Looking at her mouth, reddened by the juice, he'd known an overpowering urge to draw her into his arms. The passion of the kiss they shared had shocked him, for he had not expected it, but there was something sensual about eating warm strawberries in a country lane. Phipps had been caught by a flame that rushed through him, making him breathe harshly when he finally released her.

It was so unexpected that he could not at first credit how much he had enjoyed that kiss. He had not thought it would be hard to make love to her, but now he understood for the first time that it would be a pleasure.

What had changed? Phipps could not be certain. Yes, she had lost a little weight, but it was not that alone. He'd once had a plump mistress and she'd suited him well enough, but his feelings for Amanda were not merely tolerance now. What was it that had made him see her with new eyes? Was it the glow she carried with her, or her sense of humour that had not showed itself so much in society—or was it the freedom she had to be herself in the country amongst her own people?

She looked up at him curiously, her eyes dark with a look of smouldering desire that had been newly awakened, suddenly aware of something that he guessed she had thought little of before.

'I beg your pardon,' he said huskily. 'You looked so adorable that I could not resist. I hope you will forgive me?'

'Is there anything to forgive?' she asked shyly. 'We are to be wed and I fear I am quite ignorant in these matters, even though I am a country girl and aware of the basics of life, but…I had as lief be taught a little before our wedding night, if it pleases you?'

Phipps looked down at her, feeling an odd sensation somewhere in his solar plexus. 'It would please me beyond anything,' he murmured, his voice deep and thick with the desire that she had unwittingly aroused. 'I enjoyed our kiss very much, but we have some time to wait and I must be careful not to carry it too far too soon. I ought not to take liberties even if you are to be my wife.'

Amanda did not argue, merely lowering her gaze. He sensed a slight withdrawal and wondered if he'd hurt her in some way, though he could see no reason for it. If he held back from indulging his desire to make love to her, it was for her own sake—she must remain innocent until they wed because no one could ever be certain of the future. It would be quite shocking if something should happen to him and the marriage never happen. Had he followed his own desires… A smile touched his lips, for the picture of her lying naked in his arms was enticing; her lush curves would, he thought, tempt many a man—but there was so much more to the woman than her body.

'You caused quite a sensation,' Amanda told him, resuming her bantering chatter almost without pause as they walked on. 'Mr Greene actually told me that he could not have chosen better for me himself—and Miss Petersham said you were the embodiment of her dreams...'

Phipps laughed to hear himself so described and the slight awkwardness was forgot, though it gave him pause for thought. Amanda was so much more than he'd imagined when he'd seen her in London, for she had been in Miss Langton's shadow for most of the time and, being a modest girl, did not put herself forward in society. Here in the country, she was in her element and had changed or grown...or perhaps it was simply that he had not previously understood her.

There was, he realised, much more to the lady he'd asked to be his wife than he had first thought.

Changing her gown for one more suited to an afternoon to be spent driving, Amanda was lost in thought. Phipps's kiss after he licked the strawberry juice from his finger was something she had never encountered before. His previous kisses had been sweet and enjoyable—but that kiss... It had shaken her to the very core of her being, arousing such a whirl of fierce passions that she had been for a moment swept quite away. She'd seen something in his eyes, an answering need that made her feel that he wanted to lay her down in the sweet meadow grass and... There her mind stopped, for to imagine those sensations brought to fulfilment was shocking.

What a little wanton she was to wish that he'd given in to that urge. In her ignorance she had blundered in, causing him to retreat and make polite apologies—but she had been at fault for showing her pleasure too much. Amanda had not realised that it would repulse him if she responded so eagerly, but she'd seen the banking down of the fires and guessed that he had acted on impulse. Phipps expected her to be sensible, to be a complacent wife. She might respond to his lovemaking, but she must not initiate more or show too much eagerness.

She realised that it was going to be harder than she'd imagined hiding her feelings for Phipps once they were married. If his kiss could arouse such fire in her—a blazing inferno that had threatened to sweep away all barriers—what would happen on their wedding night? Would he be disgusted if she gave herself to him with complete abandon?

Now that was going beyond what was right and proper. If Mama guessed what was in her heart, she would not call Amanda a sensible girl. In general she was placid, slow to rise to anger. She had always done what she saw to be right, never holding back when it came to helping others, and she saw that it might be difficult to hold back enough of herself when she lay in Phipps's arms. Yet she would not have him made uncomfortable; he must not be made to feel guilty because he could not love her. However much it cost her, she would never ask him to give more of himself than he felt able…but perhaps he did not find her unattractive, for a man could not kiss like that and feel nothing—could he?

Being at heart still a sensible girl, Amanda banished all her hopes and fears as she joined Phipps for their drive that afternoon. He had brought with him a pair of beautiful grey horses, one of his servants driving them in easy stages from his home. Amanda's father had insisted on stabling them, though it had meant sending some of their own hacks to be housed at a farm nearby.

'I chose these because I thought them the most gentle of my teams,' he told her. 'You ride very well, Amanda, and your horses are spirited, but driving is different.'

She told him she was entirely in his hands and he nodded his approval. For a start he asked her to observe the way he did things, but then he handed the reins over, telling her how to hold them and nodding his approval as she took them exactly as he instructed. She was at last permitted to let the horses go and they proceeded at a stately trot with Phipps smiling and approving as she handled the ribbons with such ease that he questioned her.

'Are you sure you have never driven before?'

'Only Nanny's gig once or twice, but never a team—and never horses of this quality and breeding. I always found it easier to ride for the roads here are not good for driving, as we have seen this afternoon, and I can go everywhere on my mare. However, I do wish to learn and I am grateful for your patience, Phipps.'

'You are a quick learner and a pleasure to teach,' he said in such a way that she thought he truly meant it. 'I believe in time you will be a notable whip.'

'Thank you, I am flattered.'

'No, I do not flatter. You are a very surprising young woman, Amanda. I had not thought—' He broke off as he heard a sound and then suddenly grabbed the reins from her. 'Get down, Amanda; drop your head as low as you can and hold on tight...'

Even as he spoke, they heard the sound of a shot from close by. It seemed to have been aimed at Amanda, for it whistled over her head and, had he not shouted at her, must, she thought, have hit her. Phipps had put the horses to a gallop and they raced over very rough roads for some minutes, shaking her to the core and jolting her so that she felt she must be bruised all over. At last, when she began to feel uncomfortably sick, he reined the sweating horses in and then stopped them, turning to look at her, his mouth thinning in anger.

'Forgive me, that was Turkish treatment,' he said in a voice deep with emotion. 'I caught sight of the gun, its barrel glinting in the sunshine, and my instinct told me it was aimed at you. I am sorry for shocking you. Are you all right?'

Amanda was feeling much shaken, but she managed to smile at him. 'A little shaken, both physically and mentally,' she confessed. 'Who could it have been? I have never been shot at in my life. Do you imagine it was a poacher?'

'I very much doubt it,' he replied. 'Poachers work in stealth, mostly at night and they do not shoot at people. I have been trained to notice such things and the glinting of the sun on metal warned me, but I saw only the gun, not who aimed it.'

'But why would anyone wish to shoot me?'

'I do not know,' Phipps said, frowning. 'You have always walked safely on your father's lands, as you told me, but...' He hesitated, then, 'I should perhaps have said something before, but I had dismissed it.'

Amanda lifted her eyes to his. 'What did you dismiss, Phipps?'

'It was the night we arrived here. I was not tired and I sat drinking a glass of brandy in my room for some time, just thinking. Then I walked to the window and looked out. My candle was lit and I must have been visible to anyone outside. Just for a moment I thought something moved in the darkness, but by the time I blew the candle out so that I could see better, it had gone. I imagined it must be one of the keepers.'

'Yes, so would I,' Amanda said. 'Papa has some three or four of them to patrol the estate and I dare say he was taking a last stroll past the house.'

'Supposing that it was not a keeper but someone watching the house—watching me or you, Amanda?'

'Who…?' She stared at him, eyes widening as she saw the look in his own. 'You think it might have been the marquis…Shearne, do you not? That he might be vindictive enough to seek revenge because he believes that I ruined his chances with Cynthia?'

'I gave it but a passing thought until that rogue fired at you,' Phipps said, an angry glint in his eyes. 'Jackson arrived here this morning. He had found no trace of Miss Langton, but as we know that Brock discovered her and carried her home that does not surprise me. What he did say was that he'd heard disturbing rumours of Shearne. He went back to the inn where we met him and…' He paused, clearly reluctant to go on.

'Pray tell me, Phipps. I would hear it all.'

'It is an ugly story, Amanda. From what Jackson was told Shearne was in a raging temper the next morning and…he thrashed his servant, leaving him lying on the ground bleeding. He then tried to engage post boys and a groom to drive his coach, but when none would serve him, he took a gentleman's horse from the stables and rode off without paying his shot, but leaving his carriage and horses behind.'

'That was disgraceful behaviour, but no more than might be expected of such a man.'

'Well, the innkeeper summoned a magistrate and the owner of the horse put in a claim for compensation, such an uproar and the poor servant lying close to death in the innkeeper's chamber.'

'That is the worst of all—to treat one's servants in such a way is what Papa would never put up with. Shearne can never return to society if this becomes known.'

'You may depend that he knows it—and that is what makes him more dangerous.'

'You think that it was he who watched your room—and he that fired on us?'

'I think it likely for I am aware of no other enemies, Amanda—and you are so well known, not to say loved, by your people, that I think it can only be a man so eaten up by petty jealousy and anger that he would do anything to spoil another man's happiness. He accused me of having snaffled the best prize on the marriage mart and was so rude, as well as violent, that I was obliged to give him a leveller.'

'Yes, you told me he was drunk—but is that cause enough for hatred? To kill me simply to be revenged on you...'

'I see you find it hard to believe, but I have met men of his ilk before. You also aroused his anger when you shielded Miss Field from his amorous intentions. I dare say he dislikes you as much as he dislikes me.'

Amanda could hardly repress the shudder. She felt suddenly cold, as if a dark shadow had obscured the sun. 'That is quite horrid,' she said and twisted her hands in her lap. 'What are we to do? If Mama knew...it would quite spoil her pleasure in the wedding.'

'I shall speak to your father,' Phipps said. 'It would not harm to double the number of keepers patrolling the grounds, but it should be kept from Lady Hamilton, and Miss Field also, if possible.'

'Yes, I see that Papa must know,' Amanda said.

She reached for his free hand and took it. 'Thank you for saving my life, Phipps.'

'It was my privilege and my pleasure,' he said and grasped her hand tighter. 'I could not have done otherwise, my love.'

She smiled and then tremulously removed her hand from his. 'We should go back for tea, Phipps. Mama will expect us—and we must not distress her.'

'I would not do so for the world,' he assured her. 'But are you able to face her? This has not overset you?'

'I must admit that I wish it had not happened, but I do not see why we should let the spiteful actions of an evil man change our plans—or spoil them.'

'You are as brave as I might have expected,' he said. 'If you will give me leave, I shall send word to Brock, for though I am equal to standing up to this devil alone, I believe he would wish to know. They have history, Amanda—and if the time for a reckoning has come, Brock will want to be here when it happens.'

'Of course,' she said and smiled at him, hiding the terrible fear for the marquis that had entered her mind. 'Two heads must be better than one. If we are not to live our lives in fear of being murdered, a plan must be made and you will know how it must be done, for you are both soldiers, are you not?'

'You put me on my mettle,' he said and laughed down at her. 'I have been used to commanding my men, some of whom are in my employ still—and Jackson shall fetch them here. You shall not be shot at again, Amanda—not if I can prevent it.'

He drove them back to the house without speaking, handing the phaeton over to his groom and stopping to speak with him in urgent tones as Amanda went into the house. She ran upstairs to her room, changing quickly into a tea gown and splashing cool water on her heated cheeks before going down to join her mother and Jane in the parlour for tea.

It was not easy to smile as if nothing untoward had happened, but she did not wish to frighten either Mama or Jane, and so made herself laugh with all the ease in the world. Papa did not come in for tea, as was his usual habit unless he was detained by estate business, and nor did Phipps. She guessed that they were deep in a discussion as to how to keep Amanda safe whilst every effort was made to discover where the marquis was staying. Once they had found him, he could be watched and if he should make another such attempt…

She dismissed the pictures from her mind, accepting a cup of tea and a small cake from the hovering maid, but although she sipped her tea she made no attempt to eat. The food would have lodged in her throat and, despite all the exercise she'd done that day, she had no appetite.

'You cannot be serious?' Lord Hamilton stared at Phipps in dismay as he unfolded his story. 'Are you telling me that a rogue actually fired on my daughter on our own land?'

'As to whether he meant to hit Amanda or me I cannot say for certain, but I told her to get down, for if either of us was to be shot I had far rather it be me than her. The shot whistled over her head and must have hit her had she not obeyed me, but she did so instantly and without the slightest show of hysterics.'

Lord Hamilton smiled oddly. 'My daughter is a sensible girl, sir. She would not give way to distress over such a thing, nor would she show fear. As a child she was always ready to throw her heart over any fence and she will hold her nerve now. Her mama is another matter. We must do what we can to prevent her from hearing of this, for she might have a fit of the vapours and would undoubtedly forbid the girl to stir from the house. I shall make certain you are both watched wherever you go.'

'I have sent for some men who served under me in Spain and France. Once they get here they will search for whoever has done this thing and watch him wherever he goes. I believe it to be Shearne and if he is discovered in the vicinity it will be an easy matter to shadow him; my men are used to such work for we were engaged in special missions for Wellington, though it was not generally known.'

Lord Hamilton looked at him with a new respect. 'You must have risked more than most to serve your country, sir.'

'We all served the best way we could and my men had their methods. Until they get here, it will be best if one of us and a groom accompanies Amanda wherever she goes—though I believe

Shearne does not much care which of us he kills, for the death of either would serve his purpose.'

'He must be a vindictive devil.'

'If I was at liberty, I could tell you a story that would make your toes curl,' Phipps said, 'but it is not my secret to divulge. Let it be enough to say that if it would not have ruined a young lady's life, he should have been stricken from society years ago.'

'I can guess what you may not tell me,' Lord Hamilton said. 'It makes me shudder to think that such a man is at large—and to fear for my daughter...'

'You have my word that no harm will come to her if I can prevent it, sir.'

'Yes, I believe you.' Lord Hamilton nodded and looked thoughtful. 'Not a word to her mama then, and we'll do our best to make sure this evil man does not harm either of you.'

Phipps took his leave and went up to his own room. He too was thoughtful, for the incident had caused him to feel such a surge of anger against whoever had fired that shot that he had not been able to order his thoughts for some time. When he'd told Amanda to get her head down his only thought was to protect her, for he could not be sure who the sniper meant to shoot at—but, as he'd told her father, he had preferred that if either should be shot it should be he that took the ball. The thought of Amanda hurt or killed had been so horrifying that he had not been able to support it.

Any gentleman must needs protect the lady he intended to marry—that went without saying—but Phipps had not known how desperate the urge to protect her would be until the danger arose. A slight smile touched his mouth, for he realised that her mischievous smile, her generous manner and her courage had turned mere liking into something far more intense. She had, without particularly trying, become of more importance to him than he had imagined she could be at the start. He could not and did not call his feelings for Amanda romantic love, but he knew that she had found her way into his affections and that the prospect of a world that did not hold her in it was appalling.

The discovery left him feeling slightly bewildered, for she could never be the tall, willowy nymph, which had in the past been the type of woman he most admired. However, at the back of his mind, he suspected that sometimes those very beautiful, helpless ladies might prove tiresome after the first heat of passion had worn off—whereas Amanda would be a true companion, a woman with whom one could share one's passions and who would be a helpmeet and a staunch supporter.

He shook off his musings as he went up to change for dinner. The Hamilton family was giving a dinner party this evening and he must make sure that no one was allowed to discover his secret.

Amanda's charming manner at dinner that evening could have given no one a hint of the churning feelings in her breast. She greeted all their guests with the same warm smile as always, enquiring after their families and remembering the names of all the younger offspring, who remained at home in the nursery.

Papa's look of affection told her that he was proud of his daughter, but she was pleased to see that he introduced Phipps to their neighbours and friends with a warmth that had not been there at the start. It seemed that Phipps had found favour with both her parents and she was aware of a glow inside her.

She knew at once that their friends liked Phipps, because of the way he was asked for his opinions on various aspects of country life and answered, knowledgeably if he was able and with an apology if it was beyond him, confessing that he was but a novice in the art of estate management.

In this way he made friends, was given advice and asked if he would care to ride out to look at a neighbour's fields—and to give advice on a mare. Phipps had far more knowledge in this field and his horses had been much admired, for they had been seen about and were considered to be sweet goers. His confession that he hoped to set up a breeding sables, perhaps at Amanda's estate, brought a flood of enquiries and the offer of a mare that had good blood, but did not suit its owner as a riding horse.

By the end of the evening, the happy couple had been invited to suppers, dinners and card parties, besides a picnic to look at the charming ruins of a medieval abbey, and Phipps to take part in the local cricket derby with a neighbouring village. On being told that Phipps excelled with the ball rather than the bat, his popularity was assured.

* * *

Later that evening, after all their guests had gone, Amanda lingered in the conservatory to say goodnight to Phipps. She had taken him there to show him a beautiful and very delicate orchid that had just come into flower, but in truth, she had hopes that he might feel tempted to repeat the kiss he had given her earlier that day. However, she had no intention of giving him a hint and made polite conversation, just as if her whole body did not cry out to be held and kissed.

'You will be Mr Tompson's friend for life if you can bowl out Sir Marshall Rawlings. Every year he manages to cling to his wicket long enough to claim the winning runs. We have several good batsmen, but nary a bowler in sight.'

'I discovered my ability at Eton,' Phipps told her. 'I was never much good on the rugby field, but in the science of boxing I excelled and was reasonably proficient on the cricket field.'

'What other talents do you have?' she asked, a hint of mischief in her eyes. 'I have heard it said you are a notable whip and good with pistols.'

'In that my skill may have been overrated, but I am considered deadly with a knife—' He checked and looked at her in consternation. 'Not a fit subject for a lady's ears, forgive me.'

Amanda's curiosity was aroused, for it seemed an odd skill for a gentleman. 'When did you develop that skill, Phipps? Was it in the army?'

'I could always throw anything with accuracy,' he said, an odd smile on his mouth. 'Balls, sticks, knives. There are times when speed and silence is of the essence in war, Amanda. A knife is sometimes faster and more deadly than a ball.'

'Oh...' She looked at him, considering. 'What secrets you soldiers must have between you. It shows a new side of you, sir—one that would never be suspected in the drawing rooms of society.'

'I trust it does not give you a distaste for my company?'

'Nothing could do that,' she said frankly. 'It merely makes me more aware of what your life must have been when you were serving with the army. In London we see only the dress uniforms and think of how smart and elegant the officers look—but life cannot have been that way when you were in Spain and France.'

'No, indeed. You would not think us smart then,

my love, if you saw the state of our uniforms, which became torn and stained with mud and worse—and the way we often lived. When we were settled for a time we might find a good billet, but on the move we more often slept on the ground fully dressed and sometimes did not wash for days.'

'I had always thought that it must be uncomfortable to be at war,' she admitted. 'One hears of glory or the horrors of a resounding defeat, but nothing of the rigours endured by an army on the march.' Her eyes met his in a thoughtful gaze. 'Is that why you have sent for some of your former comrades?'

'When the war finished several of my men were dismissed, for in peacetime the army is always reduced. I found work for six of those I trusted most on my estate. We worked well together and they needed employment with someone who would understand their ways; it is not always easy for an old soldier to return to civilian life and they are glad to serve me. They will discover if Shearne is in the district and, if he shows any sign of trying to murder either of us again, he will be stopped.'

'You told Papa,' Amanda said and nodded. 'That

is why he respects you. He was unable to enter the army because his father told him his duty was to the estate, but I know he admires bravery.'

'We have reached a comfortable understanding,' Phipps said and took her hand in his, lifting it to kiss the fingers. 'As I believe we have also, Amanda. I am very tempted to make love to you, but in the circumstances I feel we must not sneak away to be alone for it might prove dangerous… and here we might be discovered at any time.'

With a sigh she tried to keep inside, Amanda acknowledged the truth of his statement, which made him laugh and bend his head to kiss her lightly on the lips.

'The time will pass, my dearest girl,' he said. 'Just think how much we are learning of each other's ways. I have come to know you much better in these past few days than in all the time we spent in each other's company in town.'

'I hope you have not been disappointed?' she said and tried for lightness, but feared she failed.

'Disappointed? Never,' he said and touched her cheek with one finger. 'I like what I see very much, my love—and it distressed me that you were in danger this afternoon.'

'You were in as much danger,' she said seriously. 'I should not have liked it had you been harmed, Phipps. I do trust that you will be careful. I know you were a soldier and snipers can hold no fears for you—but I am not as fearless as you.'

'Believe me when I say that I do not intend he shall succeed in killing either of us. I have far too much to live for to give up my life easily—and I would rather die than see you hurt.'

Amanda's cheeks heated and she was glad there was little light in the conservatory, for she would not have liked him to see how near to being overset his words had brought her.

'I believe I must go up and say goodnight to Mama,' she whispered, her heart racing wildly.

'Sleep well and do not let what happened prey on your mind,' he said. 'Once my men get here we shall very soon have the culprit behind bars.'

Amanda nodded, but made no reply. If she wondered whether the marquis taken in the act would ever make it to a prison cell, she did not question. She felt a sense of relief that Phipps had the matter in hand, for she knew that her father's keepers would do their best, but had no experience of protecting anyone against the spiteful acts of a man she thought must be a little deranged.

What other reason could there be for his attack on them? Phipps had been forced to knock Shearne down and she had cut him in the street—but surely that was not enough to cause a man to attempt murder?

Leaving Phipps in the conservatory, she went upstairs and along the landing to her mother's room to say goodnight. After a few minutes, she popped in to wish Jane a good night and then went away to her own room.

Standing in the window for a few minutes, she looked down into the gardens. There was not much light, for the moon had gone behind the clouds and she could not see far. Pulling her curtains, she refused to let her imagination run away with her. Even if the marquis had watched the house the first night Phipps had come to stay, he was unlikely to be here now. Her father had increased the patrol guarding the grounds and if anyone tried to approach the house they would be challenged and shot at.

She had dismissed her maid, because the gown she was wearing was easy enough to slip out of without help and she wanted to be alone to think. Phipps had seemed so very approving this evening and the look in his eyes almost made her believe that he had started to be just a little bit in love with her...even if he did not yet know it himself.

Chapter Ten

Amanda could not quite rid herself of the shadow that lay over her, but despite the knowledge that she was being heavily guarded and her freedom curtailed in that she could no longer go for a long tramp across the fields with only her dogs for company, she contrived to be happy.

Jane was still staying with them and Amanda spent a part of every day with her having fittings for her new gowns. Several of the dresses she had ordered in London had been delivered. Most had needed Jane's clever fingers to adjust them and the girls spent happy moments sewing and reading to each other.

Having made friends in the district, Phipps was content to ride out to visit them and to inspect horses and verdant fields. He normally spent the afternoons with Amanda, and sometimes Jane, for they were comfortable together. He had an expressive reading voice and all the ladies enjoyed it when he could be persuaded to give them a reading from one of the books they favoured.

In this way more than a week passed pleasantly, visiting friends in the evenings and receiving callers during the day. Jane was to stay for the picnic and the visit to the picturesque ruins that had been promised, after that she would go home and return a few days before the visit to Brock's family home.

It had surprised Amanda that nothing had been heard from the major, for Phipps had written to him at once, but she knew that no letter had been received in return and he had not called at the house. She supposed that he was too busy entertaining his fiancée and ceased to expect him to come. Phipps's own men had arrived within three days of being summoned and she knew that they were now searching for the marquis, though her father's men continued to patrol the grounds both day and night.

Therefore, on the day of the picnic she was able to set out with every expectation of pleasure in the treat. With so many people to watch over her as well Phipps, the marquis must have grown tired of being frustrated in his aims and had surely given up.

The abbey ruins were set in vast grounds still owned by the church, but much of the land was let out to tenant farmers. Around the picturesque walls, of which quite a few still stood, there was an area of open grassland, and set at a fair distance some shady trees and a wooden bench that had been thoughtfully set to give a pleasant view of the ruins.

Amanda's host had organised the servants to bring chairs, a trestle and board, which was soon covered with a pristine white cloth, and some blankets, which were spread on the ground for those who preferred to picnic informally.

The company, which included Amanda's mama, Jane, Phipps, two neighbours, their wives and daughters, their hostess, Lady Malden, her son, Malcolm, her daughter, Alison and two other single gentlemen.

The gentlemen amused themselves with an impromptu game of cricket, in which some of the ladies joined. Then a cold collation was served of chicken, ham, preserves, salad tomatoes and leaves, pastries, savoury pies and various sweet-meats for those who liked to nibble, all washed down with quantities of white wine, which the servants had somehow managed to keep cool.

It was a warm afternoon and after everyone had eaten their fill some of the ladies declared they wanted only to rest in the shade of the trees. A few of the gentlemen resumed their interrupted game, but Jane and Amanda decided to stroll and explore the ruins, which was after all the excuse for their outing.

'Would you like to come, Alison?' Amanda invited her hostess's daughter but she was absorbed in watching the cricket match, in which Phipps had just been invited to bowl.

'Perhaps later,' Alison said off-handedly, then clapped enthusiastically as Phipps clean bowled her father. 'Oh, well done, sir. Well done indeed!'

Amanda saw the smile on her pretty face and realised that her neighbour's daughter was more than a little taken with Phipps. She felt a little pang of jealousy, but squashed it immediately. There was no need to feel jealous because the tall and slender, rather lovely blonde was clearly giving him every encouragement to notice her.

He had responded politely each time that she addressed him, but given her no cause to harbour hope of arousing more than friendship in him.

Walking towards the ruins, which looked so picturesque from a distance, but rather dark and brooding as they approached, Amanda scolded herself for allowing even a prick of jealousy against a girl she'd known all her life. Alison's family were expecting her to marry well and Phipps would not have been their choice, even though he might have been hers had he been free. If she were to imagine an intrigue with every pretty girl he met, she would make her life miserable indeed and must stop this now on the instant.

Being a sensible girl, she did not imagine that Phipps had any intention of playing her false and put the foolish thoughts from her mind. Her arm slotted through Jane's, she talked to her of the ruins and the history of a once-great abbey. It had been destroyed at the time of King Henry VIII and left to moulder away over the centuries. The only wonder of it was that its ruined walls had not been carried away to build homes and cowsheds for the local people, but because it was rumoured to be haunted, it had been left to the elements to work their own destruction.

'Imagine what life must have been like here when the monks were alive,' Jane said. 'They would have tended their herb gardens, grown their own food...'

'I believe they made a kind of honey mead here, too, for they had a great many hives and their bees were famed,' Amanda supplied. 'It was a large industry and they used the wealth it generated for giving succour to the poor—though I often think the abbots of the time used a sizeable portion of it for their own good.'

Entering the ruins, Amanda shivered in the sudden coolness. Outside, the sun was very warm, but in here it struck through to the bones and she had an uncomfortable feeling that eyes were watching them—though she could see no one. However, the partition walls were still high enough in places to obscure the view and, though she was sure theirs was the only party visiting the ruins that day, provided a hiding place for any of evil intent. Yet the feeling she had was less of human menace than of something not...not of this earth. It was not surprising that a superstitious population would consider the place to be haunted, for if the wind whistled through the gaps in these walls at night, one could almost fancy they heard the screams of the monks as they fought to save their home.

'Where do you think that leads to?' Jane asked, nodding towards a curving stair leading upwards. 'Do you think it goes all the way up the tower?'

'I imagine it might have once,' Amanda replied. 'I think it might be dangerous for the tower looks unsafe in parts.'

'I should like to discover where it leads, should not you?'

'Oh, I think it would be unwise to venture up there,' Amanda warned, but Jane had walked away and was clearly intent on exploring.

Amanda was not a pudding heart, but she felt it would be unwise of her to follow up the stone steps lest they both find themselves in trouble. If Jane ran into difficulty, at least she could warn the gentlemen that they were needed to rescue her. However, she stood at the bottom of the stairs and craned her neck, calling up to her.

'Are you all right, Jane? Do be careful, those steps look as if they may be unsafe.'

Jane did not answer and Amanda thought she

ought to investigate for she could not leave her friend to struggle if she had encountered a difficulty. However, even as she put her foot on the first step she heard a sound behind her and froze, a chill of cold fear starting at the base of her neck.

'You will oblige me by remaining where you are, Miss Hamilton,' the man's voice said. 'I have no reason to harm your friend, but if you call to her for help I shall be obliged to do so.'

Amanda raised her head, removed her foot from the bottom step and turned to face him. 'I have no intention of asking her to help me, sir. I know very well she cannot and I do not wish her to be harmed.'

'If she stays out of my way, she will come to no harm.' Shearne's eyes glittered as he levelled his pistol at her. 'You cannot imagine how much pleasure it is going to give me to kill you,' he murmured. 'I know what you did—how you spoiled my chances with the Langton girl. You and that devil Brockley think to ruin me, but I'm too clever for the pair of you. No one makes a fool of me and gets away with it. Please step away from that stairway into the centre of the nave if you will. I have no wish to chase you up the tower, for then

I should be obliged to kill Miss Field as well—I want no witnesses.'

'Indeed, no, that would be very bad, would it not?' Amanda said, moving obligingly into the centre of the open space. 'I dare say you hope to escape unscathed, but you cannot have thought it through, sir. My fiancé will know it must have been you and he will hunt you down.'

The marquis gave a titter, his eyes moving so wildly from side to side that it struck Amanda he must have taken leave of his senses. Surely no sane man could expect to kill her when there was a party of ladies and gentlemen within a short distance. How could he hope to escape punishment?

'I hope he may.' Shearne laughed shrilly. 'His men have been hunting me for days, but I was too clever for them. I've been spying on you, Miss Hamilton. I've watched you at your bedroom window, seen your shadow as you undressed…how I should have loved to catch you then, to see the horror in your eyes as I taught you to respect your master.'

'I do not believe that I could learn anything from you,' Amanda said evenly. Her thoughts were busy as she looked about her. If she could make him look away…there were fallen blocks of stone and she might be able to throw one at his head…but he was moving closer to her and she disliked the look in his eyes. 'I should never acknowledge you as my master—so why do you not shoot me now?' Amanda did not know why she was goading him, but something bade her play for time. Inside, she knew that fear of him was almost suffocating her, but her strength of character carried her through. 'A man like you is hardly worthy of the name…' Her scorn and loathing made her strong as the pistol in his hand wavered and she saw that he was furious. She was more afraid for her friend than herself, in case Jane came back and he should take his revenge on her, and that kept her nerves steady. 'You are a fool if you think Phipps will suffer because I am dead. Why should he? I have already made my will naming him as my principal heir—so you will be making him a rich man if you kill me.'

'You scheming, lying whore,' the marquis screamed at her and made a grab for her arm. She jerked away, terrified of a man who had lost control of his senses and turned to run, but then she heard Jane's cry and saw that she had come down the stairs and was looking horrified.

Before Amanda had time to warn her to run back up, a man came through one of the archways and she saw that he had a rifle in his hand, which he had levelled at the marquis.

'Stand away from her, Shearne!' Brock commanded. 'You have no hope of escape. My men are all around you. You were followed here, but we lost you in the ruins and we but waited for you to make your move.'

Shearne ignored his command, grabbing hold of Amanda's arm and sticking the point of his pistol into the side of her neck. He gave a high-pitched cackle and she stared, fascinated, at the dribble of spittle on his chin. He must have been teetering on the edge of madness and Brock's arrival had sent him over the edge.

'Miss Field, go back up the tower and stay there until you are told to come down.' Brock shot the order at the frightened girl and silently she obeyed him. 'Shearne, I am giving you warning. If you harm Miss Hamilton, you will not live to see the hangman's noose. I shall shoot you down where you stand the moment you fire your pistol.'

'Damn you!' Shearne said. With one hand he pushed Amanda to her knees, then raised his pistol and fired straight at Brock. His ball caught him in the shoulder and he reeled back, clutching his hand to it. Amanda saw the red trickling through his fingers and tried to get up, thinking to go to his assistance, but Shearne had drawn another pistol from his pocket, a tiny one, but just as deadly, which he pointed at her head. She heard the click of the hammer as it was drawn back, saw Brock raise his rifle awkwardly to take aim, but before his finger could strike the hammer, the marquis suddenly shrieked in pain and slumped down to his knees, staring at her in shock as the pistol slipped from his hand. Amanda snatched it up and then raised her head to see Phipps approaching from the rear of the building. He must have walked round the ruins to find another entrance and come up on them unawares. It was only as he glanced down at the body of his enemy that she saw a long-handled dagger protruding from the marquis's back.

'Phipps,' she murmured, feeling a little sick and shamefully close to fainting. She suddenly realised how close to death she had come and felt an overwhelming desire to weep in his arms. However, she drew a deep breath, knowing she must not give in to the missish desire to break down and cry. Lifting her head with an effort, she said, 'I am all right. Go to Brock, he is hurt.'

'Shearne did not harm you?'

'No, you were in time. Go to Brock, we must get him to a doctor—I'll call Jane.'

She went to the bottom stair and called to her friend, who came down looking very pale and distressed. Amanda held out her hand and Jane took it thankfully.

'It is all right, dearest Jane. Phipps killed him. He was quite mad, you know. I dare say it was the kindest thing, for he would have been incarcerated in Bedlam or some such place of confinement, I imagine.'

'Oh, Amanda,' Jane said faintly. 'I was so afraid for you but I could not think of anything to do to help you…'

'Just as well you did not,' Amanda said in a practical tone. She forced herself not to give way, even though her knees felt weak and her heart was still racing. 'Poor Major Brockley was shot for his pains and, had Phipps not been extraordinarily clever, I think I should have soon been dead.'

'You are so calm,' Jane said, looking at her in awe. 'I thought I should faint, but then Major Brockley shouted at me and I obeyed him.'

'It was quick thinking on his part,' Amanda said, smiling inwardly, for she was not in the least calm, but knew she must give the appearance of being in command. 'Now, you must not faint, for I am relying on you to take Mama home and see that she does not worry too much.'

'But where will you be?'

'Mama's widowed cousin lives not two miles from here in the village we passed earlier, and I think we must take the major there. It is not expected that Cousin Sarah should nurse him, for she is not young, but nursed he must be—and I am perfectly able to do it.'

She led the way to where Phipps had supported Brock to his feet and put her plan to him. Brock was still conscious and made an unintelligible protest, but Phipps looked at her gratefully.

'It would be best not to transport him too far,' he agreed. 'Is there a doctor in the village?'

'Yes, and a good one. Cousin Sarah swears by

him. She is a generous, kind woman and I know she will take him in, but she cannot be expected to nurse him. I shall do that just at first—if you do not object?'

'I should be thankful for it. There are things I must see to once we have Brock safe and then I shall send one of the men for his own valet, who was once his batman. Franks will know what to do for the best when he arrives, but until then...'

'Cousin Sarah's housekeeper and I will manage him,' Amanda said. 'I insist on doing what I can, Phipps. He was shot saving my life and even my mama will not think it improper in me to offer my services.'

In saying that, Amanda was not quite correct, but although Mama did not quite like the idea she saw that her daughter was determined to repay a debt, and, since her affianced husband seemed to be grateful for the suggestion, she could only say that Amanda must remember her modesty and also the major's.

'I helped to nurse Papa through that fever,' Amanda said, 'and I am quite sure that Mrs Miller will make certain that nothing immodest occurs to provoke my blushes, Mama.'

'Well, I have always known you to be a sensible girl,' Mama said, secretly a little in awe of her daughter, who seemed all at once to have grown beyond her. 'Providing Cousin Sarah is willing, I can have no objection.'

Amanda thanked her calmly, ordered Phipps to place Brock in Mama's comfortable carriage and drive Jane and Mama in his phaeton. She would go with Brock and do what she could to stop the bleeding, as she had already sacrificed her pure cotton shawl by stuffing it inside the major's coat and tying her friend's shawl over his shoulder to bind him as tight as she could manage, Phipps had nothing to say except that he would not be far behind her.

Cousin Sarah was sitting in her comfortable parlour and rose to the occasion nobly. She ordered that the best guest chamber be prepared for the invalid, a smaller one for Amanda, and then sent her footman running to fetch the doctor, who, she assured them, would be only too willing to oblige them. Brock was almost immediately carried upstairs to the room hastily prepared for him, but as

Cousin Sarah told them, she always kept her beds aired just in case she had unexpected visitors.

Amanda followed the men upstairs and found that Mrs Miller, the housekeeper, had drawn back the covers in preparation. It was decided that only the major's coat and shirt should be removed, as well as his boots, of course. The coat was cut away ruthlessly, as was the shirt by a determined Amanda, with Phipps and Mrs Miller supporting him as he fell in and out of consciousness. The wound had been bleeding copiously, which made Mrs Miller shake her head and sigh over the poor man. Amanda asked for linen bandages to bind the wound and clean water.

'We have to stop the bleeding and seal the wound,' Phipps said. 'If the doctor is from home, he could bleed to death.'

'But what can we do?'

'I've taken a ball out of a man before this,' Phipps said. 'I need some boiling water, a needle and thread—and clean linens torn into strips.'

Mrs Miller hurried off to fetch what he needed, the maid following. She returned in a few minutes with the hot water. Watching with scared eyes, she retreated to the far side of the room, obviously reluctant to play any part in what was happening.

Phipps rolled up his sleeves and washed his hands; he was scrubbing them in cold water when another maid returned with everything he'd asked for.

'Would you rather leave this to me?' he asked, looking at Amanda.

'No, of course not. I shall assist you,' she said and brought the bowl containing the knife to him, together with quantities of rolled linen. 'He may come to as you cut him.'

'Yes, perhaps. Can you hold him steady while I probe for the ball?'

'Yes, of course.'

She stood by the bed as Phipps bent over his friend, pressing gently on his uninjured shoulder to hold him steady. The first slash of the knife had Brock rearing up with a scream of agony, but thankfully he fainted again almost at once. Phipps was deft and quick, finding the ball in a few minutes and flicking it out. Amanda removed it and dabbed at the blood oozing from the fresh wound.

Phipps had left the bedside and she was aware of him threading the needle with white silk. He came back to them and gathered the open flesh into a seam, sewing it quickly like the rolled edge of a blanket. Then Amanda wiped the wound free of blood again and together they pressed a pad of linen over their crude surgery and bound him tightly with bandages. Twice his eyes opened and he cursed them, but then swooned again almost immediately.

'Sorry, old fellow,' Phipps said. 'It's rough and ready, but you'll do until the doctor gets here.'

'Will he be all right?' Amanda asked anxiously. She was feeling rather weak and sat down in the chair next to the bed, not wanting him to guess how much she'd been affected. 'You were so efficient. You've done this before, I think?'

'In Spain there was not always a doctor when you needed one; they had too many badly injured men. If it was a simple wound we grew used to doing what we could. Had the wound been deeper or smashed his shoulder bone I could not have helped him—but it was no more than a flesh wound. Our main worry is infection or fever.'

'Thank heaven for it,' she said. 'I do not want him to die for my sake, Phipps.'

'You must not worry,' he said. 'Brock did what

he thought right. We must hope that there will be no fever.'

'When the doctor comes he may be able to advise us on that count...if he ever gets here. It must be half an hour since my cousin sent for him. Time enough for Brock to have bled to death had you not acted so swiftly.'

'And you, Amanda.'

'I did very little. I wish the doctor would come, though I suppose there is not much more he can do.'

The words had hardly left her lips when the door opened and Mrs Miller entered the room, followed by the doctor and the footman.

'As you see, our dear Dr May is here. And how is the poor gentleman?' Mrs Miller asked.

'Well, I see we have rather a lot of people here,' Dr May said. 'I wish only for one nurse and the gentleman to assist me, if you please.'

'We have done what we can,' Phipps told him. 'He was losing a lot of blood so I thought it best to take the ball out and patch him up as best I could.'

The doctor grunted and asked him to lift Brock, removing the bandage to inspect the wound for himself, then nodded.

'Well, you've done a decent job,' he said grudgingly. 'He may not thank you for the scar. If it festers, I may have to open the wound and cleanse it—but we'll leave well alone for now.' His eyes came to rest on Amanda. 'This gentleman is going to need nursing—is it your intention to take care of him?'

'Yes, sir. I shall stay to nurse him—' Amanda stepped forward '—and Mrs Miller will help me when she has time. What do you wish me to do for you, sir?'

'Clearly you do not faint at the sight of blood,' Dr May observed. 'I'll redress the wound with a special poultice that will take some of the soreness from the wound and help to prevent infection—but apart from that I think it is mainly rest and care.'

The bandages in place, Dr May declared himself satisfied. 'He will do now,' he said. 'I shall send you a mixture of my own preparation, which will help with the fever—he will undoubtedly suffer fever and a deal of pain when he does wake. I shall leave you the laudanum, but advise you to stick religiously to the amounts I shall show you—and on no account to give more even if it does not seem to help at first.'

'I know it can be addictive,' Amanda agreed. 'One of my uncles had an affliction, which caused him much pain, and he grew reliant on it because well-meaning servants gave him extra doses. You may rely on me to follow your instructions, sir.'

'Well, you seem a remarkably sensible girl,' he grunted. 'I shall call tomorrow—and if you need me, send your cousin's footman and I will come as soon as I am able. It was fortunate that you caught me before I set out on my rounds—but I must do so now, and so I commend him to your care.'

Amanda had taken careful note of all his instructions, for although he was an abrupt man, sometimes bordering on rude, she thought him a good doctor. After he had gone, she was alone with Phipps. She smiled up at him, and gave him a look of apology.

'I fear I must have ordered you all about at the ruins, but my concern was only for Major Brockley. It was imperative that we got him here before too much blood was lost.'

She thought that she had acted instinctively, refusing to let herself think or understand how close to death she had come. In thinking only of Brock, she had forgotten her own terror when the marquis had seemed to have her at his mercy.

'For my part I was lost in admiration,' he said. 'Miss Field has been a little faint, I understand, your mama quite out of sorts, and I really think I must leave you while I take them both home. It seems wrong to cast everything on your shoulders, Amanda, but it must be for the best. Your mama has said that she will spare us one of your footmen, who may help you in nursing Brock, for there are certainly some things that you ought not to do—and it would impose on your cousin's housekeeper to ask too much.'

'I am sure Mrs Miller would not object, but one of the footmen would be very useful, for certain tasks are beyond me, I readily admit.'

'I am sorry your day was spoiled, Amanda. We should have taken better care of you.'

'Nonsense. I am quite unharmed, and besides, I am not such a spoiled child that I shall sulk over an abandoned picnic. A man's life is far more important.'

'You are perfectly right and I can only be grateful. Some ladies would have fainted or gone into hysterics had they been held at gunpoint—not to say dealing with an incident such as this. I do not believe my mother could have handled it, though she is generally very good—at least with our childhood illnesses. This, however, I feel sure would have turned her faint for she cannot bear to see anyone in pain.'

'I fear I have no such romantic notions,' Amanda replied with a laugh. 'I have no patience with fainting or screaming when there is an emergency. I am sorry if I have disappointed your notions of gallantry, Phipps. I was very relieved when you so skilfully dispatched the villain that intended to murder me, but to have given way to faintness then would have caused you more bother. I was frightened for a while, but as much for Jane as myself. He was quite mad at the end, you know.'

'I believe there was always a queer streak in the family,' Phipps acknowledged. He looked at her in a vaguely rueful way, then inclined his head and went out.

Listening to his footsteps and then the sound of voices, she heard her mother call a brief farewell up the stairs and then everything went quiet. Finding a comfortable chair, she sat where she could keep an eye on her patient, but could also look out of the window at the garden. A few moments later, Mrs Miller brought a tray with a cup of tea and asked her if she needed anything more.

'I could sit with him for a while if you would like to walk in the garden, miss.'

'Thank you, ma'am, you are very kind and I may need to call on your services, though Phipps will return with one of our footmen before the day is out—and he will need only a pallet in this room.'

'If I may say so, you have chosen a very pleasant gentleman as your future husband, miss. He was so concerned that he was causing a trouble to my mistress and myself—but we assured him it was not so. We were glad to be able to offer our help to the poor gentleman.'

'I knew you would be.' Amanda smiled at her. 'Oh, how welcome this tea is. We had lemonade at the picnic, but nothing compares with a dish of tea, does it?'

'That's what I thought,' the housekeeper said, looking pleased as she turned to leave the room.

Amanda drank her tea and then walked over to the bed and placed a hand on the major's brow.

He felt a little hot and damp, and she dipped a clean linen cloth in fresh cool water, gently touching it to his forehead, under his chin and down his shoulders and what she could see of his chest above the covers. He moaned a little, but did not stir, and she felt certain that the doctor's medicine would hold him asleep for a few hours.

A few moments later Cousin Sarah came in, bearing a small bottle of medicine, which the doctor had sent round. It had a white label with clear instructions of the dose to give in a tablespoon and Amanda decided to see if she could get a little into her patient. At first his lips remained firmly clamped, but by dint of holding his nose, she got him to open them for long enough to pour the mixture into his mouth. He swallowed and made a sound of protest, but still did not wake.

'Oh, well done, Amanda. Is there anything more you need, my love?' asked Cousin Sarah, preparing to leave.

'I think a jug of lemon barley if you have the makings of it in the house?'

'Yes, of course, for I drink it myself all the time. Mrs Miller shall bring it up for you later, my love.'

She went away and for a while, Amanda sat and

watched her patient. Mrs Miller brought the jug and two glasses, for she said she thought Miss Amanda might like some herself. Having been thanked, she went away again. Amanda wandered over to the window and stood looking out. She was watching a thrush having a tussle with a worm when a sound alerted her. Turning, she saw that Major Brockley was staring at her.

'You are awake, sir,' she said and went to him with a smile. 'What may I do for you?'

'Miss Hamilton, what are you doing here?' he asked, seeming puzzled.

'I am here to nurse you, at least to sit with you until the footman arrives. If there is anything private you require, my cousin's man will come.'

'Thank you, I should be grateful for it later, but if I might trouble you for a sip of water?'

'Water or some of this delicious lemon barley?'

'Oh, the latter if you have it,' he said. 'I am unaccountably thirsty.'

'Yes, of course.' Amanda filled the glass to about half-full and took it to him. He tried, but was unable to sit up, so she put an arm about his shoulders, lifting him. He gulped thirstily and looked as if he would have liked more, but she thought it unwise to drink too much too soon and told him so.

'Are you always such a strict nurse?'

'Oh, always,' she said and laughed softly as he relaxed against the pillows. A fine film of sweat had broken out on his face and she could see that he was in a deal of pain. 'I fear I cannot offer you more laudanum for another two hours, sir.'

'That filthy stuff?' He shook his head. 'No, I shall do. I know the harm it can do if freely indulged in. I think that footman may be needed now, if you please.'

Amanda inclined her head and went out of the room, but hardly had she reached the top than she heard voices in the hall and then Phipps came to the bottom of the stairs followed by Jenks, one of the most obliging of her father's footmen.

'I am glad you have come,' she told him. 'The major is just awake and needing assistance. You have a free hand, but I should be grateful if you will ask me before administering any medicine.'

'Yes, Miss Hamilton,' he said. 'Mr Phipps has told me all of it, and you may rely on me.'

She thanked him and went down to join Phipps. He smiled at her, holding out his hands. Amanda took them and looked into his face, searching for she knew not what; all she saw was warmth and friendship.

'Major Brockley is awake and was thirsty. He says he does not want the laudanum, but he is in pain—though if he did wish for it, he could not have it for at least two hours.'

'If I know him, he will go through without it,' Phipps said. 'This is not the first time he has been shot and he is accustomed to the pain of such wounds.'

'Yes, for I could not but notice old scars,' Amanda agreed. 'I am glad you brought Jenks. Your friend will do well with him. I shall hardly be needed if he goes on without fever.'

'Would you wish me to take you home now that Jenks is here?'

'Shall we see how he goes on in the morning? If there is no fever, then I may as well go, but if he should become feverish it will be as well if we are both to hand. Nursing a sick man takes several persons, you know, and we cannot leave it to my cousin or her housekeeper.'

'No, that would be very wrong. Your cousin offered me a bed, but I have decided to stay at the village inn. I shall take my turn in caring for Brock, but for all of us to descend on your cousin would be too shocking.'

'My cousin would be offended if you did, dearest Phipps,' Amanda told him. 'I do believe that she is enjoying this, you know. I dare say since she was widowed she has very little male company.'

'Well, if you think so,' he said doubtfully. 'Now, are you sure you do not wish me to take you home?'

'Let us see what the morning brings. I am going to walk in the garden a little—and you may go up and speak with Brock, but do not let him drink too much all at once.'

Chapter Eleven

They did not have to wait for morning for their answer. Brock became steadily more fretful through a long evening, and by the time the long-case clock in the hall had struck the hour of eleven he was burning up with a fever. Amanda had advised a dose of the fever mixture earlier, but discovering from Jenks that Brock had set his lips and refused it, she administered a dose in her own decided manner, while Phipps and Jenks looked on in silence.

'You are a jade,' Brock muttered, but since he was hardly in his right mind, she did not regard what she knew to be an affectionate form of insult as being meant unkindly, but turned to Jenks. 'You must rest for a few hours, if you please. I know well how difficult the next few hours or days may be and we shall all need our rest.'

'Yes, Miss Hamilton. Shall I return at three?'

'Four will be time enough. I have been resting since you arrived and he had not caused me any bother before that. I think it will not be the case now.'

Brock had settled a little, but it was obvious that he was still in the grip of fever, for he threw himself about and tried to pull off the covers, his legs, now bare, protruding out of the side. Amanda removed the top quilt, leaving one thin blanket and the sheet.

'You should get some rest, too,' she advised Phipps, but he remained seated. 'I think I can manage him—and you must take your turn later.'

'Yes, but I do not wish to leave you just yet, Amanda.'

'Very well.' She smiled at him as she rinsed her cloth in cool fresh water and bathed the top half of her patient's body. 'If you wish to do the same for the lower half of him, I will turn my back and contemplate the moon.'

'And what would you do if I were not here?'

'Cover his private parts and bathe him myself.'

'Well, I shall save your blushes. Go and contemplate the moon, Amanda.'

She gave a mischievous laugh and walked to the window, looking out at the garden as the moon turned everything to silver. It was such a lovely night, a night for lovers, and for a moment she wished that she and Phipps were alone in the gardens. She was lost in her dreams when she felt a touch at her shoulder, and, as she turned, found herself drawn into Phipps's arms and soundly kissed. Responding with all the love that was in her, she gave herself up to his embrace for some minutes and then pulled away, for fear that she should be carried away and say something she ought not.

'Now you know what a shameless woman you have engaged yourself to,' she said, her cheeks burning. 'It is quite improper of me to allow you to kiss me when your friend lies ill and my cousin trusts us to behave with circumspection under her roof.'

Phipps gave a rueful laugh. 'I am the shameless one, for I was overcome by my desire to hold you and kiss you. It was very wrong of me—will you forgive me?'

'Indeed, I must,' she teased. 'How could I not? To draw back now would be most improper and lose me all your respect, after I abandoned myself to your embrace so willingly.'

He laughed, but shook his head at her. 'You are a minx, Amanda. I had not suspected it and now, as you so rightly say, we are both caught and it would cause a scandal if either of us were to draw back.'

He was teasing, as she had been, and they laughed together, feeling better, as if the intimate moment had somehow cleared the tense atmosphere. But then a fretful cry from the bed had Amanda's attention and she returned to her patient and began to stroke his forehead.

'Yes, I know,' she said soothingly. 'It is very bad of us to laugh and be happy when you are feeling so ill. I shall tell Phipps to go away, for he cannot be trusted and you must be quiet.' She glanced at Phipps, saw his brows rise and nodded. 'Yes, do go and rest if you can. I think it better that we spend time with him separately, for I promised Mama that I would do nothing that she would think wrong…and I am not sure that I could resist if you were to kiss me so charmingly again.'

Phipps smiled, touched her head as she bent over Brock, then walked from the room. She heard the door close softly behind him and almost wished that she had not sent him away, for in the moment of their embrace it had seemed to Amanda that a bridge had been crossed and they were closer than they had ever been. Yet this was not a time for making love and she knew her cousin would be shocked if it came out that she had spent the night in the same bedroom as her fiancé, even though they were nursing a sick patient.

Had Phipps remained they would have had little time for talking or for kissing, for Brock became feverish quickly, thrashing and throwing his arms and legs out of the bed. Amanda gave him a wash all over in cold water, having first slid a towel over his middle before peeling back the sheets. She bathed all his limbs and it seemed to ease him for a while, but within an hour the fever started to mount. She administered another dose of Dr May's fever mixture, but it seemed to do little good and she was on the verge of going to wake Jenks when he entered the room at precisely three o'clock.

'I woke and thought I would come, miss,' he said, looking down at the major's flushed skin.

'He looks worse, miss. Has he had the doctor's mixture?'

'Half an hour ago. I was wondering if we should send for the doctor, though I do not know what he could do other than what we have been doing all the time.'

'I shall fetch him if you wish, miss—but I think the fever is almost always worse before the dawn. If he does not cool down after I've bathed him again, and seems worse, I shall take it upon myself to call the doctor. Your cousin's man told me to wake him if necessary and I shall do so. You should go to bed, miss, if I may make so bold.'

'Of course, I thank you for you advice and will go,' she said. 'If you should need me, knock on my door. I shall wake.'

He promised to do so.

Amanda had fallen asleep on top of her bed without bothering to undress and had slept until the crowing of a cock somewhere and the sun pouring into her room brought her to her senses. She yawned, stretched, got up and poured water into a bowl to wash. Mama had thoughtfully sent her a change of gown and she was glad of clean linen and a dress that did not look as if it had been lived in a week and was stained with blood. It had been new and would have to be thrown away, but she did not regret it, for what was a silk dress when a man had risked his life for hers?

After she had made herself presentable, she went along the corridor to find that Phipps was sitting beside the bed, applying a cold cloth to Brock's brow. He smiled at her.

'You look as if you slept, Amanda. I sent Jenks to have his breakfast. Thank goodness, Brock is better this morning—still not clear of the fever, I think, but through the crisis.'

Amanda checked and discovered that their patient was indeed cooler. She thanked God for it and offered to relieve Phipps, but he said he was perfectly comfortable and told her to have her own breakfast.

Going downstairs to the parlour, she discovered that the servants were just preparing it and was offered tea, coffee or chocolate and whatever she wished to eat. Rolls and butter with a preserve of strawberry jam and a pot of tea was brought within a very short time. Amanda then took a turn about the garden, before going upstairs perfectly refreshed.

Phipps relinquished his place to her, for he had messages to send, but said he would return shortly. Amanda sat with Brock and gave him one last dose of the fever mixture; they would need more if the fever recurred, and she was about to pour more water into a bowl when she heard a moaning sound from the bed and turned to see that Brock was watching her.

'You are an amazing woman, Miss Hamilton,' Brock said, lifting his head from the pillow. 'I feel as weak as a kitten and should like something to restore me. I take it I have been in a fever?'

'Most of the night you were very hot and thrashing about,' she replied with a smile. 'I was on the verge of recalling the doctor, but Jenks advised me to wait. I do not know what he did, but when I returned this morning you were much better.'

'My arm hurts like hell, my mouth feels like ashes and I have a throbbing head,' Brock said, 'but I dare say I shall live—and I believe I owe it that I am not worse to you, Miss Hamilton. Phipps is a luckier man than he knows.'

'I thank you for the compliment,' she said and

laughed in a rallying way. 'I know you do not want to be fussed, sir—but shall I send for the doctor? Though in truth he will only give you more of that wretched stuff you hate so much.'

'No, I shall not call him out, though I dare say he will come to maul me again and change the dressings. I am not a good patient, Miss Hamilton, but I do thank you for all you have done.' He looked about him. 'Whose house am I in?'

'My mother's cousin's house, sir. She is a widow and I think she has quite enjoyed having so many people under her roof.'

'I must not impose on her,' Brock said with a frown. 'Is there an inn that would take me in until I am ready to travel?'

'Yes, indeed, there is an inn of sorts, but I assure you that my cousin would take umbrage if you were to leave too soon. Now please be sensible, sir. Your own servants have been sent for. They will surely arrive before the end of the day and then you will be comfortable. If the doctor says you may be moved, my parents would be pleased to give you a bed for as long as you need it.'

'I should then have disrupted two households...'

'Indeed, a little disruption is nothing compared

with the life of my father's daughter. I assure you he will think so and it will not surprise me if he arrives before the morning is much advanced to see how we go on.'

'Phipps saved your life, not me,' he said. 'I could not get a clear shot for I might have hit you by accident. Phipps had the advantage of the silent assassin...as we have been used to call his knife.'

'Yes, I know that it was he that disposed of that evil man, but had you not been there he might have arrived too late. Please allow us to be grateful. I understand that you were of some assistance to Miss Langton also, for which we are all grateful.'

'It was my fault...' Brock shook his head impatiently. 'I pushed him into a desperate act...but...' He lay back against his pillows with a sigh. 'I cannot fight you, Miss Hamilton. I am too weak.'

'I dare say you lost a deal of blood,' she said, and then, hearing a familiar voice, 'If I am not mistaken that is Dr May come to visit you. I shall leave you for a while, because Jenks is with him and will assist him.'

She left the room, pausing to tell the doctor that

his patient had recovered his senses, but was out of sorts and fretful.

'I shall soon have him more comfortable. I quite expected to be called out last night and am delighted that you have pulled him round between you.'

Phipps had returned to the house when she went into the parlour and told her that he'd seen a carriage approaching and thought it might be her father come to see how she did. He was proved right within a few minutes and Amanda soon had the happiness of being wrapped in his loving embrace.

'My dearest child,' he said emotionally. 'I might have lost you to that madman. Your mama has told me all and I shall be eternally grateful to Phipps and indeed to Major Brockley. How does he go on?'

'He had a bad night, Papa, but he is a strong man and seems much better this morning. I think the fever has waned, though of course it may return.'

'Well, well, we must hope not,' her father said and turned to greet Phipps and then Cousin Sarah, who had come to greet him.

By the time he had been pressed to take a glass of Madeira, the doctor had come downstairs and was brought in to give his expert opinion.

'I am happy to say that he is well on the mend,' Dr May said and looked approvingly at Amanda. 'I do not generally like to see a young woman in the sickroom, but she has played her part very well. Between them all they have brought their patient through, and unless I am mistaken the danger is now over.'

'I am glad to hear it, sir. Do you think it necessary for my daughter to remain here?'

'I think your footman very capable. I believe the major's own people have been sent for and must arrive some time today—which leaves me able to say that Miss Hamilton may consider her job done.'

Amanda would have protested, but since the doctor and her father were united there was nothing she could say, but went upstairs to take her leave of the major. He greeted her with an ease of manner that made her feel she had always known him and feel grateful that she had been of use to him.

'I shall stay here another night on the doctor's

advice, and then my servants will take me home in easy stages. I thank you for your prompt and efficient action when I was shot, Miss Hamilton. Phipps tells me it was you who took charge and stopped the bleeding as best you could before conveying me here.'

'I dare say I am a managing female,' she said with a twinkle in her eyes. 'It is because I am not at all romantic and, instead of fainting prettily, I thought it more sensible to see you in the doctor's care as soon as it could be achieved.'

Brock gave a shout of laughter, a look of admiration in his eyes. 'I wonder if Phipps has any idea of what he has taken on, the lucky devil,' he said. 'I shall look forward to your visit next month, Miss Hamilton.'

'As shall I, sir,' she said. 'Please forgive me, Papa is anxious to leave.'

She went out and found Phipps talking to her father and Cousin Sarah. Phipps had decided to stay with Brock until his own people arrived.

'If I think him ill, I shall accompany him home,' Phipps said. 'However, if he is well enough to be in the care of his servants I shall be with you tomorrow evening by the latest.'

Amanda gave him her hand and he held it for a moment. Between thanking her cousin and assuring her father she was ready, there was no time for a private word with him.

'I shall see you soon,' she said and gave him a smile that was just for him. 'Please do whatever you consider necessary and do not think of us, for we shall understand.'

Seeing her papa was anxious to leave, she tore herself away and followed him out to the carriage.

'Well,' Papa said as he handed her into the carriage, 'that was quite an adventure for you, my love, but I must tell you that I am glad it is over.'

'Yes, Papa,' she said and sighed. 'I am very glad—particularly that that evil man can no longer threaten us.'

'Yes, indeed,' Papa said as he got in beside her and told the coachman to drive on. 'That was unpleasant, my love. Now we must hope that nothing more happens to disturb your pleasure.'

The journey home was accomplished without incident and her loving mama and the servants welcomed Amanda as though she were a long-lost heroine. She found their compliments and concern almost overwhelming and was glad to escape to her room, where she could be at last alone. She had been given little leisure to consider what had happened the previous night, when Phipps had held her and kissed her so passionately. The memory of it made her tingle with pleasure and anticipation, and she could hardly wait for the next two days to pass when he would be with them once more.

Amanda had not dared to hope that her husband-to-be had anything more than a feeling of warm affection for her, but his kiss had told of something very different. Something inside her had responded so willingly that she'd kissed him without reserve, and, had Brock not been so seriously ill and they in different circumstances, she would've been happy to give herself to him completely. And that was quite disgraceful! Mama would not approve of such behaviour, even if she was engaged, and Amanda herself had never meant to lose her head.

What chance had she of hiding her true feelings when they were married if a simple kiss could cause her to abandon all modesty in such a shameless manner? What must Phipps think of her? Yet he had not seemed to feel disgust—indeed, she knew he had been reluctant to let her go when Brock's cry alerted them to his discomfort.

Could it be that he had learned to care for her? Amanda was afraid to hope lest she was disappointed. She must not look for too much, because then she would be so much more vulnerable.

A sigh left her as she realised that somehow she had to get through the intervening hours and give no one any indication of the fever of impatience running through her blood. Jane was still her guest and it was an opportunity to devote herself to her friend, and to have the last fittings for her wedding gown.

It had arrived the previous day and was something of a disappointment to Amanda, as she'd hoped it would have a long line at the waist and flare softly over her hips, which were still frustratingly bigger than she would have wished. Instead, it was loose around her waist and bunched out into a full skirt and was not at all what they had ordered.

However, Jane came to the rescue and they spent most of the day taking in the seams so that the bodice fitted her and made her waist appear quite small.

'You have the kind of figure many gentlemen admire,' Jane said when she stood back to look at her handiwork. 'No, do not shake your head, Amanda. You have full breasts, a small waist and good hips.'

'You mean I have a big bottom,' Amanda said. 'No, Jane, do not deny it.'

Jane laughed, amused by her plain speaking. 'No, no, my dearest friend. A few months ago perhaps that was true, but I assure you that your figure is good now. Curvaceous, I grant you that, but how many ladies truly are slender and willowy? Besides, some gentlemen do not like their wives to be thin—my grandfather used to say I was all skin and bone and he liked a good armful to cuddle up to at night.'

'Oh, please spare my blushes,' Amanda cried, glad that Mama was not in the room to hear. She would think less of Jane for saying such a thing, but Amanda knew that her friend was only being kind. 'Thank you for being such a friend to me, Jane. This gown looks much better now.'

'I think you look lovely,' Jane replied and a sigh

left her lips. 'I wish I might stay with you, for if I could I would take some of the fullness from that skirt—and to think that I particularly told her you wanted a slender silhouette!'

'She thought she knew best, probably believed that I would put on weight again before my wedding.'

'She should learn that her clients know best what they want,' Jane said crossly. 'I wish that I might have my own establishment, for I could design such lovely things—if only I had the chance.'

'Do you not wish to be married?'

'Perhaps, if I found the right man—but that is unlikely. Gentlemen hardly see me, Amanda, and those that do have other things in mind than marriage.'

'I am sorry you should feel that way,' Amanda said and pressed her hand. 'Do not despair, Jane. I am sure you will find someone soon.'

Amanda would miss her when she went home, but Phipps would be with her soon and in truth she wanted to spend as much time with him as she could.

To Amanda's extreme disappointment a letter was received the next day to tell her that Phipps had decided he ought to accompany Brock to his home. Although the fever had passed, Brock was feeling out of sorts and unusually weak for him.

I need hardly tell you that I think him in no danger for Shearne can no longer harm anyone. All that business has been settled and a line drawn beneath it. You, my dearest Amanda, will have nothing to say at the inquest, which should be a formality for we have several witnesses. Since both Brock and I will be needed, I thought it best to see him home and then we can arrange whatever more needs to be done, though it cannot occasion either of us the least trouble.

Forgive me for putting another's interests first at such a time. I hope to be with you within a week at the very latest.

Your affectionate and devoted servant,
Phipps

Amanda read his letter with mixed feelings. She found the terms of it agreeable, but regretted that he must spend more time away from her. However, there was nothing she could do and must bear with her mother's disapproval in silence.

Phipps would not stay away unless he thought it necessary for his friend's sake.

It was going to be hard for her to wait in patience, because things needed to be settled between them. Amanda had not expected too much at the beginning, for she was aware that she had bought herself a husband, and even though she'd made up her mind not to regard it, she could not help a few misgivings. Had she been entirely wise, she wondered, for she was vulnerable and if Phipps chose to hurt her and misuse her fortune she could not prevent him.

Her instinct bade her trust him. Papa seemed well pleased with his future son-in-law and Amanda trusted her father's judgement. He was not easily fooled and though she might be blinded by the good looks and charm of her fiancé, her father was most unlikely to accord Phipps respect unless he had deserved it.

Unable to see or talk to Phipps the doubts crept into her mind unbidden. He had probably been overcome by his feelings of gratitude for her help with his friend when he kissed her. She had read too much into his manner, for had he been as impatient as she, he might have trusted Brock's servants to care for him. She knew that they had arrived and taken charge for Jenks had delivered Phipps's letter.

While warm with affection, Phipps's letter could not be mistaken for a love letter. The more Amanda thought about it, the more she realised that she had made too much of the small incident. They had both been swept away by the emotion of the situation and the intimacy in which they found themselves had given what was after all just a kiss far more importance than it actually had.

By the time the end of the week had come, Amanda had begun to think that she'd imagined the feeling in that kiss. She was such a fool and she could only hope that her response had not given him a disgust of her.

Now that Jane had gone home, Amanda was left with little to do but visit friends and pore over the wedding lists: guests, rooms, food and wine were the subject of much discussion between Mama and Papa. Amanda took to riding out with her groom for two hours every morning because she was too restless to sit in the parlour. In the afternoons they quite often had visitors and she was pressed as to the whereabouts of her fiancé, who everyone imagined to be staying with them. Amanda knew her neighbours thought it odd and she suspected that they were whispering about her, probably pitying her because she could not keep him with her even before the wedding.

Mama thought the same and was quite cross with him. She hinted several times that Amanda might have done better for herself.

When Lord Armstrong came to visit, bringing messages and gifts from his mama, Lady Hamilton made a great fuss of him and left him with Amanda while she went away to write a letter for her friend, and pressed on him some jars of the wonderful honey their hives produced for Susanna.

He stayed with them one night, and Amanda took him on a tour of the estate the next morning. He helped her from her horse when they returned to the yard and held her hand for some minutes, looking down at her gravely.

'When I heard from Miss Field what occurred at those ruins I told Mama I must come and make certain that you were not harmed. You must know that I have a great regard for you, Miss Amanda.

I should have been devastated had anything more untoward occurred.'

'Thankfully, due to Phipps's quick thinking I received no more than a few bruises.'

'Yes, one must thank Providence for that,' he agreed. 'One does not necessarily approve of his methods—a knife between the shoulder blades is not the chosen weapon of a gentleman. One wonders why or how such a skill was developed.'

'Oh, I think he made good use of it in Spain, against the enemy, you know,' Amanda said, a sparkle in her eyes. 'You must not show disapproval of him to me, sir. I was very grateful, for otherwise that man would have killed me. He did intend it.'

'How very shocking and dreadful that would have been. I do not think I could have borne it,' he said and pressed her hand again. Looking at her oddly, he added in a soft voice, 'I did wonder if all this had given you a distaste for the lieutenant and his friends? To have involved the lady he intended to marry in such a dangerous encounter seems careless to me—if not scandalous.'

'I assure you that it was not Phipps or Major Brockley who brought the marquis's wrath to bear on me, but my own attitude towards him. He was rude and encroaching towards Miss Field and I spoke harshly to him for it.'

'That is all very well,' he said. 'I dare say there can have been nothing in it for you are not yet married...though it might have been otherwise had the wedding already taken place. I would advise you to be careful, Miss Hamilton. I believe there was a lady he was very fond of but unable to marry because he could not afford her—marriages on the rebound are not always the happiest. She is recently widowed, I understand. With a fortune at his command...'

Amanda's eyes took fire. It was with difficulty that she restrained herself, and only the knowledge that his mother was Mama's best friend held her back. Was he indeed hinting that Phipps would be happy to see her die if they had first been married? How dare he! It took every ounce of self-control to answer him civilly.

'I do not know what you imply, sir, but I can assure you that Phipps's only part in this was to protect me from harm.'

On that note they walked into the house and parted. Amanda was seething underneath. Had he dared to suggest that Phipps might have let her die? She was so angry that she barely spoke to him when he took his leave later that day, and when Mama said how good it was in him to visit her she had nothing to add.

How could he imply that Phipps only cared for her fortune? Amanda was so angry that she wanted to scream and shout, but of course she had kept her frustration inside. It would be foolish to allow his insinuations to destroy her happiness.

She had no way of knowing if it was true that Phipps had once loved a lady whom he could not marry for lack of a fortune, nor if he still cared for her. Amanda had never considered such a thing, because he had paid attention to her and also to Cynthia the whole Season. Cynthia had withdrawn and Phipps had chosen to ask Amanda— why would he do that if his old love had suddenly become free once more?

No, she would not believe Lord Armstrong's spite. She did not know why he should wish to marry her—or why he would stoop to underhand tactics—but thought the less of him for pursuing it now that she was engaged.

Deciding that it was merely pique at being overlooked in favour of another, Amanda decided to put the unpleasant incident from her mind. She did so wish that Phipps would come back and resume that kiss where they had left off.

Chapter Twelve

Phipps was obliged to attend two meetings with the local magistrate before the affair was finally finished. Brock had been too unwell to give his evidence for some days, but after they made the journey to the court and swore their testimony, they were told that no more would be heard of the matter. Further investigations had proved that Shearne was in financial difficulties and there was some evidence of his being responsible for a young man's death. Apparently, a gentleman had lodged a complaint of his son's having been cheated and ruined, a circumstance that led to his taking his own life. Once this was known, and the marquis's general bad character had been established, the magistrate no longer doubted that Phipps had acted lawfully in saving the life of the lady he was to marry: even though, in his considered opinion, a knife in the back was not the act of a gentleman.

As Brock observed to him on the way home, had the magistrate been in charge of the raiding parties Phipps had led on enemy positions, Wellington would have lost the war. Amanda's life had been in peril and anyone but a fool would have hailed him as a hero.

Phipps had arranged to leave Brock's home to journey to Amanda's the next day, when the letter arrived for him. Its contents were so shattering that he hardly knew what to do for the best. His elder brother had been brought home from a riding accident and was not expected to live. Phipps's parents wanted him home immediately. They apologised for dragging him away from his friends, but his mother was prostrate on her bed and his father did not know what to do to comfort her.

Phipps took his leave immediately. His plan to join Amanda as soon as he could complete the journey was at a standstill. His brother had always been a good friend and the shock of learning that Alex was close to death was devastating. Obviously, his first duty was to his parents at this time, though he knew Amanda must be fretting and he wanted to be with her. This should have been a time of celebration, a time when the young couple got to know one another and received the congratulations of their friends.

Amanda's family had the wedding plans already well under way, and now Phipps was not even sure that it would go ahead without some lengthy delay. If his brother died…how could he go ahead with celebrations when his family was in strict mourning? It was a terrible blow and he could not think straight.

He ought to write to Amanda and tell her of his disappointment, but for the moment he had only one thought in his head, and that was to reach his home as quickly as possible.

Surely, this was all a nightmare? He would wake up and discover that he had dreamed the whole. His elder brother was such a fine strong man and the pride of his father, the favourite child of his mother. They would be devastated. Phipps could not desert them to go off and marry Amanda and take her to Paris for a honeymoon, as he'd planned.

He must write to her father and explain, also

to Amanda to tell her how very sorry he was—but those letters must wait until he was home and knew exactly what the situation was.

Phipps had never been more shocked in his life than when he saw Alexander lying unconscious against the white sheets. Little colour remained in his cheeks and his breath was so shallow that he had to lean closer to assure himself that his brother did indeed live. Placing a hand on his brother's forehead, he felt quite cool. He was not suffering from a fever, but showed few signs of life.

'What does the doctor say?' Phipps asked of Lord Piper. 'Does he give Alex a chance?'

'As yet he will not commit himself. I know he is worried because your brother shows no sign of recovering consciousness... He told me straight that I must prepare myself for the worst, Peter.'

'Surely you won't just give up? Have you sent for Knighton from London? These blows to the head are not always fatal, sir.'

'No, but sometimes it's worse,' Lord Piper said. 'He might live and yet never come to his senses—or be something other than he was...'

Phipps saw the pain in the older man's eyes and knew that that eventuality would be the end of his hopes that his elder son would do something special with his life and make him proud. They had hoped that Alexander would become the Whig leader and Prime Minister of the government or excel in some other way, perhaps at court as an adviser to the Crown. Alexander had been the clever one, the son who had won five firsts at college and been his father's pride and joy ever since he was a young lad. Phipps could never hope to follow in his footsteps, but if Alexander died... he would be the heir.

'You mustn't give in to these fears,' Phipps said to his father in a rallying tone. 'Alexander isn't a quitter. He would not just give up his ticket like that, you know.'

'Oh, why did it have to happen to him?' Lord Piper asked, a shudder going through him. 'Your mother—well, if he dies, I don't think she can bear it.'

'We must pray that he lives,' Phipps said. 'I shall send for Knighton. We need a second opinion— old Masters is well enough, but he hasn't kept abreast of modern thinking.'

'You know as well as I do that if a head injury is serious nothing can be done,' his father said harshly. 'You are going to have to face up to the fact that you may have to step into his shoes.'

'I've no taste for politics, Father.'

'I didn't mean that,' Lord Piper said heavily. 'I'm well aware that you won't follow that path. No, I'm thinking of the estate. You will have to give up that rackety life you lead in London and come home.'

'Oh, I say, sir. I wouldn't say I'm rackety. Besides, I am getting married soon and I shall be busy with Miss Hamilton's estates. You are not ready to give up the reins here, I think?'

'No one said I was, but Alexander has been learning to run the estate since he was a lad. You've never had the chance and I suppose that was my fault. I never thought I should see this day. It is a terrible thing when a man has to face the prospect of his elder son's death.'

'Alex hasn't curled up his toes yet,' Phipps objected. 'I shall send for Knighton if you won't—and I'm not going to usurp his place until I know there's no hope.'

His father looked at him thoughtfully. 'You're a

good brother. You've never thought of taking his place, have you?'

'I am well aware that I could not,' Phipps said ruefully. 'I fall a long way short, sir. Besides, I'm content for him to inherit the title and the estate. It is his right.'

'Yes, his right and his mother's and my wish, but if he is unable to take up his position, then you have no choice but to step into his shoes.'

'Yes, I do see that, but I shall continue to hope and pray for his recovery. If you don't mind, sir, I'm going to send off some letters. I must send to London for my own people—and I shall have to let Lord Hamilton know that the wedding has to be postponed.'

'Postpone your wedding?' Lord Piper frowned. 'That is a curst nuisance, but I do not see what else can be done in the circumstances. While your brother lies here in a coma...'

'Yes, Father. We could not attend a wedding while he lies so ill—and I should not feel like taking Miss Hamilton to Paris until I know he's through the worst.'

'And what if the worst happens?' Lord Piper asked. 'Will Miss Hamilton accept a delay of some months—or perhaps a very quiet wedding with no celebrations or fuss?'

'I don't think we could ask that of her,' Phipps said reasonably. 'Brides always look forward to a wedding, and even though she doesn't want a large one, her father and mother do. Lord Hamilton is proud of her and wants to show off his wealth.'

'You do not want to lose her,' Lord Piper said. 'Of course you won't exactly need her money if… your brother dies, but still, it is always useful.'

'Yes,' Phipps agreed, not meeting his father's look. 'It may surprise you to know, sir, that Miss Hamilton's money isn't the only—or indeed the main—reason why I asked her to be my wife.'

'Your mother says she's a little dumpling, no figure or beauty to speak off. She has it on the authority of your cousin Mildred, who met her in London at some ball or other.'

'Miss Hamilton has many qualities to recommend her and I've grown fond of her.'

'Well, you know your own mind best,' his father said with a little tutting sound. 'I'm sorry you must suffer a delay to your plans, but there it is.'

Phipps went away and sat down to write his

various letters, first to the eminent surgeon begging him to come without delay, then to his valet and personal servants to join him here—and then the more difficult letters to Amanda's father and Amanda.

The letter of apology to Lord Hamilton was difficult but straightforward: he was a man of sense and would understand that the wedding must be postponed, at least until Alex's condition became clear. Writing a letter to Amanda was fraught with difficulty. Impossible to say to her the things he wanted to say, for the confessions he wished to make could only be said to her face. He needed to look into her eyes and have her look into his, for words written on paper could often sound otherwise to the way they were intended.

In the end, he wrote an apology for having to delay the wedding, and begged her to forgive him. He said that he was impatient to see her and wanted very much to talk to her about something important, promising to make the journey as soon as he could.

Brock is expecting your family and Miss Field next week as arranged. If you hear nothing from me before then, please continue as we intended and I shall join you there if I am able. I have sent for an eminent surgeon from London and hope that he may have something favourable to say to us.

Hesitating, he thought carefully before adding,

If my brother—God forbid—should die, it would mean that my father would require us to live here. I am not sure how you would feel concerning the alteration to our plans.
Please believe that I would understand, whatever your decision, and I remain, as always, your affectionate Phipps

For a moment he almost destroyed the letter, for it did not in the least convey his feelings, but the facts must be faced. Amanda expected that he would devote his life to her interests, which, if he became his father's heir, would become of secondary importance. Although he would naturally oversee her estates and keep an eye on things, he would be tied up here more often than he liked. This was grossly unfair to his future wife and if she decided that she did not wish to accept the situation…

Phipps sighed. His father was relying on him, but so, too, was Amanda. Yet surely there was more between them than a business agreement, though it had certainly started out that way. It was a tangle and Phipps could only pray that his brother would recover.

Amanda sat staring at the letter for some minutes. She had read it in haste and then again at her leisure, but discovered that she could not get the meaning behind the words. Of course the wedding must be postponed, and as frustrating as that must be to poor Mama, who must put off all her extravagant plans, it was no more than what was right and proper. If Phipps's brother were to die, it might be several months before they could marry, unless they had a very quiet affair with few or no celebrations. For herself Amanda did not mind a quiet wedding, though her father and mother would be extremely disappointed. However, Phipps's statement that if she were unhappy with the situation was disturbing…for what was she to make of it?

If his elder brother did die, Phipps would be the heir and that was a very different situation. His father's title would be his, as would the estate. Amanda's fortune might be more than equal to his and her father's title was respected, though not as old as Lord Piper's—they went back in an unbroken line to the Conqueror—but as the heir he did not need to marry for money.

Amanda thought that if the accident had happened before Phipps proposed to her he might very well not have done so. She knew that he had not been in love with her at the start and, even though she believed he felt something for her now, given a fresh start he might choose not to marry her.

If Phipps became his father's heir he could have any woman he wanted—and that might not be Amanda. The thought ripped through her like a knife through butter, making her cry out in distress. While she could give him a fortune and the chance to make something of his life, she had something to offer—but what could she give if he already had all that?

Phipps was an honourable gentleman. Even though his circumstances might alter vastly, he would not jilt her. It would be beneath him to do so, but he might be glad if she were to cry off...

The thought was so lowering that she felt like bursting into tears. She could bear the disappointment of having her wedding postponed, but the idea that Phipps was trapped in an unwelcome engagement nearly tore her in two. She could not do that to him; she cared for him too much.

No, no, she was being a fool, she thought as she reread the letter and puzzled over it. He had something important to say to her, but would not write it in a letter—what could that be? Of course to write that he wished her to withdraw would seem so heartless and she knew him to be a kind, thoughtful man. He wanted to break it to her gently…for all she knew his father might have urged him to find a way of extricating himself from a match that would do well enough for a second son, but was not brilliant enough for the heir.

How extremely distressing this was, Amanda thought, folding her letter and putting it away. Had she not been a sensible girl, she might have begged Mama to take her to Phipps's home immediately to enquire what was in his mind. Of course she could not do so. Her presence at a time of family crisis would be a nuisance. If she could perhaps have been of use to Phipps or his family…but she was a stranger and could be of no help to a woman whose eldest son was believed to be dying.

How very sad it all was! Amanda hardly knew how to compose herself when Mama came to her full of complaints about all her arrangements.

'Phipps did not wish for this, Mama,' she said at last. 'He is very distressed, for he is fond of his brother…only think how you would feel if it were my brother.'

'You are very understanding, Amanda.' Mama sighed. 'I suppose the wedding can be arranged again, but it does make things so awkward.'

'Yes, I know, and I am very sorry for it. Perhaps we shall know more next week.'

'Perhaps. I suppose we must go to Lord Brockley's, as we'd planned, but I tell you, Amanda, I am most unhappy about this. Had you consented to take Lord Armstrong I am sure he would not have been so disobliging.'

Amanda bore this and a great deal more with patience, but, after her mother finally left her, gave way to a bout of tears. The wedding did not matter, for she could have waited without rancour, feeling only sympathy for the family in such distress, but she had an uneasy feeling that if Phipps's brother did die, he would hope that she might be brought to withdraw. And, of course, if he did wish for it, she must give him what he asked and that would break her heart.

Until the worst happened, she must keep a brave face and carry on as if nothing had happened to disturb her peace, but the glow of happiness that had warmed her after that night in Brock's bedchamber had now faded as if it had never been.

There was nothing for it but to take up the reins of her old life. She would visit all her friends at the neighbouring villages and Papa's cottages on the estate. It would not do to let her own distress make her forget what was due to others and she would be going away for the next three weeks.

'Amanda, why do you not eat your puddings?' Papa looked at her across the table one evening. 'I do not like to see you picking at your food, my dear. You were always so partial to chocolate puddings, as I am myself.'

She smiled at him, hiding her sigh. Papa had always loved his food and he had a sweet tooth, sometimes eating as many as three different puddings at one sitting. As a child she had copied everything Papa did and consequently it had had its effect, for while a large active man could comfortably eat as many sweet things as he wished without putting on the least weight, his diminutive daughter could not.

'I am not hungry, Papa,' Amanda said. 'I ate a peach, which was delicious. These days I find I prefer fruit to sweet puddings.'

'That isn't like my little princess,' he replied, frowning. 'I do hope you are not pining because we've heard nothing from that young man of yours?'

'No, Papa, of course not,' Amanda said. 'Phipps told me he might not be able to write. He begged me to go on with my plans to visit Lord Brockley and promised to join us if he could. Since Jane is so much looking forward to the visit, I do not think we should withdraw.'

'Certainly not,' Papa said. 'I dare say Phipps would not want you to curtail your pleasure because his family is in trouble, my love. You are a sensible girl and I should not like to think you were sulking over the delay to your plans.'

'Sulking? Oh, no, Papa, how could you think it?

I know very well that Phipps will come as soon as he can—and this is not in the least his fault. I am just sad that he and his family are in such distress. I would wish to be of use to them, but I do not see what I can do.'

'There is nothing, of course. How could you?' Mama said. 'Jane is arriving tomorrow. I dare say she is looking forward to the treat. It is a pity that Lieutenant Phipps cannot escort us, as we planned, but Lord Armstrong has also been invited and says he would be delighted to offer his services.'

'Oh…' Amanda looked at her mama unhappily, but could raise no objection. She might have known Mama would communicate the whole to her friend, and it was like Susanna to have offered her son's services. 'Well, that is kind of him.'

'Indeed, I thought so,' Mama said. 'Such an attentive man. If…Phipps becomes the heir, he may not wish to marry for a year or two, Amanda. If you were to part by mutual consent…'

'No, Mama. I could not think of it, please do not ask me.'

'Well, it was just a thought,' Mama said. 'I dare

say things will turn out for the best and Phipps's brother will recover...'

Amanda inclined her head, but did not answer. She was glad when the evening had passed and she could retire to her room.

Oh, why did Phipps not write to her and tell her what was happening? Or were things so bad that he could not bring himself to do it?

Phipps watched as the eminent surgeon lifted his patient's eyelids one by one and then waved a lamp to and fro before them; he replaced the lamp on the bedside chest, held the limp white wrist in his hand and frowned as he consulted his gold pocket watch. Eventually, he straightened up and looked at Phipps gravely.

'I have been making a study of these cases, as you may know,' he said. 'It is my belief that in cases of severe head trauma there is often bleeding inside the skull, which forms a clot and presses on the brain. If this could be successfully removed it might mean the patient recovered, but there would, I fear, be significant damage to the brain itself.'

'That is what my father fears,' Phipps admitted.

'I know surgeons have performed crude brain surgery in the past, but it always leads to some loss of the senses, does it not?'

'One day in the near future I believe such operations will come to pass and in many cases without too much damage to the brain, but that is for the future. I would not care to undertake such a procedure—particularly in the case of such a clever man, as your brother was, sir. It would be a pity to see him much reduced, as in those patients undergoing a lobotomy. In any case, I saw signs of recognition in his eyes when I held the light before them.'

'What does that mean?'

'There is hope that he has merely severe concussion and may recover in his own good time.'

'After three weeks of lying there unconscious?'

'I have heard of a case where a young lad was in a coma for three months and then woke up and wondered why everyone was crying over him. He declared himself starving and his mother went to church and thanked God for a miracle.'

'As well she might,' Phipps said. 'So you would not advise removing the blood clot, even if you could...?'

'Had I some means of seeing inside his skull to determine where it is, how large or even if it is there at all, I might undertake it—but to blunder in and remove the skull like some clod-hopping fools that call themselves surgeons... No, I would not risk it. I believe your brother would not thank me for it if he were to live out his years as a dribbling fool.'

'No, indeed, he would not,' Phipps said with a shudder. 'Father swore he would not allow it, but I hoped that you might...be able to do something more than our local man.'

'My advice is to get a good nurse for him,' Knighton said with a smile and a shake of his head. 'He must be kept clean and given liquids—and if any signs of recovery are seen, send for me.'

'My brother shall not be neglected,' Phipps vowed. 'I only wish that Amanda might be here. She was so good with Brock when he was wounded.'

'I recommend you to fetch the lady, if she is willing to come. Is she your old nurse?'

'No, she is the lady I am to marry,' Phipps said. 'I know her to be a kind and efficient nurse. I shall consult with my mother, but she...she cannot bear to look at Alex. Every time she enters the room she starts to weep.'

'Then by all means send for your fiancée. It is a pity you were not already married.'

'Yes,' Phipps agreed. 'I shall speak to my parents—and then, if they agree, I will go and ask Miss Hamilton immediately. In the meantime, I must thank you for your advice, sir.'

'I am only sorry I can be of no real assistance,' Knighton replied sombrely. 'However, I have seen worse cases recover so do not give up hope.'

'Do you mean that, sir? Our local man was confident that Alex would die—indeed, he expected it before this.'

'We have many such as he in our profession. If it were left to those of his ilk we should still be in the dark ages. There is progress in surgery all the time, but, unfortunately, head wounds still remain an unsolved mystery. I intend to write a paper about the possibility of relieving blood pressing on the brain by draining it out—but that would mean an operation almost as soon as the accident occurred. I am not yet sufficiently advanced in my theory to attempt it, but had I been consulted at the start and your father willing…'

'Yes, I wish that you had been instantly consulted, but my father did not tell me immediately and it was a while before he would consent to your being called in.'

'And I was not immediately available,' the eminent doctor agreed. 'However, I do not believe all lost—though these things can happen suddenly. Prepare yourself for the worst, but live in hope, sir.'

With that Phipps had to be content, for Knighton was anxious to leave. He had a busy practice in London and his rich patients did not like to be kept waiting.

After seeing him to the door, Phipps went back to his brother's room. Lord Piper was sitting with him, looking as if he were sunk in gloom. He glanced up as Phipps entered, shaking his head.

'Did I not tell you how it would be? They can do nothing without risking either his death or such damage to his brain that life would be a torture to him.'

'Knighton says that if there is a blood clot on his brain it might be relieved by removing it, but admits that it might cause severe damage.'

'As I told you…'

'He does not despair of Alex, however. He says there were signs of recognition to light and he thinks he might just be deeply concussed.'

'For three weeks? I do not think it.'

'He says we must be sure to employ a good nurse. I was thinking that Miss Hamilton might be willing to help with him, sir. Naturally, his man will tend to his bodily needs, but Miss Hamilton is so patient...so sensible. She would sit with him for hours. He must be made to drink and the maids will not bother if he simply lies there. Mother might, but she is too distraught to think clearly. We need a clear head.'

'Would she come? Surely it is too much to ask of her?'

'Had we been married, I know she would have been more than willing. If you could spare me, sir—I should go and fetch her myself.'

'Well, there is little you can do here. I had thought your mother might respond to you, but all she does is lie there and weep.'

'Miss Hamilton might be of help to Mama also.'

'Very well, fetch her—but you must not delay your return. If he should die...'

'Yes, I understand,' Phipps said. 'I shall be needed here.'

'Is she at home?'

'No, she will have joined Brock at his family home. It was arranged in London and I begged her to go ahead with her plans.'

'Very well, you have my permission to bring her here. Perhaps, if her family agree, a quiet ceremony could be held here?'

'I shall speak to her about it,' Phipps promised.

Perhaps he ought to send word ahead of his coming, but driving his own curricle he could be there almost as soon, and he could not wait to see her again.

Amanda was shocked by the change in Cynthia. She seemed to have lost much of her sparkle and spent most of the time staring into space and sighing. Only when Brock entered the room and spoke to her did she come back from wherever she had been. Amanda had tried to sympathise with her, but met with a stony look for her expressions of regret for what had befallen her. It was obvious that she intended to stick to her story of having had a fall and there would be no confidences. She was perfectly polite to Amanda, but kept her at a distance and did not speak to her with the warmth she had when she'd considered Amanda an ugly duckling to be patronised by the beautiful swan.

Amanda remained friendly towards her, but did not try to break down the barrier Cynthia had erected; instead, she spent her time enjoyably walking about the beautiful grounds and enjoying her hosts' lavish hospitality. That her pleasure in the visit was dimmed by Phipps's absence could not be denied, but she hardly ever gave way to tears and always in the privacy of her bedroom. No one who did not know her well could have guessed that she felt so very unhappy.

Mama looked at her critically when they had been at Lord Brockley's palatial home for a few days.

'Are you sure you are eating enough, Amanda? You look so pale and thin, my love. I dare say you meant to lose a little weight so that you would look elegant at your wedding, but that dress begins to hang on you—and it was new before we left London.'

'Yes, Mama, I know, but it just happened. I eat as much as I wish for, but I am not hungry.'

'Your papa thought you were pining for Phipps. I hope you are not so foolish, Amanda? You must know why he asked you to marry him, and if you have fallen in love…I fear you are destined to be disappointed in your marriage.'

'No, Mama, I am not pining,' Amanda assured her, though it was a terrible lie. She felt sometimes as if her life was over and knew instinctively that if Phipps had changed his mind she could never love again.

'Lord Armstrong is leaving in the morning, my love,' Mama said. 'It is not too late to fix your interest with him. You could tell Lieutenant Phipps that you have changed your mind…after all, this business of his brother may make it impossible for you to marry.'

'No, Mama.' Amanda lifted her head. 'Please put this nonsense from your mind. I do not care for Lord Armstrong and would rather live my life as a spinster than wed him.'

Mama looked at her in annoyance, but the subject was dropped. However, the next morning, when they were sitting in the parlour with Jane, and Lord Armstrong came to take his leave, she insisted that her daughter take a stroll outside with him to say her farewells.

Not wishing to make a fuss, Amanda allowed herself to be persuaded and they went out into the sunshine. For a few minutes they walked in silence, Amanda enjoying the scents of lavender and roses, but wishing that this interview might soon be over.

'Miss Hamilton…Amanda,' Lord Armstrong said suddenly. 'I must and will speak. I cannot bear to see you so unhappy. I fear that you are nursing a secret sorrow—can it be that your engagement is at an end?'

'No, sir. As you are aware, Phipps's brother is very ill. He has been delayed and the wedding cannot take place while his brother is in danger of his life.'

'Yet I fear that he has let you down and you may not trust him. Please, my dearest Amanda, let yourself think of turning to another… I am willing to wait until you extricate yourself from this sorry situation.' He seized her hands and covered them with passionate kisses. 'I adore you, my angel.'

'No! You must not, sir. I beg you…' Amanda

cried, but he was lost in his passion and took her by the waist, drawing her close and, holding her so that she could not escape, he kissed her. She gasped, thrust him away and slapped his face as hard as she could. 'How dare you! I forbid you to touch me again. You disgust me—and I despise you. Please leave me now.'

Even as he hesitated, someone came out of the house and began to run towards them. Turning, Amanda recognised him at once and gave a glad cry, rushing towards him and throwing herself into his arms.

'Oh, Phipps...' she wept emotionally '...I am so glad you have come.'

'What did he do to you?' Phipps demanded, his eyes glittering with fury. 'Damn his impudence!'

'He proposed to me, and he—he forced a kiss on me...' she said, but caught his arm, as he would have gone after Lord Armstrong. 'No, let him go, Phipps. I hit him as hard as I could and after what I said...I do not think he will approach me again.'

'I should thrash him,' Phipps said, fury smouldering in his eyes. 'But I do not have time to waste on such things. Amanda, my brother is so ill—and Knighton says he must have a sensible nurse. I could not think of anyone who would be more capable…would you come and help me care for him?'

'Of course,' she said, though her heart sank. He had not come because he could not bear to be away from her another moment, but because he thought her a capable nurse. 'I have wished that I might be of use to you, dearest, but felt I could not push myself forward.'

'My mother cannot bear to look at her adored son and my father walks around in an angry daze. I need you there with me so much, Amanda. I should like to be married quietly at my home— unless you would prefer to wait?'

'Oh, no,' she said and prayed that she would not come to regret her rashness. 'I shall come with you now. Perhaps your father would write and invite my parents and then we may be married very quietly at your home. I do not particularly wish for a big wedding…but I should like to invite Jane to be my bridesmaid, if your family would not mind her staying with us?'

'I am sure they would be delighted to have her,' Phipps said and kissed her hands. 'Oh, Amanda, I am so glad to see you. You cannot imagine how awful it has been at home. I think I would by far rather be ill myself than see Alex lying there like that.'

Chapter Thirteen

Mama was a little reluctant at first, but as she could see that Amanda was determined, she was forced to give way. She complained that it was rude to leave Lord Brockley's house before the visit was due to end, but Brock was concerned for his friend and insisted that he would escort them to Phipps's home.

'I should not dream of standing in your way,' he said. 'You must of course go, Miss Hamilton. I think Phipps a lucky man to have secured you for his bride—and as for the celebrations, I shall be there to stand as his best man. When things are back to normal, which we must all pray for, you can give a large ball. I may be married myself by then…we have not yet decided. Miss Langton's mama prefers an engagement of some months, but we shall see.'

Brock took his leave of his betrothed in private. Amanda did not know what he said to her, but Cynthia came to say farewell and wish her happy. She apologised if she had been distant, but she was not feeling quite well. In the future she hoped they might be friends again.

Jane was quite happy to be leaving. She had seemed very quiet the past few days, but when asked denied being in any distress.

'You may find it very quiet at my home,' Phipps said to her when he helped her into Lady Hamilton's carriage. 'I would not have taken you away but that Amanda would like you at her wedding—which is now to be very quiet.'

'Oh, I shall be perfectly happy, sir. If Amanda will permit me, I intend to spend my time sewing. Her clothes need altering again and I shall enjoy being of service to her—I love her dearly, you know.'

'I am sure she is extremely fond of you.'

The journey to Phipps's home was not long and easily accomplished by teatime. They were greeted by Lady Piper, who had roused herself sufficiently to entertain her guests to tea, though she looked pale and wan and was happy to allow herself to be taken up to bed by her woman later to lie down for a while before dinner.

'This is very kind of you, Miss Hamilton,' Lord Piper said, his brows a little arched as if surprised. 'I cannot apologise enough for imposing on you— and for causing your wedding to be postponed. I wish I had not had to ask Phipps to put his own happiness aside for a time.'

'We have settled on a quiet wedding, sir,' Amanda said and smiled. 'As Brock said, we may easily give a ball when your eldest son is recovered.'

'I wish to God that I might think it possible, but I fear the worst.'

'I do hope not, sir. I do not claim to have any nursing skills above the ordinary, but I am patient and Phipps seemed to need my help.'

'And so you came. What a very good sort of girl you are, Miss Hamilton! I did not realise quite how lucky my son was in his choice.'

Amanda blushed and disclaimed, but was warmed by his genuine welcome. She could only hope that she might be of some real use to the family in its distress, though Mama was certain that nothing was to be done in such cases.

Phipps took her to his brother's chamber after tea and she felt her heart stir with pity as she saw the young man lying so pale and still. He was like Phipps to some extent, but his hair was almost black and it curled at the ends. Its colour made him appear very white and she realised that he was a very attractive man, with a look of intelligence about his lean features. Instantly realising what the loss of such a son must mean to his parents, she understood his mother's total collapse. Her own mama might be much the same if her son had been brought home in such a state.

'Oh, Phipps, I am so sorry,' she said. 'I will do all I can, though I do not perfectly understand what I can do. His valet keeps him clean and I have no real nursing talent...'

'I know. I simply needed you here,' he said. 'You were so very kind to Brock and—I fear that the servants may neglect him. Knighton said we should make sure he swallows liquids... Oh, and he said talking might help. He thinks Alex may just be concussed.'

'We must pray he is right,' she said and went

over to the bed, placing her hand on the patient's brow. 'Oh, he is a little too warm, I think. Has he had a fever?'

'Until now I think not,' Phipps said and followed her example. 'By Jove, there has been a change since I left him to fetch you... I do not know whether it is for good or evil.'

'At least it means I may be of some real use,' Amanda said in her practical tone. She could see that Phipps was very disturbed and wished to save him what pain she could. 'Is there water in the jug? Ah, yes, I can bathe his forehead—but I do not see a jug of drinking water. Could your cook make some iced lemon barley for us, do you think?'

'I am sure she could,' Phipps said and smiled at her in such a way that her heart flipped. 'Oh, Amanda, I am so thankful you are here, my love. I think I can bear anything now.'

Amanda felt the sting of tears and her throat caught with emotion. She told herself not to be foolish and set about the task of bringing the patient's fever down. As Phipps left the room she cautiously peeled back the covers. Alex was wearing long pants, which covered his modesty. They would have to be removed when his man came, because he needed something less enveloping. He was sweating profusely and, as she began to soothe her cool cloth over his heated flesh, she heard him moan. Unsure of what he said, she soothed his hair back from his forehead.

'Yes, sir. I dare say you feel very ill, but the mercy of it is that you can feel, you know. Poor Phipps was in terror lest you die and that would be very bad. Everyone wishes you to get better.'

She turned with a smile as Phipps returned with the barley water.

'Try not to worry, dearest,' she said. 'I am here now and we shall nurse him together.'

Alex was burning up by the time the doctor arrived. He shook his head gravely and gave it as his opinion that this was the onset of a death fever and that the patient could not live long. It was useless to force him to take medicine and kinder just to leave him to die—giving him liquids would merely prolong his agony.

After he had gone, Amanda let free the rage that had consumed her.

'What a prosy fool he is,' she said. 'No wonder

your poor mama is having hysterics and your father is sunk in gloom. I should write to Mr Knighton and beg him to come at once—and in the meantime I shall ask Mama to make up her own remedy.'

Mama was agreeable and, after she had visited the sick man, went away to beg the housekeeper for the necessary ingredients. She watched Amanda administer the first dose and said she was proud of her, then left her to go down to dinner. It was her duty to make sure that Jane was not left alone, and, since Lady Piper had made the effort to dine with them, she could do no less. Amanda said that all she required was some tea and a slice of bread and butter, which she would eat here.

Amanda and Phipps decided to share the nursing with Alex's valet, who was accustomed to shaving him and was able to wash the parts that would have been a danger to Amanda's modesty. She was perfectly content to leave such intimate duties to the valet, who seemed very capable, and agreed that she would need help when administering the medicine and giving the patient drinks.

She and Phipps sat up together through the late

hours, and the valet took over in the morning while they went away to their separate rooms to sleep.

In the morning, Jane came in as she was eating her breakfast and sat on the edge of the bed.

'I should not mind sitting with him for an hour or two so that you and Phipps can walk in the gardens—such lovely gardens as they are. I went for a walk this morning as far as the lake. I can sit and sew in his room as well as the parlour, you know.'

'Oh, Jane, you are such a good friend—and you've done so much for me.'

'Not as much as you have done for me. I never had a friend before and I have been about so much more than if I had not met you. Had I gone home without an offer I do not know what would have become of me—perhaps the curate might have offered…'

Amanda laughed. 'You are far too pretty to marry the curate, Jane. I know we shall find you a husband one day, my dearest friend.'

'I have thought, if you should like it,' Jane said, 'that I might take your wedding gown to pieces and make something simpler. You will not wish to wear such an elaborate gown for a quiet affair.'

'It is much too grand and was never what I hoped.'

'Besides making you look like a dumpling with all those skirts and that train—but the good thing is that I can cut it into a very simple dress, rather like the white muslin you look so well in.'

'You are so clever with your needle,' Amanda said. 'I shall leave you to do whatever you think—just make it a surprise. Papa is coming at the end of next week and I believe Brock has gone to get a special licence for us. When he returns we shall have the ceremony and a simple dinner here.'

'Oh, you are to have a cake. I heard Lady Piper discussing it with your mama.'

'Well, I suppose Papa would not like it if some celebration were not made. Poor Papa, he did so want to show everyone how proud he is of his daughter.'

'Well, you may have a ball when things…are settled.'

'Yes.' Amanda smiled at her. 'Thank you for being here, Jane.'

'Oh, I shall be sorry when I have to go home.'

Jane looked wistful. 'To live in a house like this…
it would be a dream come true.'

'I should prefer to live in a house that belonged
to Phipps and me,' Amanda said. 'If we have to
live here…but that depends. We can only pray
that Alex will get better.'

Alex was in a fever for three long days and
nights. It gradually mounted and he began to
writhe and call out, but nothing he said made
sense and that made his father look grave and
brought a look of fear to Phipps's eyes. Everyone
dreaded that a crisis was coming and Amanda
was relieved when Mr Knighton arrived from
London.

He came into the bedroom just as Amanda was
bathing her patient's arms and talking to him in
a soothing voice. Alex quietened as she spoke to
him and the doctor watched her for a moment or
two before addressing her.

'Yes, I see why Lieutenant Phipps thought you
should be called on,' he said. 'You are doing just
as you ought, just as I advised. What have you
been giving him?'

'Barley water and the tisane Mama makes. The

local doctor told us that we were merely prolonging the agony. Have I done wrong, sir?'

'Not at all, though I think my own mixture may help—and, when the patient is able, I shall recommend some restorative jelly, which will give him a little strength. No hot wine, if you please, or spirits. A little thin gruel if you can get him to take it—but the fever should break soon enough and then we shall see.'

'Do you think he will come to his senses?' Amanda asked as he straightened after examining the sick man.

'I have every hope of it. There is already an improvement. Had Phipps not called me in—and fetched you, Miss Hamilton—I fear his grieving family would have allowed him to die with dignity. We must thank God that Phipps had the sense to override his father.'

Amanda felt the sting of tears. 'Oh, thank heaven,' she said. 'Do you think he will be as he was?'

'That I cannot say, but I am certain he will live. The fever is a blessing in disguise, for it has made him fight—or perhaps you did that...' He smiled at her. 'I am going to stay here for a few days, and you may send for me at any moment of the day or night.'

Amanda thanked him profusely and he went away. Jane came to take her place while she ate a light nuncheon and then walked in the gardens. When she went up to Alexander's room, she discovered that he was sweating profusely. Jane said it had started after Phipps gave him the second dose of Mr Knighton's fever mixture.

After Jane had gone to take a turn in the garden, Amanda gently bathed her patient's brow and then went to pour a little barley water into a glass. She brought it back, lifting him slightly with one arm and pressing the edge to his lips. He gulped thirstily and then muttered something, which sounded like, 'Thank you.'

Amanda replaced the glass on the bedside table, placed a hand on his forehead, which seemed slightly less clammy. She was about to take up her seat again when she heard a groaning sound from the bed. Turning, she saw that Alexander's eyes were open. She noticed they were very blue and then he spoke, clearly this time. 'Do I know you?'

Her heart beating so fast that she could scarcely

breathe, she approached the bed and looked down at him, hardly daring to hope that she'd heard him.

'I'm Miss Hamilton, Phipps's fiancée,' she said softly. 'Are you feeling very poorly?'

'Damnably so,' he muttered and fell back against the pillows, closing his eyes.

Amanda placed her hand on his brow. He was quite dry now and much cooler. It seemed that the fever had broken and she thanked God for it. Tears had started to her eyes, running down her cheeks. She brushed them away, but they would not stop.

Turning, the tears still upon her cheeks as the door opened and Phipps entered, she was unable to speak at once for the emotion that overcame her. He came to her at once, a look of fear in his eyes, and took her hands.

'Oh, my poor darling, is he dead?'

'No, the fever has broken. I think he is sleeping…' She clasped his hands tightly as she began to tremble. 'Oh, Phipps, he spoke to me—asked me who I was.'

'He spoke sensibly to you?' Phipps stared in wonder. 'You are certain it was not just something he muttered in a fever?'

'No, for first he thanked me for the drink I gave him and then he opened his eyes and asked if he knew me. I told him who I was and asked if he felt very poorly and he said—damnably so...'

Phipps stared, unable to speak at first, and then, in a choking voice, 'That is always his expression. Father does not like it—but I think it is the sweetest thing I ever heard. Thank you so much, my dearest Amanda.'

'I did nothing,' she said and smiled as he suddenly grabbed her and held her close to him, just holding on as if in the grip of extreme emotion, as if he would never let her go. 'I can't be sure, but I think he must be going to recover, Phipps. Oh, my poor love, do not cry.'

'Forgive me,' he said, choking off and laughing. 'What a poor specimen I am to weep at such news. It's just that we thought...we thought he was going to die.'

'Mr Knighton said there was an improvement,' Amanda said. 'He believes that Alexander's body was healing itself while he lay in a coma and said he detected signs of a change when he examined him.'

'Yes, I know, but just think what might have

happened if I had not brought you here. My father, good soul though he is, would probably have let Alex die with dignity rather than have him face life as an imbecile.'

'Who are you calling an imbecile?'

The voice was still a little wavery, but when they turned to look at Alex he was regarding them both with interest. Phipps gave a snort of laughter and moved towards the bed.

'It was that fool of a doctor of ours, Alex. He thought you would not recover and advised us to let you die, for he thought if you recovered consciousness your wits would be lost.'

'Always was a damned fool,' Alex said. 'My head aches damnably and I should like to sit up, but I feel so weak. How long have I been in this damned bed?'

'Almost a month. It was nearly three weeks before Father allowed me to send for Knighton. He said you must be nursed and I fetched Miss Hamilton. It is she who has somehow managed to get both liquids and a thin gruel into you, besides bathing your forehead when the fever raged.'

'So long? Good grief, no wonder I'm damnably hungry.' His blue eyes turned to Amanda. 'How do you do, Miss Hamilton. I fear I was abrupt with you when I first woke. I must thank you for your kindness and say that my brother is a lucky dog to have found such a treasure in his future wife.'

'I thank you for the compliment,' Amanda said, feeling unaccountably shy as she dipped a curtsy. 'May I have some soup brought up to you, sir?'

'I should much prefer some good rare beef and pickles,' he replied and laughed as he saw her set her face. 'No? What a dragon you are, Miss Hamilton.'

'It is Miss Hamilton, but you may call me Amanda. I think we are to be brother and sister, sir. There is no need to stand on formality. I will have some soup and a little buttered toast sent up for you—and I will consult with Mr Knighton on how soon you may have red meat, pickles and I dare say a glass of wine, but I fear it may not be yet.'

'Remarkably fine girl you have there,' Alex remarked as the door closed behind her and Phipps settled him against the pillows. 'You had been crying—so you didn't care to step into my shoes, then?'

'I should damned well think not,' Phipps said.

'Besides, Amanda has many properties of her own. I shall have my work cut out looking after them without the estate, that's your job.'

'You always were a good brother,' Alex said. 'I feel like hell and my mouth tastes of sawdust. Be a good fellow and fetch me a glass of brandy and—'

'No, not until Knighton says you are able to stomach them. Amanda has given up her wedding for your sake, Alex. You might at least respect her judgement—and that of Knighton.'

'Oh, well, I suppose I must submit,' he said. 'She's quite a determined little thing, isn't she? Someone told me she was a dumpling and not attractive, but I thought her quite taking myself. I hope you didn't propose solely for the money? If you were in trouble you could have come to me.'

'Wouldn't dream of it,' Phipps said. 'I always liked Amanda, but since I've come to know her, I… Well, the truth is—'

Phipps was not destined to finish what he had to say, because the door flew open and their mother entered. She looked wild with emotion and, as she saw her eldest son sitting up in bed, apparently talking to Phipps, burst into tears.

'Is it true what Miss Hamilton said? Have you recovered your senses—not, not an...'

'Mama, I should prefer not to be called an imbecile, if you do not mind,' Alex said and threw a look of appeal at his brother, as his mother appeared to consider whether to throw herself on to him or faint. 'Phipps, old fellow, take Mama away and talk to her. I should like to rest before I eat...'

'Mama, Alex truly is better,' Phipps said and took her arm, steering her from the room. 'Come, control yourself. He may be recovered from the coma, but he is exhausted. We must allow him to rest.'

Closing the door firmly behind them, he took his mother down to her own parlour and settled her in a chair, before pouring her a small glass of brandy and compelling her to sip it because she seemed in danger of hysterics.

'There is no need to distress yourself,' he said gently. 'You may visit when Alex is feeling better, but he doesn't need an excess of emotion just now. He is still weak and tired, and it will be a while before he is better.'

'I am not a child, Phipps,' she said and sniffed into her handkerchief, but then took a sip of the brandy. 'Go back to your brother. I'm sure he wishes to talk to *you*.'

'Well, I am probably going to feed him, because I doubt he can drink his soup from a spoon.'

Smiling at her, he went away, but encountered his father just come in from the stable. Lord Piper had that minute spoken to the footman and started forward.

'Is it true? Has he recovered his senses?'

'Yes, he woke up and spoke to Miss Hamilton and then fell asleep for a few minutes, and when he woke he was perfectly sensible, Father—just as Knighton hoped he might be.'

'Thank God you had the sense to send for him,' his father said. 'May I see Alex?'

'I think and hope he is about to have some soup. I shall see how he feels after that, but he may wish to rest. Perhaps later, when he feels more the thing. I believe Mama may need you more at the moment.'

Leaving his father to consider his words, Phipps returned to his brother's chamber and discovered that Amanda and the valet had Alex propped against his pillows and he was being encouraged to drink his soup from a small cup, which the valet was holding for him. Amanda had just poured a glass of barley water, which she placed on the chest beside him. She smiled at Phipps and then turned to address his brother.

'Now, sir, your valet and your father's servants will care for you in future. It would not be proper for me to do so now that you have recovered and I do not fear a relapse, for Mr Knighton says it is unlikely. I shall visit you when you are up and about again, so if you will forgive me I shall leave you to your excellent man. However, I do beg you to take Mr Knighton's advice. He says you should stick to broth and bread for two days and then you may eat a little cold chicken.'

'Oh, are you deserting me?' Alex gave her his charming smile. 'I am sorry for it, for I know you have done so much for me. I was aware of you talking to me; you have such a comforting way with you. May I say again that Phipps is a lucky man.'

Amanda blushed prettily, smiled at Phipps, saying softly, 'I shall walk in the rose gardens. Perhaps you will join me later?'

'Yes, of course,' he agreed and opened the door

for her, returning to the bed as Alex pushed away the almost empty cup.

'Had enough? Was it foul stuff?'

'No, rather good, but I find I can't stomach too much. Amanda was right about the beef and pickles, much though I should fancy it.'

'I dare say you will be up and eating whatever you want soon enough.'

'Is Mama all right?' Alex said, thanking his valet as the man helped him back against the pillows once more. 'Thank you, Sorrel, that will be all. I shall ring when I need you.'

After the man had gone out, Alex looked at him for a moment, then, 'I should like to give your bride a present she would really like, Phipps. Have the goodness to discover what I may give her, if you please.'

'I've been looking for some good horses for her to drive—and you have a splendid pair of chestnuts in your stable that I think just right...'

'Then present them to her with my compliment, and I wish it were a hundred times more, Phipps. I did not at first realise it, but it was her voice that guided me back... I was in a far place, you see, and I could not find my way towards the light, but then she kept talking and she would not let me rest, so I followed the sound and…then I woke up and saw her.'

'And we thank God for it. Will you see Father yet?'

'No, not just yet. I should like to sleep if you do not mind. You must go down to find…' Alex frowned. 'Did you tell me she had given up her wedding for me?'

'Yes, her father was to have given her a splendid affair, but it had to be postponed and we meant to marry here by special licence—just a quiet affair.'

'No, that will not do,' Alex said firmly. 'You must set in train all that her father had planned, Phipps. If I am able I shall come to it—but if not, then it must still go ahead. Every bride should have her special day and she is rather lovely. She must be allowed to shine.'

'Lovely?' Phipps smiled fondly. 'Yes, she is—but do you see, I hardly know whether she is slim or plump or even pretty; to me she is the sweetest darling I have ever met and…in plain truth I adore her.'

'In that case, I should waste no time in going after her to tell her,' Alex said, 'and now I am going to sleep off that chicken soup.'

Chapter Fourteen

Amanda was sitting on a bench in the rose garden when she saw Phipps walking towards her. She had been enjoying the warmth of the sun on her face, for she had taken off her straw bonnet and it lay on the grass at her feet. The only sound to be heard was the buzzing of honey bees and she had been quite at peace, feeling that she could not ask more of life than to know that she had played some small part in bringing Phipps's brother through his fever. She looked up and smiled at Phipps as he came up to her, unaware that all the love she felt for him was in her face or that he felt himself bathed in its warmth.

'Is he sleeping?' Phipps nodded and sat down beside her. 'I thought he would. He is very tired, but Knighton says that is to be expected, and with rest and care, which his valet will give him, he will be perfectly well soon.'

'Yes, I know. I spoke to Knighton. He says he will stay one more night and then return to London, but he does not expect a relapse.'

'It is a miracle,' Amanda said. 'We must thank God for it.'

'No doubt God played His part,' he murmured, taking her hand in his and beginning to play with the fingers. 'But I thank you and Mr Knighton; he for having the good sense to say what was needed was a good nurse—and you for your devotion. Alex says you guided him back; I do not perfectly know what he means, but he does and that is all that matters.'

'I am glad he is restored to you, Phipps.'

'Yes, for now your father may set all in train again for the wedding.'

'That would please Papa,' Amanda replied, a little frown on her brow. 'But are you sure? Will you not wish to stay with Alexander for a time?'

'He insists on it, my love.' Phipps lifted her hand to his lips and kissed each of her fingers in turn, noticing that her ring was a little loose. 'I must get you the ring I promised—and have this made smaller. I thought it was a good fit.'

'Yes, it was, but my finger has got smaller.' She did not wish to tell him that she had lost a lot of weight in case he had not noticed.

'Well, it can soon be altered,' Phipps said. 'Alex has asked me to give you a pair of his thoroughbreds as a wedding gift from him—and I have had a light phaeton made for you. We shall be able to begin your lessons as soon as we return from Paris.'

'Are we going to Paris?'

'Yes, for a few days, though we may travel on to the coast for it is very beautiful there—but every bride should buy a few gowns in Paris. I have thought that your dressmaker does not always do you justice, my love.'

'Jane says the same. She has been fashioning me a new wedding gown... It may be a little plain, Phipps, for I thought it to be a quiet wedding.'

'I care not for gowns, only to please you—because I owe you a debt I can never repay...'

'Oh, please, do not. I did so very little...'

'You will have it your way,' Phipps said and drew her up. He looked long and hard into her eyes and then pulled her against him, bending his head to kiss her lips. His kiss was sweet but intense and deep, shaking her with the force of his passion. Looking up into his eyes, Amanda saw that they were dark with emotion. 'I can only tell you that I adore you, Amanda. When I asked you to be my wife, you knew that I admired you and thought we should deal well together—but I had no idea of the woman you were inside. There is no way for me to put into words what I feel now.'

'You are grateful, I know…' she began, but was seized ruthlessly, her lips crushed beneath a kiss of such force and heat that she could not speak when he let her go, the look in his eyes such that she was surprised into speech. 'You really care for me…do you not?'

'You have become so much more to me than I could ever have thought. I love you so much that if anything were to happen to you I believe I should not wish to go on living.'

A happy peal of laughter rang out as she threw herself back into his arms and kissed him, letting herself melt into him as their embrace became more intense and overwhelming. Her body trembled and she knew a desire to lie in his arms and become one with him. Phipps loved her—truly loved her—and she had not thought that it could ever happen to a girl like her.

'Then now you know how I feel,' she whispered when they could at last stop kissing. 'I do not care what anyone says or does now that I know you truly love me.'

Phipps stroked her cheek, then frowned. 'Did someone speak ill of me to you?'

'He said that you had proposed only for the money—that there was another lady you had loved, but she would not have you, because you were but a second son.'

'It was true that there was once someone I thought I loved,' Phipps told her. 'But when she chose a despicable old man for his money and refused my love, I saw her for what she was. I have not thought of her for years—and I never felt about her as I do you, Amanda.'

'Then we shall not speak or think of her again,' Amanda said. 'Are you coming with us when we leave, Phipps?'

'I shall escort you naturally,' he promised. 'Alex will come to the wedding if he can, and if not, my parents will leave him once they are assured that he is recovering. You must tell your parents to go on exactly as they had planned, for there is surely nothing to stop us now.'

There had been nothing to disturb their plans for the wedding. Amanda had had the happiness of taking Phipps to visit all her friends and neighbours, and the wedding gifts had poured in for days on end. News from Phipps's home had told them that his brother was well and gaining in health, and her papa was in his element, sparing no expense to make sure that Amanda's wedding was fitting for the daughter he loved.

Amanda had been secretly a little anxious about her wedding dress, for Mama expected a creation of satin and lace with yards of skirts and a train behind that would be encrusted with small diamonds and shout its cost at the world. Jane had kept the creation she was making a secret and she did not reveal it until the morning of Amanda's wedding, when she brought it covered in plain white linen to her bedroom.

Having breakfasted on two rolls and a little honey with a cup of coffee, and now dressed in her petticoat of fine silk, Amanda felt flutters in her stomach as she waited for it to be unveiled. It was as she had expected: very plain and simple with what appeared to be a seamed, elongated waist, but no waistband or sash of any kind, and a slender skirt with a demi-train behind. There was a swathe of fine embroidery over one shoulder and down one sleeve, and this was sewn with the tiny diamonds that had been on the wide skirt, but no lace or other ornament, the neckline a soft swathe of tulle that skimmed just above the swell of her breasts.

Gasping in shock and not knowing what to say, Amanda allowed Jane to slip it over her shoulders and then turned to look in the cheval mirror. What she saw there made her stare, unable to utter one word.

Jane looked pale, fearful. 'Have I made it too plain for you, Amanda? I thought it would suit you...' She faltered as Amanda turned to her, tears in her eyes.

'Is that really me?' she asked. 'Surely it cannot be? I look...slim and...beautiful. Oh, Jane, thank you so very much for your wonderful gift to me.'

Jane gave her a kiss on the cheek, but did not hug her because she did not wish to crease the fine silk. 'I'm so glad you like it. I know it is a trifle plain, but I think you look wonderful—and I think you will set a new fashion. And it is not just the gown or being slimmer, Amanda. Your hair shines with health, your eyes are bright and— oh, it is as if a light shines out of you, my dear friend. I think it must be love—or happiness. I do not think that being thin makes anyone beautiful. Indeed, I should like to have some of your curves—but happiness certainly makes you glow.'

'And my beautiful gown sets it all off. I should imagine I shall be plagued for the name of my seamstress.' Amanda opened the box on her dressing table. 'Phipps gave me this simple pearl-and-diamond pendent. I think I shall wear that, for anything more elaborate would look out of place.'

Jane fastened it about her neck, then helped Amanda's maid secure a lace veil over a tiara of diamonds that her father had bought her as one of his many wedding gifts. She wore no bracelets, for the sleeves came to a diamond-encrusted point over her wrists and she did not wish to spoil the line, but her shoes of white satin had diamond-studded heels, another of Papa's presents. On her left hand she wore a ring with one splendid diamond, which Phipps had had made for her.

Jane picked up her bouquet of white roses and a tiny blue forget-me-not, bound with lace to frame them and a silver posy holder, and placed it in her hands.

'Now you look as you deserve,' she said softly. 'You are lovely, Amanda, you always were, but for some reason you allowed yourself to become too plump and then you wore hideous clothes to hide in.'

'It is very strange, but I have lost my sweet tooth, much to Papa's dismay, but since I shall now be living in Phipps's house he will not notice it—and though with the years and bearing children I may become plumper, I shall never let it destroy me again. I have learned to value myself for what I am, not whether I am fat or thin—and because Phipps values me I cannot think less of myself.'

A knock at the door heralded Amanda's mother. She entered and stood looking at her daughter in silence. 'Good grief,' she said at last. 'I... You look lovely, Amanda. You really do.'

'I hope Phipps will think so,' Amanda said. 'But

in truth I do not think he much cares. He loves me, you see, fat or thin, and for better or for worse.'

'Men always talk nonsense,' her mother said. 'Believe me, allow yourself to become fat again and he may start to look elsewhere. They all have a roving eye, Amanda. Make the most of your honeymoon, for it soon wears off, believe me.'

Amanda kissed her mother's cheek, but ignored her. Once upon a time her mother's careless remarks might have hurt her, but she could no longer be hurt by them—or anyone else's spite. Phipps loved her as she loved him. She knew it, had felt it to the core when he was making love to her in secluded places, where they had kissed and touched until it had become very hard to wait, but Phipps would not anticipate their wedding night, though both had been tempted to it.

'We must go down,' Mama told her. 'Your father keeps checking his watch, and you know what that means…'

'Yes, Mama.' Amanda laughed and turned to wink at Jane. 'Be sure to catch my bouquet when I throw it. We shall have you married next if I can arrange it. You shall come and stay once we are back in England, dearest Jane—and thank you so much for my gown.'

Jane blushed and looked pleased, picking up her own bouquet and following behind the mother and daughter.

At the foot of the stairs, Amanda's father was talking to her brother, Robert. He turned to look at her, frowned as if displeased that her dress was not worthy of her—and then his eyes widened and he checked the hasty words on his lips.

'That is an odd sort of dress to get married in,' he said, 'but it suits you, puss. I always knew you were a pretty girl—but damn me if you ain't beautiful in that.'

'Jane made it for me out of the one the seamstress made,' Amanda said, 'that fit me ill and so Jane restyled it for me. I think it is beautiful, Papa.'

'You are beautiful,' he corrected her. 'I shan't say it don't look well on you, for it does, but I should have liked something a bit more showy.'

Amanda went into a peal of laughter for she had known what he would think: Papa always looked for more for his money, and he would have liked to see her decked out in yards and yards of the most expensive lace money could buy with a stiff underskirt of satin, which, because she could not mend her height, would merely make her look plump when she wasn't.

Phipps heard the music start and could not resist the temptation to turn and look as his bride walked down the aisle towards him. For a moment he was stunned, because he had never seen a gown that was so simple and yet so breathtakingly lovely. It was a few seconds before he took in the fact that his bride was slender, the dress that had a long line skimming her waist and hips in a way he had never seen done before and he admired it. Amanda looked entirely different. Many fashions of the day were caught up beneath the breasts and allowed to fall straight to the ankle, with more fullness for the plumper girl than the slender ones. Amanda had worn hers thus and it had hidden the truth from him—not that he had been looking for it.

As she took her place beside him, Phipps reached out and turned back the lace veil, smiling down into her eyes. He had been thinking her beautiful for a long time, so was not surprised that her eyes sparkled to rival her diamonds and her colour was a delicate rose, her lips soft and delicious. He was tempted to kiss them, but the vicar was calling them to order so he contented himself with smiling at her and reaching for her hand. Plenty of time to tell her later how beautiful she was.

Amanda was shining with happiness when Phipps led her from the church as the bells pealed out. Young children came to present the bride with posies and a love charm that made her blush, since she was told it would make sure her first child would be a son.

As they ran for the carriage to take them to the house for the reception, friends and relations showered them with rose petals and rice. Laughing, Amanda held on to Phipps's hand as he lifted her up into the carriage and told the driver to move off.

'Alone at last,' he said and reached out to draw her to him. 'I've been wanting to do this since the moment I saw you.' He bent his head and kissed her deeply, making Amanda laugh up at him and kiss him back.

'Oh, dear, you will crease my lovely gown,' she said. 'Do you like it, Phipps? Jane made it for me after the seamstress sent me something that made me look like a sack of potatoes.'

'You could never look like that,' he murmured in amusement, for she did not change and he did not wish that she should. 'Brock told me that he envied me—and Alex says that if he had seen you first he would have cut me out.'

'No, he could not do that,' she said and nestled up to his chest. 'I am so happy, Phipps. It was wonderful that Alex felt able to come—and your parents looking so proud and happy.'

'They've always been proud of him, that is why they could not bear to lose him.'

'I meant proud of you, Phipps. You look so handsome—and no one could have done more for your brother than you did. Most younger sons might be glad to step into their elder brother's shoes, but you did all you could to make sure that it didn't happen.'

'Well, I care for him,' Phipps said gruffly. 'Besides, Alex knows he owes his life to you.' He laughed as she raised her eyebrows. 'Well, he says it and I know I owe mine to you so I shan't argue with him. I was a feckless fellow before I met you.'

'Oh, no, I never thought so.'

'Well, I cared little for anything but soldiering and then when the war was over I hardly knew what I should do with my life—but it is devoted to you, Amanda, and to looking after your interests.'

'Our interests,' she said. 'Money is for making life better, not for hoarding, Phipps—and, if we have enough for ourselves and our family, then we should do what we can for others. Do you not agree?'

'Perfectly, my darling,' he said and smiled. 'We shall go to your house this evening and stay for a few days before we leave for Paris—and you shall begin your driving lessons, my love.'

'Oh, lovely,' she said and put her arms about him again. 'To think that I might have died that day at the ruins—and now we have so much. You know I want to make sure Jane is not left to slide into her old life, and—do you think Brock and Cynthia are quite happy?'

'What makes you think that they are not?'

'I don't know,' she said, knitting her brows. 'It was just something he said at our dance the other evening…but here we are. We must look after our guests and I mean the people from the estate as well, Phipps. Papa has set up a marquee in the garden to house all the neighbours and workers who were not invited to the reception, and we must be sure to go and see them, I think, before we greet our other guests.'

Phipps laughed. 'I do believe you will keep me on my toes, my love. I shall never have time to be bored.'

Chapter Fifteen

Amanda was reluctant to change out of her wedding gown, but knew she must for she could not travel in it. The carriage gown of blue velvet became her well enough, but she did not know if anything would ever make her look quite as she had in Jane's creation.

'Thank you for everything,' she said to Jane as she kissed her goodbye. 'I shall see you when we return, I hope?'

'Yes…it is rather unexpected, but Lady Piper has asked me if I will go down and stay with her for a while. We got on very well when I was there, you know—and she admired your dress so much that when I told her I had designed and made it, she wanted me to make some gowns for her and I think I shall.'

'You must not think of becoming a seamstress

though,' Amanda begged. 'I shall see you wed to a good man one day.'

'Yes, perhaps you will,' Jane replied and blushed prettily. 'No, I must not say more, for I cannot be certain...'

'Well, I shall not tease you, but I must be the first to know.'

'I promise you shall be one of the first,' Jane said and kissed her cheek. 'Be happy, Amanda.'

Amanda left her to join Phipps. They ran for his travelling carriage again and were showered with rose petals once more, their friends laughing and waving until they could no longer see one another.

Phipps lounged beside her in the carriage, his hand reaching for hers as she sat back against the squabs. He smiled down into her happy face and then untied the strings of her bonnet, laying it on the other seat.

'We must not crush such a pretty thing, my love, but I want to kiss you. I think I shall never have enough of kissing and touching you, Amanda.'

Amanda gave herself up to his kisses, feeling that she had found something so precious that she had never believed could be hers. Mama had prepared her to expect at best courtesy and kindness from her husband, to be complaisant and never make a fuss when he left her to visit town on business. For Mama was of the opinion that few ladies were ever truly happy and few husbands ever entirely faithful. Amanda wondered briefly what had happened between them that led to the breakdown of trust.

She'd never doubted that her father loved her, for he had always doted on her—but perhaps it was because Mama did not show him the love and trust he deserved that Papa had devoted all his affection to his daughter. She had truly been spoiled and could only hope that now she was no longer at home Mama and Papa would find a way to fill the gap in their lives.

However, the slight shadow this thought had cast could not blight her happiness, which increased as the miles sped by and Phipps devoted himself to entertaining her in the most delightful ways.

Because Amanda's inherited estate was but twenty miles distant they arrived long before it was dark. The servants had been warned to expect them and lined up to greet their new master; normally it was the groom's privilege to take his bride to his home, but they had decided on this alternative, because it was not too far to drive the first night.

Phipps had had the chestnuts Alexander had given his bride as a gift walked by easy stages to the estate, and promised her they would visit them in the morning. After drinking a glass of the champagne that Phipps had ordered for them, she went upstairs to let her maid prepare her for her wedding night, choosing a diaphanous nightgown of fine silk that revealed as much as it concealed.

Phipps came to her as soon as he'd spoken with the butler, entering softly and startling her timid maid. Smiling at the girl's nerves, Amanda sent her away. She herself felt no apprehension whatsoever and got up to go to his arms at once.

'Weddings are all very fine,' Phipps said as he clasped her to him, 'but I sometimes think that they go on far too long.'

'Papa likes to be lavish with his hospitality—and he was saying goodbye to his little girl, remember.'

'Oh, I remember well enough and I do not grudge him his moment of triumph,' Phipps said.

'When your dress was seen it caused a sensation for it had a look of the medieval about it.'

Amanda laughed and nodded, looking up at him with love. 'It was so fitting, Phipps, because I was a maiden locked in an ivory tower and you rescued me, setting me free from the bonds that held me.'

'Ridiculous girl,' he said, but his eyes sparkled with laughter. 'I believe you will set a fashion, my love. Everyone was saying how lovely you looked; there was not a little surprise and jealousy, I can tell you.'

'Cynthia told me how happy she was for me, Phipps. She was everything that was kind and begged me not to forget her. She ought to be happy, for Brock is everything that is kind and courteous, but I could not rid myself of the notion that there is something amiss between them.'

'I am sorry for it if it is so,' Phipps said, looking down at her with a mixture of love and laughter in his eyes, 'but just at this very moment I am not too bothered by their thoughts.' He bent down and scooped her up behind the knees, carrying her to the bed. 'As light as a feather. You won't disappear altogether, will you, my love? You have become so slender that a puff of wind might carry you off.'

'Now, don't you start fussing,' Amanda warned, but with a twinkle in her eyes as he looked at her before setting her down. 'I had enough of that from Papa. I have never starved myself—but I no longer need the prop of sweet sticky things and somehow it all just melted away without my trying.'

'As long as you are well and happy. You do not need to be as slender as a reed for my sake, I liked you well enough exactly as you were.'

Amanda did not reply. Not because she had no answer, but because she had no time or inclination. His kisses were so sweet that they aroused her to feverish impatience, and she could hardly wait until both of them had shed their nightclothes and were lying pressed flesh to flesh in the vastness of the four-poster bed.

'My sweet lovely angel,' Phipps said as he began to stroke her, to kiss her in all the secret places that she would once have felt ashamed for any eye to see other than her own. 'It is you, the person inside, that I love, Amanda, and I always shall.'

And, as she thrilled to his touch, a gasp of

pleasure escaping her as he took her to the dizzy heights of desire that she had never known could be, she believed him.

Mama might say what she wished of men, others might try to spoil her happiness with spite, but the ugly brown sparrow that had once been Amanda had become a bird of Paradise. She shimmered in the haze of her own perfect happiness, and as she gave herself to her lover with all the passion that no one but he would ever see, she knew that whatever life brought in the future they would never lose this bond that held them now.

* * * * *